Our Lives Are the Rivers

rayo *An Imprint of* HarperCollinsPublishers

Our Lives
Are
the Rivers

A NOVEL

JAIME MANRIQUE

HarperCollins books may be purchased for educational,
business, or sales promotional use. For information, please write:
Special Markets Department, HarperCollins Publishers,
10 East 53rd Street, New York, NY 10022.

FIRST EDITION

Book design by Shubhani Sarkar

Printed on acid-free paper

Library of Congress Cataloging-in-Publication Data
has been applied for.

ISBN-10: 0-06-082070-5
ISBN-13: 978-0-06-082070-1

06 07 08 09 10 DIX/RRD 10 9 8 7 6 5 4 3 2 1

FOR JOSEFINA FOLGOSO,
IN MEMORIAM

ACKNOWLEDGMENTS

IN APPRECIATION OF THEIR SUPPORT I would like to thank the MacDowell Colony, the Medway Writers' Retreat, the New York Foundation for the Arts, the Foundation for Performance of the Contemporary Arts, and the John Simon Guggenheim Foundation.

My Splendors are Menagerie—
But their Competeless Show
Will entertain the Centuries
When I, am long ago,
An Island in dishonored Grass—
Whom none but Beetles know.

EMILY DICKINSON

AFTER THE EMPIRE

IN THE FIRST TWO HUNDRED YEARS following Christopher Columbus's arrival in the New World, the Spanish Empire spread so widely over the confines of the earth that it was said the sun never set on it. But by the 1820s, after a series of corrupt monarchs, Spain had lost most of its Latin American territories and had entered a period of chaos and irreversible decline.

Under the leadership of Venezuelan-born General Simón Bolívar, known as the Liberator, five South American nations—Colombia (which back then was known as Nueva Granada and included present-day Panama), Venezuela, Peru, Ecuador, and Bolivia—had achieved their independence after decades of bloody warfare. Bolívar had a dream of uniting these five countries to create one great and powerful nation named Gran Colombia.

CONTENTS

book

ONE

The Spaniard's Daughter

I

QUITO, ECUADOR
1822

I was born a rich bastard and died a poor one. That is the short story of my life. What it felt like to be Manuela Sáenz, the love child of my parents, Simón Sáenz de Vergara y Yedra and Joaquina Aispuru, is a longer story. But the story I want to tell you, the story of my love for the Liberator, Simón Bolívar, began long before I met him. It began when I was a young girl in the school of the Concepta nuns in Quito, where my mother's family kept me imprisoned until I eloped with the first man who said he loved me.

While my classmates memorized endless romantic poems to recite at family gatherings, I learned by heart long passages from Simón Bolívar's proclamations. On my visits at the end of the school year to my family in Catahuango, I would search out copies of his latest speeches and manifestos and smuggle them back to school to read during the few hours of the day when I could escape the nuns' surveillance. I read everything

I could find about Bolívar in the few newspapers that arrived at the school library, and I drank every word of the tales about him that were so much a topic of the conversations of the adults. To me Bolívar was the noblest man alive. Although he had been born into the richest family in Venezuela, he had given up his fortune to free South America. In my eyes, sacrifice made him even more heroic. His wife died just after they married, when they were still newlyweds. It was said he grieved for her so much that he lost his will to live. Bolívar's savior came in the form of revolution.

He had been exiled from South America to Jamaica after his first defeat by the Spanish army. He soon returned in triumph. His proclamations had the power to move people with the mighty force and truth of his words. He was a poet, a warrior, a great lover. Wherever he went, women threw themselves at him. And who could blame them? I was convinced he was the man South America had been waiting for, the man who would lead the continent to independence. The moment I first heard of the Liberator's intrepid feats, I pledged my life to his cause.

By the time I was old enough to understand that we *criollos* could not attend the best schools, or enter the most prestigious professions, or export and import goods from countries other than Spain—in other words, that we would never have the same rights in the eyes of the law as the Spaniards—and would just plain never be treated as equals and with dignity, simply because we were born on the American continent—I began to dream of the day when we would be free of Spanish rule. Thus each one of Bolívar's victories—victories that freed more and more South American territory from Spain—made me delirious with joy. When I learned his army had suffered a defeat, I felt as if the loss were inflicted on my own flesh—I would take to bed for days, screaming from the pain of my headaches. If members of my family dared criticize the Liberator in my presence, I would explode with anger. "You ungrateful race," I said at dinner one night to my aunt and grandmother, tears pouring from my eyes. "Bolívar has given his all to set us free, and all you can do is mock him. If the future of our nation lies in the hands of the likes of you, then we're doomed." As far as I was concerned, the man was perfect, and one could either love him and believe, or be his enemy and live without meaning. My friends and family quickly learned to be cautious whenever Bolívar's name was mentioned in my presence.

It was not until I was a married woman that our paths first crossed. In 1822, I had returned to Quito from Lima, determined to sell Catahuango, the hacienda my mother had bequeathed to me. In order to leave James Thorne, the Englishman my father had sold me to, the man I had been wife to in Lima for the last five years, I decided I must liquidate my only valuable property. My marriage to James had made me one of the wealthiest ladies of Peru, but more than a life of luxury, I wanted my freedom, and attaining this depended on selling the hacienda.

My entrance to Quito, accompanied by my slaves, Jonotás and Natán, caused a commotion. I rode into town wearing on my breast the highest honor Peru bestowed upon civilians—the gold medal of Knight of the Order of the Sun, which General San Martín had awarded to me for my contributions to the independence of Peru just the year before.

Natán and I had barely begun to unpack my trunks in my old bedroom in my father's house when Jonotás burst into the room, shouting the news that Simón Bolívar and his troops had reached the Avenue of the Volcanoes and would enter the city the following day. She informed us preparations were under way to receive the Liberator with a parade and a ball. Just the year before Bolívar had proclaimed the formation of Gran Colombia, which included the provinces of Nueva Granada, Ecuador, Panama, and Venezuela.

I could not have timed my arrival in Quito better even if I had had knowledge of Bolívar's plans. His imminent arrival was a fateful sign. I was determined to meet *el Libertador* at last. I immediately wrote a note to the authorities of Quito asking for an invitation to the ball in his honor. In the years that had passed since I first became obsessed with Bolívar, my admiration and loyalty had only grown. It was in part the blind admiration I felt for him that gave me the courage and conviction to work clandestinely on behalf of Peru's independence. The news of his impending arrival in Quito rekindled every adolescent emotion I had: I burned at the thought of his presence. In the past, Bolívar had seemed as far removed from my immediate world as a distant planet. Now, for the first time, we would be in the same city—in the same room. The trip to Catahuango to see my aunt about my inheritance would just have to wait.

I BARELY SLEPT that night. The invitation to attend the ball had arrived and today I knew I would meet him. I rose from bed and gave orders to prepare my bath. I immersed myself in a steaming bathtub full of fragrant herbs. Jonotás scrubbed every inch of my body, lathering it with French milled soap. I washed my hair with French shampoo. After the bath, I slipped on a simple white dress cut to leave my arms exposed. Natán wove my hair in braids—which gave me the appearance of a schoolgirl. In case he saw me before the ball, I wanted to exude the virginal essence I was sure would beckon him to me.

The victory parade would pass in front of my father's house. I enlisted everyone in the house to make crowns of laurel to throw to the patriots from my balcony. I waited all morning, never too far from the balcony, smoking cigars, refusing all food, monitoring the cheers of the crowd as they grew louder and louder, announcing the approach of the Liberator and his army of heroes. The bells of the churches of Quito had just tolled noon's twelfth bell when Bolívar appeared in his general's uniform, glorious on his white horse, Paloma Blanca. As he passed under my balcony, I tossed a laurel crown in his direction. I misjudged the force of my throw, and the crown hit him squarely on his forehead. The startled general yanked at his horse and Paloma Blanca reared up, nearly unseating him. I froze, stunned by the commotion I had created. Bolívar shot an angry look in the direction of the balcony and our eyes met. I smiled and cheered, *"Viva el Libertador!"* He did not return my smile or wave back, but I was sure I saw a gleam in his eyes signaling he forgave my incautious behavior. I knew then, almost immediately, that I could use this incident as a pretext to approach him at the ball later that evening and apologize for my faux pas.

As the hour for the ball approached, I chose my dress, gloves, fan, shoes, necklace, bracelets, earrings with such deliberateness as if I were preparing for my wedding. As a finishing touch, I proudly fastened to my black sash the glittering medal of Knight of the Order of the Sun. How many women in Quito could compete? I was going to make sure that once the general laid eyes on me, all the other women at the party would fade into the background.

At the ball, after the speeches and toasts, Bolívar asked to see a performance of an Ecuadorian folk dance. I volunteered immediately. This was my chance. As a girl I had been infamous in Quito society for my dancing. Unlike the other girls of my social class, who danced with precision and modesty, I had spent my childhood dancing with Natán and Jonotás who taught me to move with the abandon of their African bloodlines. I would have one chance to make an impression, and I would do it with my dance steps, my eyes, my hands, my smile, and the wiggle in my hips. I would have his total attention only once. There are some nights, and there are not too many of them in one's life, when you are perfectly illuminated, as though on stage, and for that instant you are the cynosure of all life around you. I had to seize that instant.

A partner was chosen for me. I barely looked at him. He might have been tall or short, handsome or ugly, I never noticed. I performed a *ñapanga*—not for my dance partner but for the general. I raised the hem of my dress above my ankles, thrust my shoulders and head back, and gyrated my hips. I twirled, flounced, strutted, and swayed. When it was over, I heard the rustling of dresses, the sound of ladies' fans stirring the air, the clinking of glasses, a polite cough or two, throats clearing, whispers creeping into the moment. My dancing had not been well received by the women, but I only cared about what *he* thought. I dared not look in his direction. I had never heard his voice, but when I heard someone exclaim *"Brava,"* I knew, because of the authority it commanded, it could only be his. He began to clap, and every one in the room joined him.

I was sipping a glass of champagne and receiving compliments from a group of unmarried men when one of the Liberator's aides-de-camp approached me and said, "Señora de

Thorne, the general requests the honor of your company." I felt dizzy as I followed the officer.

"*Brava,*" Bolívar repeated once I was in his presence. "Thank you for the pleasure of watching you dance. That was splendid."

"My general," I said, curtseying, avoiding eye contact, "I am Manuela Sáenz *de* Thorne," I emphasized the *de*, so he knew I was a married woman. Blushing, I added, "I'm the woman on the balcony who almost killed you with my laurel wreath. My dance was meant as an act of contrition. Will you ever forgive me?"

He laughed, full and throaty. "I know who you are. You are not only a marvelous dancer but also a heroine of Peruvian independence. We need more women like you, Señora *de* Thorne. Will you do me the honor of joining me for a drink?" His eyes bore into me as he offered me his arm. "It's very stuffy in here. Shall we go out on the terrace for some fresh air?" His voice rang with the complete confidence of a man who was used to getting what he wanted. What did I care what people thought? I placed my hand on the general's arm. I could feel his muscles under the fabric of his jacket and felt my blood rush to my head.

Followed by a steward with glasses of champagne, we walked out of the ballroom and onto the terrace overlooking Quito's plaza. In honor of the occasion it was illuminated with torches and various bonfires, around which soldiers and the people drank and sang songs of independence. The black of the sky was vivid, as if made of the finest black silk, and the shimmering frost of the stars looked as if it had been painted over with diamond dust.

Bolívar and I stood next to each other, alone, Quito at our

feet. The night air was brisk, and I shivered. He placed his glass of champagne on the railing of the balcony and said, "Allow me, *señora*, I don't want you to catch a cold because of my desire for fresh air." He removed his gold-embroidered red cape and draped it around my shoulders, his fingers brushing my bare arms. I could smell him, his perturbing maleness.

I wanted to be natural; I wanted my admiration to shine in my eyes so he could see it. "How long does Your Excellency plan to stay in Quito?" I asked, lapsing into my socialite role.

"I don't know," he said. "It depends on several things. But now that I've made your charming acquiantance, I'm not sure I want to leave Quito so quickly."

I pretended not to have heard his compliment. I did not blush nor did I giggle flirtatiously. I had to make him understand that I was different from the women he usually met. "While you are in Quito, my general," I said, "if there is anything I can do to advance the cause of independence, no matter what, no matter how small, all you have to do is ask. I'm ready to give my life for your ideal."

"My, my, are you always this . . . intense . . . this serious, Señora de Thorne?"

I was acting like a fool. I laughed.

"Actually, you *can* be of help to me," he said and looked at me with a seriousness which for a brief moment almost frightened me. "I understand you know General San Martín. I am interested in your impression of him. What kind of man is he?"

When General San Martín had entered Lima after the defeat of the Royalist forces, I was one of the patriots he had asked to meet so he could thank me for my work on behalf of our drive for independence. San Martín and my best friend, Rosita Campusano, who had first involved me in the struggle, had become lovers, and I was later invited to small dinners at the palace.

"Though I have met His Excellency," I said, "I would not presume to know him. However, one can learn a great deal about a man not from the way he is with strangers, in public, but from the way he treats those close to him. General San Martín treats his servants well, his men with respect, and the woman he loves as an equal."

"Very interesting." He sipped from his glass and looked away. He was still gazing into the distance when he said, "What was your sense of his plans for Peru? Is he a true republican, or does he want Peru to become a monarchy?"

"We're fighting these wars to do away with monarchies, Your Excellency."

"Yes, we are. But do you think San Martín wants to become king of Peru?" His sharp tone and the directness of his question surprised me. At that moment I caught a fleeting glimpse of the ruthlessness of the man who would stop at nothing to get what he wanted.

"I hope not," I said. "It would be a betrayal of our ideals. I don't believe he himself would want to be king. Yes, there are murmurs that he would like to bring to Peru a European prince to rule as monarch. That's what his enemies say. But I wouldn't presume to know what General San Martín's plans are for Peru."

"I am told you and the lady he loves are inseparable," Bolívar said, continuing his line of questioning.

"Rosita Campusano and I have been like sisters since our days in school here in Quito."

"Do you correspond with her? Has she written to you about the political situation in Lima?"

"I have heard this is a delicate moment, Your Excellency. Independence is still fragile. There's fear that the Spanish forces ensconced in the sierra could rally and attempt a take-over once more." I tried to hide my confusion. Did he want me for a spy and not a lover? Because of my intimacy with Rosita I was the only person in Quito who could provide him with the information he needed about San Martín. I was better informed of the situation in Peru and of San Martín's intentions, than anyone in Bolívar's camp. Perhaps this was how I might win his confidence—I was only too happy to do it. If Bolívar wanted me as a political ally, I would show him the honor would be mine. The longer I was in his presence, the more I could make him love me. Of this there was no doubt in my mind. Bolívar was my key. In aiding him I would no longer care about pursuing my inheritance, about escaping to Europe. Being with him was another way of setting myself free.

"Señora de Thorne," he continued, totally unaware of my thoughts, "my sources confirm what you've told me: the Spaniards are reorganizing their armies for an attack on Lima. General San Martín has sent emissaries to me, asking for my troops to come to the aid of the Peruvians. San Martín wants to rendezvous with me in Guayaquil, to discuss the future of Peru." Bolívar paused. "Can I trust him?"

"You can trust General San Martín," I said without hesitation. "From the few occasions I have met with him, and from what Rosita has told me, he doesn't appear to be a man blinded by ambition and glory. There's a real decency and honesty about General San Martín. I don't think he's the kind of man who would ask you to meet with him and then betray you. If he gives you his word of honor that he means peace, then by all means go."

"Thank you, *señora*. You have been most helpful."

Was he looking at me now in a different light, as someone of value, as an asset? Behind us, in the ballroom, the band played the first bars of a waltz.

"*Señora*," Bolívar asked, "would you do me the honor of dancing with me?"

I took his arm and we walked toward the center of the ballroom floor. We stopped under a chandelier ablaze with candles. Quickly, a wide circle formed around us. I could barely control my excitement. Bolívar took my hand in his and placed his arm around my waist. His hand on my back felt warm under my dress. He gently squeezed my hand. As I placed my hand on his shoulder, the aroma of his cologne aroused me. My face was burning; I looked away so he wouldn't see. Instead, I saw all eyes riveted on us, and then little else, as we spun around the dance floor. The grip of his hand was firm, as if he were already claiming me. From the first steps we took, our bodies were perfectly attuned, as if we had been dancing partners for many years. I could tell he loved to dance as much as I did: his eyes were charged with light as the music crescendoed. When our waltz ended, the guests applauded. Bolívar bowed and kissed my hand. I curtseyed, thanked him for the dance, and began to walk away. He caught my hand before I could leave and said, "Señora de Thorne, it's been a long time since I've enjoyed a waltz so much. Would you do me the honor of sharing the next dance with me, and then the one after that?"

Many of the guests joined us on the dance floor. As we twirled among them, the general plied me with questions about them. I told him I had just returned to Quito and that some in the crowd were unknown to me, but my lacking information did not stop our conversation. We held the floor for hours, laughing, stopping only for more champagne.

It was well past midnight when the Liberator invited me to join him in his room. I felt reckless from drinking, from his lavish attentions, the dancing, the pure intoxication of being close to so much power, to a man who was already a legend. I knew what the invitation meant for him. Another conquest. The general's conquests were not limited to the armies of Spain on the battlefield but included countless women, in his bed. The names of many of his lovers—Josefina Núñez, Isabel Soublette, and Fanny de Villars, among others—were well known across the Andes. What would he do if I refused him—for this night? Would I ever get another chance to be alone with him? I would have to proceed with caution. I was, after all, a married woman. I was determined to leave my husband, yet could I afford to live solely by my romantic impulses? I had done it once, eloping with Fausto D'Elhuyar when I was a student in the nuns' school, and the repercussions were grave. On the other hand, if I said yes to the general, a life I had long envisioned for myself might await me. I knew what to expect of my marriage with Thorne—with Bolívar the possibilities were infinite. And I would never find out the scope of those possibilities unless I acted on my desire. As for the people of Quito, I had already scandalized them once. To scandalize them once more, especially if it meant making happy the greatest man I had ever met, was an insignificant issue.

2

LIMA, PERU

1875

Natán

I am a woman of average intelligence, unlearned, an ex-slave at that. But unlike most slaves, I lived at the center of extraordinary events and greatness in the form of the people who liberated the countries of the Andes from Spain. I believe I have the right to tell my version of what happened because I lived the events, in my own flesh, and I am still alive.

It was always Jonotás did this, Jonotás did that. Without fail, my name is mentioned right after hers. Even now, fifty years later, when Manuela, Jonotás, Mr. Thorne, and General Bolívar are all dead, and those days have become part of the history taught to my children and grandchildren in the schools that teach the history of our march toward independence, my name still rates no more than a footnote.

But in truth, I never resented my background role. My life as a shadow. Early on, when we were still girls, I realized my best hope of survival was to play sidekick to the two of them.

Anyway, that was my nature, how God made me. Jonotás and
Manuela were creatures of extremes, scorching flames. I was
born to tread the middle. Jonotás used to say that the house
could burn and fall around me and I would stand there, immo-
bile as a rock. I wasn't extravagant like the two of them, but I
don't think even they appreciated, or could explain, the natural ease with which I took in the drama of that tumultuous
time.

As I am the only survivor of their legend, now and then I
am visited by young students of history who knock on my door
in search of my version of those times. I'm an old woman, with
few years left. Who's to prevent me from telling my own version of what happened? I learned about politics and history
by spying on the enemies of Manuela and the Liberator; serving Manuela and the general their meals (when they talked as
if we weren't there); cleaning their chamber pots; helping
Manuela to bathe, dress, and undress; serving drinks and emptying ashtrays at the *tertulias;* stoking their fires and washing
the bodies of their dead. This is how I came to know what I
know.

For over thirty years I followed Manuela as only a slave
will follow her mistress. Jonotás and I were seven years old
when we were taken to Catahuango to look after Manuela, who
was then three. Manuela's mother purchased Jonotás and me
at a public auction in Quito. We had been brought to Ecuador
along with our mothers and a group of slaves from our *palenque,*
San Basilio, on the Pacific coast of Colombia, formerly known
as Nueva Granada. San Basilio was founded by a band of run-
away slaves in the Chocó jungle on a strip of land by the sea.

These families—my family—had escaped from their owners in the provinces of Santa Marta and Cartagena.

We were ordered to shadow Manuela's every step in the house, in the garden, in the orchard, to make sure she did not harm herself in her restlessness. The hardest thing for Manuela to do was to keep still. Any chance she got she bolted into the fields like a wild filly. Even then we could tell her spirit was impatient with the daily routines of the hacienda. It was only a matter of time before she would outgrow us.

I saw a white person for the first time the day of the assault on San Basilio, which was the first day I knew as a slave. I knew white people existed beyond the jungle and on the other side of the sea because my family still lived in fear that their former owners would send bounty hunters to find them and take them back in chains. We knew the white people would not come from behind the mountains, because to get to the sea they had to wade through rivers and streams teeming with piranha, anacondas, and caimans, and forests infested with deadly vipers, bloodsucking bugs, and man-eating jaguars. Only Africans dared venture into the forest. So we lived in peace in San Basilio: the men fishing the sea, rivers, streams, and lagoons, hunting monkeys, birds, deer, and wild game; the women tending the fields of plantains, yucca, and yams; the children helping our mothers and bathing and drying our bodies under the afternoon sun. Sometimes we were visited by traders from nearby towns, Africans who had escaped to the Chocó, like us. They brought alarming news of slave ships that came ashore to raid the coastal palenques, of traders who made every effort to take our people back into slavery.

Some people make a point of forgetting the bad things that happened to them, and that's how they survive. All my life I have made it a point never to forget how my people were taken back into slavery.

When it happened, the men were taking their siestas in the hammocks hanging under the mango trees, the women and children were napping inside the houses on straw mattresses spread on the cool floor. I was dozing next to my mother and my little brother when I was awakened by a *prum, prum,* so loud, as if thunder had struck nearby. Then I heard people screaming: "*Ay, Ogún!* Protect us!"

"Come, come, get up," Ma said, pulling my hand. She lifted Juanito from the mattress and held him tightly to her breasts. I'd never seen such a look of fear in Mama's eyes. "We have to hide. Run," she said pushing me out of the house in the direction of the plantain groves behind our home. Outside, our people were running in all directions, screaming and crying. I saw white men wielding swords and machetes, some pointing their muskets at us; other men held back huge barking mastiffs with boiling red eyes. The powerful dogs on short leashes dragged the men behind them. The white men commanded, "Don't move. Stay where you are or we'll shoot."

The invaders herded us in the direction of the town's plaza, as we did with our own burros and pigs at sunset, so the jaguars would not eat them. The older women, who remembered their years as slaves, wailed inconsolably; and their children cried even louder, the terror in their mothers' eyes a sure sign their lives were changing forever. The men were quiet, a stunned fright in their eyes, like the glaze over the eyes of the unfortunates who glimpsed the evil spirits in the forest. I marched with Mama and Juanito, my father ahead of us.

We were corralled in the square. Moncho Corso and Ramón Eparsa, two of our men who had been wounded in the raid, were dragged to the middle of the circle. The mastiffs, with their big jaws, thick foamy tongues, pointed teeth and mad eyes, were let loose upon them. While Ramón and Moncho screamed in pain, the hounds tore the flesh off their bones. When the mauling had ended, the mastiffs fought each other, the earth beneath them black with blood, over the wriggling and squirming arms and legs that, although lifeless, still moved—like the severed tails of lizards, snakes, and iguanas, or like cut pieces of the giant earthworms that came out after the rains. I hid my head between my legs. Ma tapped on my shoulder and said, "Don't close your eyes, Natán. Look and remember. Remember always what white people will do to slaves."

The hungry mastiffs gorged themselves until they were so full they began to vomit chunks of flesh. Every time someone in the crowd moaned or started praying for mercy, one of the white men would scream, "Shut up, or the dogs will rip open your throat."

While the beasts devoured Moncho and Ramón, we were chained and ordered to remain seated on the ground. We sat there for hours, under the burning sun, thirsty, watching the long lines of red ants carry back to their mounds small pieces of bleeding flesh, and the vultures circling, a dark cloud overhead, waiting for the chance to reap their share of the scraps. We watched as the white men went into our homes and took our tools, the fabrics we made, the gold nuggets we found in the streams near our village.

At twilight, flocks of *alcaravanes* in the trees at the edge of the forest sang a mournful and angry song, as if they were saying good-bye to us. Night fell and with it came swarms of mosquitoes that bled us until the sun rose. My consolation was that I'd been chained next to Mama and Juanito, though Papa had been separated and chained with a group of men.

An overcast sky hid the moon. The mosquitoes, the hooting of the owls high in the trees, the cries of night birds, and the flapping wings of the bloodsucking bats that flew over our heads kept me awake. Close to morning, I fell asleep, my head against Ma's shoulder. The first rays of the sun and the renewed crying of the women and children opened my eyes. The air was filled with the smell of decomposing flesh. With every breath, we took in the airborne remains of the people we loved.

Later that day we were transported to the ship waiting for the haul offshore. Only the old and the sick were left behind in San Basilio. Strung in chains, each of us like a dark-colored bead in a necklace, we were thrown belowdecks. There we remained, rocked by the waves of the ocean, cold, wet, and seasick, covered in our own vomit and excrement. People who died on the voyage were thrown in the sea only when their maggots threatened to invade the ship's provisions and the smell was so bad it made the men who fed us sick. In the darkness, day and night became one. We all wondered if we'd ever see land again. An elder said he thought we were sailing toward Panama City, on our way to the provinces of Santa Marta and Cartagena. The people who had been slaves said they wished they had died in the raid rather than go back to the life they were once lucky enough to have escaped from.

Now and then we received a cup of water and a soggy biscuit, which kept us from starving. When the ship finally docked, we emerged into the sunlight looking like human sores. My little brother, Juanito, collapsed into a sack of skin and bones, all the blood sucked from his body. We were not in Panama but in Guayaquil, Ecuador. The men who'd captured us were not bounty hunters taking us back to Nueva Granada, my father said, they were slave traders who planned to sell us in Ecuador. "We're cimarrones," Pa said. "Nobody wants to buy cimarrones because we always try to run away the first chance we get. But here people won't know that, so they won't have trouble getting a good price for us."

Nobody had to tell me the happy days of my life were over. Guayaquil was a large port town, its bay clogged with sea vessels of all sizes. Whites, Indians, people who looked like both, slaves, and people with hair the color of gold, who spoke in languages I did not understand, rushed about. I had seen only our homes in San Basilio, but there were many big buildings in Guayaquil. My pa, who had been a slave in Cartagena, explained to me the different kinds of people and what each big building was for. When I heard the bells of a church toll for the first time, I screamed—it felt like my head had been filled with dry coconuts knocking against each other.

Our people were confined in a corral in the outskirts of town. The sick were tended to, and we were given plenty of water to wash ourselves and abundant food. They wanted us to look like our former healthy selves. People came to gawk at us, inspecting our legs and arms, as if we were valuable animals. Outside the corral, vendors congregated to peddle their wares. My father was taken from that fattening pen and sold to someone who, I would find out, put him to work in the Amazon.

Soon after, many of the women and their children were put in wagons and each one given a potato sack. We were told to hold on to them because we would need them to protect us from the cold. The wagons started in the direction of the sierra, and we soon entered a cold, misty world, a land of ice-capped mountains and smoking volcanoes where instead of monkeys, jaguars, and *alcaravanes*, I saw for the first time llamas, alpacas, guanacos, and huge condors. It was a land of Indians, chestnut-colored people of small stature who spoke in their own language. These Indians were not like the easily scared ones who lived in the forest beyond San Basilio and who avoided us. The Andean Indians were everywhere. Underneath their taciturn ways I could see that they, like the slaves, were full of hatred for white people. Their eyes said it all. They were also suspicious of us.

At the end of the long journey, we were sold in the main plaza of Quito. Jonotás and I were separated from our mothers, and fate blessed us by allowing us to be sold together. For many years I cried, remembering the day. I stopped crying when I finally understood that tears would not change anything; that I had to conserve my energy if I wanted to survive.

At first, Manuela treated us with the affection she showed her lap dog—something lovable that wasn't quite human. As her slaves, we were supposed to bathe, groom, feed, and play with her. Her favorite game was to dress us up in costumes, as if we were her living dolls. The other slaves and Indian servants in Catahuango often reminded Jonotás and me that we were lucky, because house slaves did not have to toil in the fields doing backbreaking work, and we did not have to live with the other slaves in flea-ridden and rat-infested huts on Negro Row, sleeping one on top of the other like dogs do to keep warm on cold nights. We got to eat the scraps of meat that were left from the family's table, not the boiled potatoes and roasted corn that the other slaves lived on. At night we rolled out straw mats on the cold wooden floor by Manuela's bed, in case she woke up crying, thirsty, or needing to use the chamber pot.

Manuela's mother, Doña Joaquina, was the saddest woman I'd ever seen—like a lost soul in purgatory. From her bed, she tried to run the affairs of Catahuango, and made sure Manuela was well cared for. She was so ill with consumption that Manuela was seldom brought to her bedroom to see her. Doña Joaquina was known among her slaves and Indian servants on the hacienda as a kind mistress. Fortunately for Jonatás and me, Manuela was her mother's daughter in that respect.

Just months after we arrived in Catahuango, Doña Joaquina's illness got worse, a doctor arrived from Quito, and two days later she was dead. The day Doña Joaquina died, her mother and sister and brother arrived in Catahuango to take the body back to Quito, where they buried her. Manuela's aunt, Doña Ignacia, and grandmother, Doña Gregoria, settled in Catahuango to raise Manuela and run the hacienda. After they moved in, it was as if the icy top of a volcano had formed over the hacienda.

When Manuela asked about her mother, she was told Doña Joaquina had gone to Quito to see the doctor and that she would return soon. Manuela cried and cried, but neither her grandmother nor her aunt knew how to comfort her. At first they tried to quiet her down by giving her toys, then a puppy, but as the days came and went, and Manuela continued crying for her mother, they were happy to let Jonatás and me comfort her. As long as we kept the crying child out of sight, we were allowed many small freedoms.

Jonatás and I discovered that if we sang to her, Manuela would fall asleep quickly and peacefully. In her bedroom, at night, after everyone went to bed, we sang so softly nobody heard us. We remembered a few songs we'd learned in San Basilio.

"Sing the one about your mothers," Manuela would request. After she learned the words, she sang with us:

> *O Mama, O Mama, where are you, Mama?*
> *Good-bye, Mama; good-bye everybody.*
> *Good-bye to our people.*
> *Good-bye to the* platanal.
> *Good-bye, Hallelujah.*
> *Good-bye, Mama, sweet Mama.*
> *Good-bye to your kisses*
> *And the sweet sea where we bathed.*
> *Good-bye, sweet-milked* cocoteros.
> *Good-bye, dear Mama.*
> *Good-bye, dear friends.*
> *Good-bye all, good-bye.*

After Manuela fell asleep, Jonotás and I would huddle in the darkness and shed tears for our own families. We reserved our sadness for the darkness—if we were caught crying in daylight, we'd be punished for being ungrateful.

The more time that passed, the blurrier my mother's features became. It was as if I saw her through a curtain of fog; the sound of her voice and the smell of her breasts as she hugged me became fainter, the feel of her fingers on my head as she combed my hair looking for lice before she braided it faded. Jonotás and I used to play a game. We'd say to each other, "Tell me what my ma looked like," and then we would recall details about the other's mother. One day I realized what I remembered was not Ma, but Jonotás's version of her.

I never stopped longing for Mama. Years later, when we were brought from Catahuango to Quito to live in Don Simón's house, every time I saw a Negro woman of a certain age walking the streets I'd follow her for a few blocks, wondering whether or not she was my mother. Sometimes in the market, I would see a Negro I didn't recognize, whether a man or a woman, who looked as if he or she had been brought to Quito from Nueva Granada. I would approach these strangers, introduce myself, and ask if they knew a Negro woman named Julia, about forty years old, married to Nemesio, from the *palenque* of San Basilio in Nueva Granada. People always shook their heads—no one knew anything. It was as if my mother had been thrown into the mouth of the smoking volcano I now lived near and had turned to dust. I refused to give up the hope that my mother was somewhere in Ecuador, perhaps not even far from Quito. When I found her, I would ask Manuela to buy her from her owners and bring her to live with us.

MANUELA STOPPED ASKING about her mother, and only once in a while would she cry at night, calling for Doña Joaquina. Manuela's aunt and grandmother did not try to console her. It was as if the sight of her reminded them of something bad. When Manuela sensed that the Aispurus would never give her affection, she turned to us. It was then that we became her family, the only people at Catahuango she could trust, and we grew to love her, and she us, despite the difference in the color of our skin.

Jonotás and I were young girls but we knew that slaves were bought and sold, and that the defiant ones were branded with hot irons; the women were branded on their foreheads and cheeks with their master's initials. We had heard about cruel masters who routinely killed their rebellious slaves, without having to answer to the law. We understood that our best chances of living the most tolerable life a slave girl could expect would come from Manuela's protection. We belonged to her by law, and only Manuela could dispose of us.

Those few years after Doña Joaquina's death, and before Manuela, at age seven, was sent away to Quito to board with the nuns, were—despite the loss of our families, despite our not being free—among the happiest years of my life. With Manuela we were allowed to play, to be children, to sing and laugh. As long as we kept Manuela out of trouble, we were fed, clothed, and spared the angry lash of the slavemaster's whip, the ultimate sign of the hellish life of a slave.

QUITO AND PANAMA

1800–1817

Manuela

I have only one blurry memory of my mother: bedridden and gaunt, eyes dilated, clutching a handkerchief spotted scarlet. One day my mother was taken to Quito and I was not allowed to say good-bye. Eventually I understood that my mother was never coming back to Catahuango, that she was dead. A heavy lock was placed on the door of her bedroom, never to be opened again, at least not in my presence. I longed for something that reminded me of my mother—a cameo, a lace handkerchief, a ring, a fan, but all her personal objects disappeared. Worse, her name was never spoken, as if she had never existed. I cherished the only measure of her existence, that one memory of her, sickly and in bed.

Of my father, on the other hand, I had no memory at all. I grew up wondering who he was. I waited and waited for my relatives to tell me about my father. They never did. I was afraid to ask, afraid of the answer. Was he dead, too? And if he was alive, why didn't he come to see me?

Shortly after my sixth birthday, I finally summoned the courage to question Aunt Ignacia about him. "Manuela, you ask too many questions," she snapped. The way Ignacia spoke, as though any mention of my father were a taboo subject, instantly silenced me. I would have to figure out another way to find out who my father was, and where he lived.

One day, playing with Jonotás and Natán in the orchard, I asked them if they knew where their parents were.

"They don't tell slaves where they take their families after they sell them," said Jonotás.

"Was my father sold, too?"

The girls giggled nervously. Natán said, "No, Manuela, you're white. You are our mistress. White people are not sold. Your father was not a slave."

I pondered why some people were bought and sold and others were not, but it seemed like too big a question to ask. "I know my mother is in heaven. But where is my father?"

Jonotás said, "I don't know." She screwed up her face in that way she had that told me she was thinking. "If you like, I can try to find out from one of the servants."

That night, in my bedroom, after the candle was snuffed, Jonotás got up from her mattress on the floor and climbed into my bed. She whispered in my ear, "Cook says your *papá* lives in Quito." I embraced and kissed Jonotás and thanked her for this news. Happiness and curiosity kept me wide awake that night.

The next morning, during my daily reading lesson with Aunt Ignacia, shaking with excitement and fear, I said, "*Tía*, I know my father lives in Quito. I want to meet him."

She clapped shut the catechism we were reading. "Who told you that?"

"Nobody," I said, not wanting Jonotás to get in trouble. Before my aunt had a chance to question me further, I flung the book against the wall, stomped on the wooden floor, and screamed, "I want to see my father! I want to see him!"

"Listen to me, Manuela," Ignacia barked, "your father has a wife and children of his own. He doesn't want to see you. You're his illegitimate child. You're an embarrassment to him. Just like you are to us."

"You're a liar! My father loves me!" I yelled. I got up from the chair, shoved it aside, disregarding whatever punishment Ignacia would surely devise for me. I bolted from the room and ran out of the house to the orchard, where I found a grassy spot under a peach tree, threw myself down, and sobbed, while tearing out clumps of grass with my hands and teeth. Jonotás and Natán found me, and Jonotás took me in her arms, and Natán stroked my forehead, but I continued shaking and screaming until finally I collapsed, exhausted.

That night, by the candle in my bedroom, I composed the first of countless letters I would write to my father. Dipping a quill in the inkwell, I wrote: "Dear *Papá*: I am Manuela. I live in Catahuango. Can you come to see me? Your daughter."

I blew my breath on the ink to dry it, folded the letter, put it inside an envelope I had taken from my uncle's office, and used his seal to close it. When this was done, I realized I did not know how to send a letter. Worse, I realized I did not know what my father's name was. I felt as insignificant in this world as a tiny ant. My heart filled with venom for Aunt Ignacia.

The day she told me the truth was the first time I heard the words "illegitimate child." From then on, until I became a grown woman, those words, more than any others, had the power to wound and humiliate me. I would hear them used against me by the nuns at school. They used "illegitimate" as a way of setting me apart from the other girls, as a way of marking me tainted, impure. As I grew older, I understood that all of us *criollos* were "illegitimate"—and therefore inferior—in the eyes of the Spaniards. It was from this that my lifelong contempt for the Spanish Crown grew. Long before I knew there were battles being fought in South America to liberate my people, the descendants of the Spaniards born on South American soil, I wanted more than anything else to see the Spaniards, with their smug superiority, with their hypocritical Catholicism, thrown off our land and sent back to Spain, humiliated. I wanted them to have a taste of the shame and disgrace I suffered at the hands of my family and the nuns. I became convinced even as a child that I would never be free of the label of illegitimacy until we were free of Spain.

WHEN I WAS seven, my aunt informed me that I was being sent to Santa Catalina, a school in Quito where the daughters of "good" families were educated by the Concepta nuns. "We had to pay them a fortune," Ignacia said at dinner the night before I left Catahuango for school, "so they would overlook the circumstances of your birth. Make sure you do well in school, Manuela. We're making a great sacrifice for you, and I'm not sure you deserve it. But it's the least we can do. After all, you carry our name."

I was sad to part from Jonotás and Natán, but I looked forward to moving away from my loveless relatives and meeting other girls my age. I had hopes that the sisters, who were married to Christ and devoted to doing good works, would be kind and maternal. I so longed to have a mother. My hopes were quickly dashed. In class, when I raised my hand if I knew an answer, other girls were called on first. I never received any praise for my homework, even when I consistently got the highest grades, and I never got treats at dinner—a piece of fruit or a pastry—like some of the other girls did.

The Virgin Mary, Mother of God, was my only consolation. I prayed to her, so full of love for all humans, to ease my misery. If no grown-up showed me affection, she would be my source of love. I became a devotee of the Virgin, and learned many prayers to her. Often, during our daily noon break, when all the other girls went out on the grounds for some fresh air, I would head for the chapel and pray on my knees to the Blessed Mother, begging her to make the nuns treat me as kindly as they treated the girls of "good" families.

During my first year in school, as May, the month devoted to the Virgin, approached, preparations were made for daily celebrations to be held. All the girls were assigned duties to perform, to show their devotion to the Virgin. Some were put in charge of arranging the flowers on the altar, or changing the water in the vases every day, or lighting the candles in the chapel and scraping the wax of the candles that melted onto the wooden floors. I waited and waited for a task to be assigned to me, but I was one of the few girls who was not chosen to serve in the Virgin's name. Even though the nuns frightened me—I had seen them use a length of cane to spank the few girls who dared to raise their voices in protest—I went to see the Mother Superior in her office. Dizzy with fear, I heard her say, "Come in."

"Manuela Sáenz," she said frowning, "what are you doing here? You're supposed to be in class."

My knees were knocking against each other, but I had to speak. "I want to know why I haven't been chosen to serve the Virgin Mary during the month of May, Reverend Mother," I piped.

"Come here," the Mother Superior said, motioning me to approach her desk. I felt faint. When I was so close I could feel her breath on my face, she said, "Children like you, Manuela Sáenz, born of unholy unions, are not worthy of serving the Mother of God. The Virgin only accepts girls who are innocent. You're lucky that we took you in. But I'm warning you, if you're going to be a troublemaker, we will send you back to your aunt. Understood? Now, for the rest of the time you're a pupil here, I forbid you to mention this subject again. Remember, you're an unfortunate girl unworthy of serving the Holy Mother of Our Savior Jesus Christ. Go to class—at once."

My hatred of the Catholic Church was born that very day. I stopped praying to the Virgin after that. If it was true that I was unworthy of serving her, if she could not protect me from the cruelty of the nuns, why should I spend hours on my knees asking for her help? With the passage of the years, that poisonous feeling evolved into the conviction that there could not be a God if he allowed so much suffering and injustice on earth. And if he did exist, then what good was he to us?

FOR THE NEXT TEN YEARS, the black-veiled bloodless Conceptas kept me on my knees, every day for hours praying and reciting the rosary, sometimes for weeks at a time, during what should have been the most carefree days of my life. The nuns believed in mortification of the flesh: cold baths in the winter and hot baths in the summer, and endless fasts, as if we were training to be fakirs, or soldiers in the armies of Sparta.

The school day began at five-thirty, when every object we touched was still coated by an icy film left by the glacial night air. After we washed our faces in cold water and got dressed, we were herded into the chapel for a period of introspection, which was followed by the Holy Mass. By the time mass was over, I was grateful to receive my one cup of chocolate and slice of unbuttered bread.

There were two more masses during the day: one before the noon meal and the other one at vespers. To cap the day, before we went to bed we had to say an interminable rosary. We had to endure this torture to learn how to embroider gold on silk, to knit and darn stockings, to make ribbons and lace, to sew on buttons, to stitch shirts, skirts, shawls, and all sorts of white plain undergarments, to indicate virginal purity. The nuns also taught us to read Latin so we could recite archaic prayers, and study pious texts about the lives of saints who mortified their flesh.

Those days in school were like being interred in a chilly mausoleum. Indeed, in many parts of the building, one could smell the faintly sweet stench of the nuns buried in the convent. Each day we had to pass through the terrifying galleries hung with large portraits of dead nuns, painted in their coffins, their faces withered, severe. Though the nuns were wearing crowns of flowers and lavish shrouds, they did not look as they did in life, but as if they had been mummified for centuries. Almost without exception, an expression of contempt for the world showed on each of their faces, which seem to be saying, "Life is suffering, the world is a terrible place."

The nuns' favorite texts to instruct us with were hagiographies of other nuns, especially those who had become holy saints, a reward for their terrifying visions of mortification. We memorized long passages from these books and recited them in class every day. These visions were violent, bloody, filled with cannibalism and dismemberments. They gave me nightmares. During the day, when I found myself alone in the chapel or walking down a corridor with a portrait of a beheaded saint, my throat would close and I could not breathe. Of all the visions, none was more hair-raising than those of Jerónima, a nun who had lived sequestered in a convent in Santa Fe de Bogotá. Her vision of being placed inside an oven ablaze, watching her own body charring, but feeling her heart still beating, made me ill. Often, before we were put to bed, Sister Carmenza would read us one of Jerónima's visions, just to remind us that we were put in the world to suffer. Nightly, before the candle was snuffed, we listened to Carmenza repeat in a lugubrious tone: "You do not know death, you yourselves are death; it has the face of each and everyone of you, and you are nothing but the reflections of your own death. What you call to die, is to finish dying and what you call to be born is to begin to die and what you call to live is the slow death of dying."

Many years later I discovered that the great poet Francisco de Quevedo had written that passage. Yet the nuns had managed to take out of context his poetic words and turned them into something so harrowing that I often cried myself to sleep.

Most distressing of all was that the shutters of all the windows of the school that faced the street were nailed shut. This was to prevent us from setting our eyes on men other than the priests who visited the school. The nuns explained that the only way for us to pray to God in a state of purity was to never be tempted by images of men. Our souls must be like stainless crystals, they said, so that our prayers could reach Christ's ears. Seeing men, even from afar, would prevent us from hearing the secret voice with which Christ—our intended husband—spoke to his future wives.

IT WAS DURING THIS TIME that I learned my father had been born in a hamlet in the region of Burgos, that he had left Spain as a young man and settled in Ecuador, where he prospered serving as tax collector of the bishopric of Quito and president for life of the Council of the Catholic Church. He was married to Juana del Campo, a lady from the city of Popayán, in Nueva Granada, with whom he had several children. All this news was gathered by my only friend at school, Rosita Campusano, a girl from Guayaquil who on weekends went to see her guardian in Quito. As our friendship grew, Rosita confided in me that she, too, was "illegitimate." Like me, she had been accepted by the nuns because of her family's wealth. In order to get an illegitimate girl accepted, the family had to make a large monetary donation to the school. Our education, like our lives themselves, was nothing more than the end result of a series of corrupt choices.

WHAT GIRL DOES NOT love her father, even if he is a bad one? I would daydream in class about the day—soon, very soon—when he would come see me and explain the reasons for his silence. My father would be kind and loving, and he would rescue me from the Aispurus and be my protector for the rest of my life. Rosita found out his address and I wrote to him, introducing myself and asking him to visit me at Santa Catalina. Whenever we received our mail, I held my breath, hoping there would be a reply from him. But though I wrote to him many times, begging him to take me away from Santa Catalina, I never got a word from him.

How could my own father be so cold and uncaring? Were not all fathers supposed to love their daughters? As the years passed, my longing to see him lessened and evolved into a rancorous desire for revenge. One day I would become the most important woman in Ecuador and my father and his family would finally acknowledge me and seek my company. I would then publicly humiliate him and his family, treating them as strangers.

It dawned on me that even if nobody believed in me, or encouraged me, it was up to me to forge a great destiny for myself. My chances were good, I knew. I was more intelligent than most of my dense classmates; and everyone, even the ungenerous Aispurus, praised my beauty. Furthermore, I knew with certainty that I was heir to my mother's fortune. Once I came of age, Catahuango would legally belong to me. With my wealth, I would devise my own future: I would pick and choose any husband I desired. I would sell the hacienda and move to Paris. There I would open a salon where all the great people of the age would be regulars. Novels and plays would be written about me; lovestruck poets would dedicate books of sonnets to me. A European prince, a king—or at least a duke—would fall in love with me, and I would command the full respect saved for European royalty. This is where my dream got complicated. Even then I hated the idea of inherited titles, which I saw as one more despicable legacy from Spain. The only nobility I ever acknowledged was that of the men and women who achieved great deeds. The German explorer and scientist Alexander von Humboldt was my idea of nobility. Perhaps I might even meet von Humboldt, and he would take me on as a disciple and teach me everything he knew. And I would become an explorer, and write scientific books, and climb the highest volcanoes in Ecuador. In 1802 he had almost succeeded in climbing to the top of Chimborazo, which was thought to be the highest mountain in the known world—and a mountain that no man would ever conquer. But, most important, I adored von Humboldt because I had read, in a subversive newspaper Rosita brought me from the outside, that he had said that the South American continent was ripe for revolution.

Rosita and I became close friends because, as the only illegitimate girls in school, the nuns treated us as outcasts. Two other bonds united us: our passionate love of reading and our interest in anything the nuns did not teach us. Rosita and I pooled our allowances so that she was able to buy books and bring them from the outside. Rosita had bribed a servant in her guardian's home to buy her novels and books about history. Most books that dealt with contemporary issues were forbidden and were sold clandestinely.

The other bond we shared was that even at that early age we both dreamed of the day when South America would become free of its Spanish chains. The time for revolution was now. Though the papers could not publish any commentary that was critical of the Spanish monarchy, and news from Spain took months, sometimes years, to reach South America, once it reached the continent, it spread through the land like lit gunpowder.

Even the Royalists in Ecuador could not hide their alarm at the decadence of the Spanish court. Carlos IV and his promiscuous wife, Queen María Luisa, were hated by their own people, whom they kept in dire poverty and ignorance. Rumors reached Ecuador that the heir to the throne, their son Ferdinand, was a monster who had already tried to poison his own parents. That this prince was beloved by the Spanish people could only mean that the reign of the Bourbons was as decadent as the last days of the Roman Empire. So in 1808, when Napoleon Bonaparte installed his brother Joseph on the Spanish throne, it became obvious that Spain would soon be all too consumed by its mounting crisis to be able to contain the growing sentiment for South American independence.

It was around that time that, among the printed materials Rosita managed to smuggle into school by wrapping it around her chest and back under her clothes, we read "The Declaration of the Rights of Man and of Citizens," written by the National Assembly of France. I had heard about the French Revolution, though both at home and at school it was always deplored as an example of the unfortunate consequence of allowing the masses to govern themselves. I memorized the seventeen points of the manifesto, though perhaps I only understood the first one: "Men are born, and always continue, free, and equal in respect of their rights." That was enough to sustain me during those years when I was made to feel inferior because of the circumstances of my birth. Those first words of the French "Declaration of the Rights of Man" would seal my fate.

I LIVED FOR the school holidays when I could leave the convent for Catahuango, where I'd spend my days horseback riding with Jonotás and Natán. We were inseparable; we called ourselves the Three Musketeers. Jonotás, my favorite, had grown into a wiry, vivacious girl with a thatch of black curls, a long neck and torso, and the strong legs of a mountain climber. She was also an irrepressible prankster who, encouraged by me, loved to mimic the Aispurus.

Natán, though shorter, was the prettier one. She had big, golden eyes and features so delicate they seemed drawn with a sharp-tipped pencil. Natán was not a boisterous tomboy like Jonotás; she had the demure manners of a lady. But despite her quiet nature, she was a willing collaborator in whatever mischief Jonotás and I instigated. She understood that Jonotás and I had a special bond and did not seem jealous of our intimacy. Natán seemed content just to be included. Her dream was to one day live an independent life and have her own family. I promised her that when I grew up I'd free her. I loved Natán's sweetness of demeanor and felt more protective of her than of Jonotás, who was quite capable of fending for herself.

Though the Aispurus disapproved of my attachment to the girls, they were relieved not to have to look after me all the time. When I returned to the convent, I spent many cold nights wide awake reliving the happy times with my girls, my true family.

On Sundays, when most students left the school for the afternoon with their parents or relatives, or their guardians in Quito, I remained in Santa Catalina, reading in the library. Aunt Ignacia only took me home for the major holidays. I sought in books the knowledge that was withheld from us girls. I found solace in the forbidden activity of reading novels, ro-

mantic and exciting tales that transported me far away from
the convent's clammy, chilly walls. I read and reread Rousseau's *La Nouvelle Heloise*, which Rosita had smuggled into
school. Like Rousseau's heroine, I longed to be struck by passion, to violate the strictures of society, and be redeemed by
love. Reading sustained me, confirmed my belief that there
were other worlds larger and more thrilling than the one I
lived in.

Now and then other girls invited me to visit their homes on
Sunday, but the nuns forbade it. They never provided an explanation, yet I knew it was because of my bastard status. This
was another way of reminding me of my inferiority, that I was
one with whom girls from proper families should not socialize. The nuns' enforced shunning had its intended effect—
loneliness became a habit for me. To allay my suffering, I lived
for the day when I would get away from the nuns, from my
relatives, and from Quito itself.

One Sunday afternoon, four days before my fifteenth
birthday, Sor Lorena came to the library, where, as usual, I was
reading and told me to put on my best clothes because I had a
visitor. I noted that Sor Lorena said "*a visitor*," so it couldn't be
Jonotás and Natán, who usually came together once a month,
carrying a basket of fruits, butter, cheese, and pastries from
Catahuango. They also brought the toiletry articles I asked my
aunt for in letters.

In my room I rinsed my face and hands, brushed my hair
and tied it back with a ribbon. I was excited by this surprise in
my routine. In the room where visitors were received, a lone
gentleman sat in a chair near the window. I took two steps in

his direction and then stopped. The man had my oval-shaped face, my alabaster complexion, my abundant and glossy black hair, my copious eyebrows and large black eyes. As he rose from his chair neither of us moved. I stopped breathing until he spoke.

"Come here, Manuela."

I stood in front of him and curtseyed.

"I'm your father," he said, confirming my intuition.

I sat down across from him, mute, and looked out the open window into a courtyard with a dry fountain in the middle of a garden with a solitary fig tree. This was one of the few windows in the school that was not shuttered, perhaps so that visitors would not find it too oppressive. On each corner of the square that formed the garden was a small bed of pinkish carnations. In the dim, misty light, the garden had a deathly look. To the north, above the red clay tiles of the convent, Cotopaxi's icecap was swathed in an ashen shroud of mist. I kept staring at the volcano, as if mesmerized. I bit my lower lip to fight the tears rushing into my eyes and clasped my hands to stop them from trembling. I was afraid that if I opened my mouth to speak to him I would spew toads, vipers, scorpions. My heart was beating so fast I could hear it pounding.

My father remained standing. I heard him say, "Manuela, you've certainly inherited your mother's beauty."

I turned to look at my smiling father. "Sir," I said coldly, "why have you come? I do not need you now. As for my beauty, I played no part in it. And my mother's beauty only ruined her."

He sat down, took out a perfumed handkerchief, and blew his nose. I wanted to run from the room, hide in my bedroom, bury my face in my pillow.

"Manuela, please believe me when I say I could not have

come earlier. I am a married man with a family. My wife would not have understood."

"But she understands now? Is that what you're saying, sir? Well, did you ever stop to think the shame your silence caused me? Or how much I would suffer because of your carelessness? I am afraid you've come much too late." I wanted him to feel all the loathing I had for him, for his horrible wife and children.

"You do need me, *hija mía*," he said, ignoring my anger. "In a few years you'll be of marrying age, and no man from a good family will want you for a wife unless I acknowledge you publicly as my daughter."

So, was he here because the Aispurus had asked him to come? I wondered how much money they had promised him if he would acknowledge his paternity. "Let me assure you, sir," I heard myself say in a shrill voice, "that I have no desire to marry—if that's what concerns you. When I come of age, I'll have my own money. I won't need a husband to take care of me."

"Stop talking nonsense, Manuela," he said. "I am your father and you owe me respect. Beginning next Sunday you'll come to my house for the day, and you'll spend school holidays with us. My wife and your brother and sisters look forward to embracing you as one of their own. It's true I have been a bad father," he said as he rose to leave, "but all that has changed as of today. I hope you will come to love me in the same way I already love you."

Now that I had met him, I hated him even more for his hypocrisy. How could he claim to love me after spending only a few minutes with me? This was not a man I could trust. This was a man who could say anything, whether he meant it or not, in order to get what he wanted. That was how he had ruined my mother.

I BECAME A member of the Sáenz del Campo family. Though I was predisposed to dislike my stepmother, I found no serious reasons to complain about Doña Juana del Campo. She treated me, the awkward new addition to the family, with formality; and my sisters, the sisters I had known from afar and been envious of for years, welcomed me with courtesy. Clemencia and Josefa were two and three years older than I, and were solely interested in talking about new dresses, parties, and young men who were good marriage prospects. My first Sunday at my father's house, my half sisters left to visit a friend and did not take me along. When my father discovered what had happened, he summoned my sisters in my presence and told them that from that day on, without exception, they had to include me in all facets of their social life. Clemencia turned to me and, her voice dripping with insincerity, said, "We apologize, Manuela. Believe us that it was just an oversight. We did not mean to slight you." I suspect that this forced apology caused them to feel even more resentment toward me, though they behaved with a measure of grace and never excluded me again.

My sisters' silliness was bearable only on account of my brother, José María, who had been born the same year as I. From our first encounter I recognized, from the gleam in his eye, that he was a dreamer like me. And he loved riding as much as I did. It was during our rides together that our intimacy grew into a loving bond. His devotion to me also meant that my sisters had indeed to accept me as a permanent addition to the clan.

Although the seed of revolution already grew in my heart, the love of my new brother was so genuine that I forgave him for enlisting in the Royalist army. Given time, I told myself, I would convince him that the only defensible position for a patriot was to join the *independentistas* fighting to end the rule of the Spanish Crown. Still, I envied the male freedom that allowed my brother to leave the stifling family home—even if it was to join the abominable army of Spain.

I began to look forward to the Sunday visits at my father's home. After the early dinner that followed noon mass, José María and I, if the weather permitted, rode to the foot of El Panecillo, where we tethered our horses and then hiked to the top of the mountain. On clear days, gazing at the snowcapped volcanoes, we let our imaginations roam free and dreamed of glorious futures where we'd be happy, in love, and could prove our valor in battle. I saw myself fighting in the great battles for independence, felling the enemy with my gun, charging with the cavalry, wielding a lance against the Spanish troops, nursing our wounded soldiers. Though my desire to one day prove my bravery on the battlefield amused my brother, he did not laugh at my illusions, peculiar though they were. Nothing was said of the fact that our fantasies found us fighting in opposite armies.

MY FIRST APPEARANCE with the Sáenz del Campo family at Sunday mass created an awkward situation when, after mass,

the other families gathered on the steps of the cathedral to socialize. I was introduced as my father's daughter—no other
explanation was offered. Most people were cool but acted cour-
teously enough, out of deference to my father. By my second or
third appearance, quiteños got used to the idea that I was a permanent member of the family, although I was certain they
continued to question my status behind my back. I was sure I
was an object of gossip and scorn.

My father now represented to me my best hope to leave the
nuns and get away from the Aispurus, who would have been
just as happy to see me take vows and be forever immured in a
convent. As if to make up for the years when he was absent,
Father made sure that Quito society knew how sincerely proud
and defensive he was of me. Any young man who came near
me was the subject of severe scrutiny. His custodial zeal made
me uncomfortable. Sometimes I felt my sisters resented the
way in which I came to take such a prominent place in our father's affection. He constantly praised my beauty and intelligence, and would not deny me any of my wishes.

I decided to exploit his guilt. At the time of our sixteenth
birthday, the nuns allowed each student to have a personal
maid who brought her food from the outside, cleaned her cell,
washed and ironed her clothes, and helped her get dressed. At
the end of the day, the maids went home. I asked Father to
bring my girls to Quito to look after me, and he granted my
request. From then on, they only returned to Catahuango for
visits, much to their relief. Jonotás became my personal maid,
while Natán became an indispensable housekeeper in my father's household.

Though I still could not forgive Father for all the unneces-

sary pain his neglect had caused me, I did begin to call him
"*Papá*" instead of "Don Simón." I wished, though, that when I
called him "*Papá*" it came from my heart.

MY FRIENDSHIP WITH Rosita Campusano made the years in
the convent bearable. Though we were the same age, Rosita
was shorter and smaller in every way. She was perfectly pro-
portioned, like a miniature doll. Rosita's father was a Spanish
businessman who owned stores in Guayaquil, Quito, and Lima.
His shops sold fabrics, buttons, ribbons, laces, hats, and other
feminine accessories, which meant that Rosita never lacked
for such things and generously shared them with me.

Rosita was my ally against the nuns, who never stopped reminding us that they were doing us a favor by allowing us to
study with our betters. The Mother Superior's favorite form of
humiliation was to ask me each year to present proof that my
father had legally acknowledged me as his daughter. At the
beginning of each school year I was called into her office to be
warned that I might not be invited to return to school the following year unless I produced such a document. That trans-
lated into Aunt Ignacia each year having to make larger and
larger contributions to the nuns' charities, of which my aunt
never tired of reminding me. When my father appeared in my
life, I requested he produce this legal document. "I can't do
that, Manuela," the coward said. "My wife would never allow
it. That would make you one of my heirs by law, and that would
be unfair to your sisters and José María. Remember, one day
you'll be richer than all of them when you inherit your mother's estate."

It was not what I wanted to hear. Only his reminding me of

the future money that I would inherit, which would allow me to pursue my true destiny, comforted me. It was a crude but potent solace.

AS WE GREW OLDER, Rosita and I became more curious about the nocturnal activities inside the walls of Santa Catalina. The two of us wanted to find out the provenance of the strange noises we heard echoing in the gloomy, drafty corridors late at night, which the other girls in the convent believed to be ghosts. The ghosts turned out to be hooded priests who came and went in the midnight hours. Rosita and I began to spy on them as they skulked down the corridors to enter the cells of the younger nuns, most of them novices. At turns transfixed and giggling, we stood by the doors of the sisters who received nightly visits, and heard muffled moans.

"Manuela, I'm not sure what they're doing in there," Rosita whispered to me one night, "but I don't believe they're saying the rosary. What do you think?"

"And they're not studying the lives of the saints, either," I said.

Months later we saw these young nuns swell up, their cheeks become full moons, their stomachs more prominent. Some of them died suddenly, from causes that no one would explain to the school or to the dead novice's family. Later, Rosita and I learned that the young sisters died of infections as a result of crude abortions induced by potions made from the shavings of the peels of green avocados and performed in the convent. The fetuses and stillborns were burned in the crematorium in the back of the convent. Once in a while a nun would hide her pregnancy so well that she would bring the baby to full term. The crying infant, still covered in blood, would be taken away, wrapped in a blanket, and left at the door of Quito's home for foundlings. Rosita and I began to fear that the fate of these young and most often desperate nuns might be awaiting us.

One day, after class, I wondered aloud to Rosita, "Have you noticed how there aren't any happy saints? How come at least one of them, just one of these many thousands of poor suffering creatures, couldn't become a saint for making people smile?"

Rosita laughed. "You are right, Manuela. Do the sisters really expect us to be uplifted by stories of crucifixions and burnings at the stake, of people starving to death, or getting stuck with arrows, their limbs torn off their bodies?"

"Exactly," I said. "Why isn't there just one girl who became a saint for wearing beautiful gowns that made people feel good when they saw her?"

We strolled down the corridor, giggling, until Sor Jacinta, having heard most of our conversation, bolted out of a classroom, wielding her length of cane. "Manuela Sáenz," she called, her eyes bulging, her features distorted with censure, "I curse the day we accepted you in our school. This is not a place for the likes of you. And you, Campusano, if you don't want to end badly, I strongly suggest you put an end to your friendship with this one."

ONCE MY EDUCATION with the nuns was completed and after I turned eighteen years old, I had two choices: to leave the school or to enter the novitiate. Of course, only the first was within the realm of possibility. I wanted my independence, and I had no desire to live in my father's house.

Although I knew I would incur my father's wrath for bringing up the subject, one Sunday, after dinner, when Father was in the library smoking a cigar and reading the newspaper, I decided to make my hopes known. If this was going to be a hard-fought battle, why wait?

I sat down across from Father. He put down the newspaper and said, "Yes, Manuela?"

"*Papá*, may I pour you a drink?" I began, hoping to buy some time, regretting what I had started. Maybe I should wait a few more months. After all, I did not want to alienate him. Since he had taken me under his roof, the nuns were a little nicer, and Aunt Ignacia and the Aispurus were less insulting. Nobody wanted to offend the daughter of an important official of the Spanish Crown.

"You didn't come here to pour me a drink. Something's on your mind. What is it, Manuela?" He smiled, encouraging me to speak. I intensely resented his condescending smile. It spoke of duplicity, and for the rest of my life I could never trust a man who smiled all the time.

"*Papá*," I began quietly, "I want to leave the school as soon as I graduate next year.... I don't want to become a nun. I have no religious vocation whatsoever..."

"Don't think I haven't noticed your lack of a religious temperament. If you want to leave the convent, you have my blessing."

"Thank you, *Papá*," I said and sat staring at my hands, mulling over how to say what I really wanted to discuss with him. There had been no doubt in my mind that Father would approve of my desire to leave the nuns. But how would he feel about my desire for financial independence?

"Is there anything else you want to discuss with me?"

"*Papá*, please, I want to talk about what will happen to me after I leave school."

"There's nothing to talk about, Manuela," he said. "You are my daughter, this is your family and your home. You'll live with us until we find a suitable husband for you."

"But, *Papá*," I pleaded, "I don't want to enter into an arranged marriage. I want to marry for love."

"Fine, then," he said, exasperation creeping into his voice. "You are the most beautiful young lady in Quito. I'm sure among your many suitors—and there will be many suitors—you'll find one you love."

"Before I get married, there are other things I want to do."

"And what is it, exactly, that you have in mind?"

"I want to sell Catahuango and move to Europe...with my girls."

He laughed, as if this were too incredible to take seriously. "Manuela, you don't know what you're saying. You forget unmarried women don't travel alone anywhere, much less to Europe."

I grew emboldened, as I always did when I encountered opposition. "I didn't say I was planning to go to Europe by myself. I said I would take Jonotás and Natán with me."

He gave me a puzzled look, as if I had spoken to him in Greek.

I would not back down. "I know my rights, *Papá*. The hacienda is mine and I can sell it when I become of age. I don't mean to make you unhappy. I just—"

"Listen to me, Manuela," Father said softly. In his eyes I

detected something akin to pity for me. "Catahuango is yours because it was your mother's property." He spoke in a steady tone, enunciating every syllable to make sure I would not misunderstand him. "But when you were born, your mother registered you as a foundling. That means that according to the law your parents are unknown. Legally, you can inherit Catahuango only after the Aispurus die. It's true that someday you'll be a wealthy woman, but only after your aunt and uncle are dead."

My bachelor uncle, Domingo, was in poor health, and his end might be approaching. I couldn't wait for him to die. I had no love for my uncle, who had always kept me at a distance. After his death only Ignacia stood in the way of my becoming the sole heiress of Catahuango. Still, Ignacia could live for a long time. By then, I might be an old woman myself.

"Everyone knows I'm my mother's daughter," I said.

"Your mother's dead. She can't corroborate that."

"But you can. Besides, in case you haven't heard about it," I quoted, " 'The right to property being inviolable and sacred, no one ought to be deprived of it, except in cases of evident public necessity, legally ascertained, and on conditions of a previous just indemnity.' "

Father gave me his condescending smile again. Whenever he disliked anything I said, there was the smile. This was his way of silencing me, of making me feel invisible.

"What's this subversive nonsense you're parroting? I wonder if you understand a word of what you said?"

"I understand perfectly well every word I said. For your information, it's item seventeen of 'The Declaration of the Rights of Man.' "

"The rights of man," he sneered. "Not the rights of woman.

When are you going to understand that men and women do not have the same rights? That they are not equal? That a good daughter must always obey her father? And unless you want to be shot by a firing squad, if I were you, I wouldn't go around quoting the 'Rights of Man.'"

I felt as though I were about to choke for lack of air in the room. Knowing that someday I would inherit Mother's wealth and live the life I envisioned was the great hope that kept me going during my time in that wretched school. He was denying me that hope. I felt a flare-up of my old animosity toward the man who sat there in front of me, whose seed had brought me into the world.

I made up my mind that very day. As soon as I could manage it, rich or poor, I would leave my father's house. My life was mine to control. Not my family's. Not society's. And certainly not the law's. I felt crushed but not defeated. I would have to find a way out of my predicament. A way that would give me what I wanted, without having to answer to anyone ever again. Never would I have guessed, that my answer would come in the form of first love.

4

I first set eyes on Fausto D'Elhuyar, a lieutenant in the Royal Guard of Toribio Montes, the president of the Royal Audiencia of Quito, on a Sunday *tertulia* at Father's house. José María's army friends were regulars at the *tertulias*. Many love matches were made at these gatherings. The most eligible young men in the city and the daughters of the best families got to know one another there, under the close chaperoning of their parents.

Clemencia, the eldest of my half sisters, was keen on Fausto. Who could blame her? He was prettier than most girls I knew. His sleek, powerful body exuded confidence. He seemed fully aware of the effect his glittering flaxen hair, exquisitely groomed mustache, green eyes, and long lashes had on people. Everything about him proclaimed that he was destined for a brilliant career in the Spanish army. Judging by the eagerness with which my father and stepmother behaved toward

Fausto, it was apparent they considered him a good match for Clemencia.

The *tertulias* ended at seven in the evening, and some of the guests would then say the rosary with the family in the living room before they left. It was during a rosary that I noticed Fausto stealing glances at me while the rest of the company prayed with closed eyes. I did not encourage the flirtation, but I didn't discourage it, either. Whenever our eyes met, I would look at him blankly, as if his look meant nothing. Though I was flattered that the handsomest man in Quito seemed to admire me, the last thing I wanted was to create trouble with Clemencia or with Doña Juana, who, despite her surface hospitality, always made me understand I was not the equal of her daughters.

THE SITUATION WITH Fausto did not escalate because I left to spend part of my school holiday at Catahuango, where my uncle was gravely ill. The usually grim atmosphere of the house was made even more oppressive by the proximity of death. Aunt Ignacia behaved as if Uncle Domingo were already dead and now dressed exclusively in black. She forbade laughter and singing, as well as visitors, in the house. I tried to spend as many hours as possible outside, and, regardless of the weather, every day went riding with Jonotás and Natán. To start preparing for the day Catahuango would belong to me, I took a new interest in the activities of the farm. I visited the corrals where the cows were milked, the lambs sheared, the pigs fattened. Accompanied by the overseer, who answered my questions, I learned about the crops we grew for sale in Quito.

My busy days, however, did not prevent me from thinking

of Fausto often. I had grown up in a world without men. In Catahuango, besides my infirm uncle, the only males were the Indian laborers and the African slaves; and at school, the lecherous priests. Fausto was the first man of my own class to catch my attention.

Everything I knew about love, I had learned from reading the delicious romantic novels Rosita smuggled into the school. One morning I woke up feeling my skin crying out to be caressed, and the first thing I thought about was Fausto's face. I knew from my reading that this meant I must be in love. I decided to keep those feelings to myself. There was nothing wrong with thinking about the handsome lieutenant, after all. It helped me to while away the silent hours when I sat embroidering with my aunt, the only activity we had in common. Aunt Ignacia made a point of teaching me everything she knew of the matter.

When I embroidered flowers and fruits and birds, I pretended I was making a picture of Fausto's face. When I looked out the window, the color of the mountains, the leaves on the trees, the hue on the hummingbirds' breasts reminded me of his emerald eyes. When I walked outside at sunset, the light draping the mountains reminded me of his golden hair. I longed to hear his voice, his laughter. Entirely new were the daydreams of his hands touching me. I had touched his hand a few times in greeting. Now, thinking of him, I took my right hand, cradled it in the left, and kissed my palm tenderly, pretending I was kissing the warmth he had left on my skin.

One afternoon when we were walking in the fields, Jonotás said, "Something's troubling you, Manuela. You're distracted all the time. What are you hiding?"

"Nothing," I replied.

"Then why are you blushing? You can't hide anything from me, Manuela. But I'll understand if you don't want to tell me." She looked hurt.

I had never kept a secret from Jonotás.

I started walking faster, to outpace her. She called after me, "I know what it is. You're not fooling me. It's about a young man."

I ignored her remarks and walked faster still.

"It's about a certain lieutenant, isn't it?"

How could Jonotás know about Fausto D'Elhuyar? I myself had not been aware of my feelings for him until I had arrived in Catahuango. Perhaps my relatives were right: Jonotás was a witch and had supernatural powers. She could read people's minds. I turned around to see her running toward me.

"Is it about that attractive Lieutenant D'Elhuyar?" Jonotás said, trying to catch her breath.

I flushed. "Are you crazy, Jonotás? He is Clemencia's intended."

"He *was* interested in Señorita Clemencia. Make no mistake about it, now he's interested in you."

"Why do you talk such nonsense!"

"Well, maybe because he stopped me in the market when I was running errands and asked me questions about you."

I turned to face her. Could this be true? "About me? Why? I haven't given him any reason to think I'm interested in him."

"Manuela, when two people like each other, they know it. He even asked me if I'd take a letter to you. I refused."

"You did? Why? I didn't tell you to do that."

"Because Doña Juana fancies Fausto as Clemencia's husband, Manuela. If she finds out you and Fausto like each other, she'll lock you up in a convent and throw the key down the mouth of Cotopaxi," she said, gesturing in the direction of the volcano. "And my teeth will bleed before you get out again. As for what she'll do to me if she catches me serving as a go-between, more than my teeth will bleed."

"He's handsome," I said dreamily.

"That he is," Jonotás concurred. "But besides looking good in his uniform, what about his brain? Does he have one?"

We laughed together as if on cue. I slipped my arm through Jonotás's, and we skipped down the meadow, giggling.

CONFIDING MY SECRET to Jonotás broke the grip of my ob-session. I decided that, as flattered as I was by Fausto's inter-est, I would not risk alienating my family. Their displeasure could make life a lot harder for me. The world was full of Fausto D'Elhuyars, I decided. All I had to do was wait until I became an independent woman, and then there would be plenty of handsome lieutenants to choose from.

At the end of the holiday, I returned to the nuns. Jonotás came to my cell each morning, after we said mass and had breakfast, and left late in the afternoon. We did not mention Fausto again. If I thought about him, I immediately shook my head to expel his image from my mind. Fausto stopped appear-ing at the Sunday *tertulias*. I was puzzled by his absence, but there was no one I could ask about him.

One morning, Jonotás came in carrying fresh laundry and the sweets Natán had made especially for me. She pulled out an envelope she had tucked under her turban and handed it to me. I studied the handwriting—it was not from Father or my stepmother. Jonotás turned her back to me and began making my bed.

I took from my desk a gold letter opener Father had given me for my sixteenth birthday and opened the envelope.

Dear Manuela,

You may have noticed that since you returned from your vacation I have not been coming to your parents' home on Sundays. I have deliberately deprived myself of the great pleasure of seeing you because I have come to realize it is you, not Clemencia, I love; you, Manuela, whom I want for my wife.

When our eyes met at your father's house, I thought I detected a warmth toward me. Could it be possible that you feel toward me the same way I feel toward you? If this is the case, I will be the happiest man alive.

Manuela, I write because time is of the essence. In sixty days, I will be transferred to Guayaquil, where I will stay for at least a year. This transfer is an important step in being promoted to Captain of the Royal Guard. At the risk of displeasing your father, will you come with me to Guayaquil, where we can be married and where we will live as husband and wife?

Yours,
Fausto

I handed Jonotás the letter, which she greedily read.

"He's *loco*," she said. "I brought you the letter because he promised me that if I did he wouldn't bother me again. Every day since we got back from Catahuango he waits for me to ask me to bring you a letter."

The letter was thrilling and frightening at the same time. "Next time you see him, Jonotás, tell him you gave me the letter and that you have no answer for him."

"What should I do if he gives me another letter?"

I thought about it for a moment. To accept his letters was a tacit agreement that I reciprocated his feelings. Yet the idea of receiving love letters was too romantic a notion to abandon so quickly. "Take it," I told her. "If he asks you whether I've read the letters, say you don't know."

"If you say so, Manuela," Jonotás replied, in a tone that hinted nothing good could come from this.

JONOTÁS BEGAN TO deliver Fausto's letters daily. I did not answer them; I wanted to test his constancy. My silence, however, was not enough of a deterrent. On the contrary, it seemed to make him ever more determined to get a response from me. "Just a sign from you," he wrote. "Take pity on my suffering." He was no great writer, that was obvious. The sentiments he expressed seemed so ordinary. I wanted his letters to make me tremble and swoon. Instead, they were repetitious. Yet although his power of eloquence was small, he did seem sincere and appeared to have fallen in love with me quite blindly. This romantic side of his nature appealed to me—he was like one of the adventurous male heroes in my favorite novels, and I could not stop thinking about him.

One Sunday, following noon mass, as I was leaving the cathedral with my family, I caught a glimpse of Fausto. Standing alone by the fountain in the Plaza Mayor, he looked splendid in his uniform. That afternoon, I waited with feverish anticipation to see him attend the *tertulia*. He did not. It was decent of him not to encourage Clemencia. The next time Fausto appeared at my father's house, he would have to make it clear that he was there not to see Clemencia, but me.

That night, back in the convent, the image of Fausto's dap-

per figure in the plaza kept me feverishly awake. I finally fell
asleep, but when I woke up the next morning, I found I was
still thinking about him—and kept thinking about him when
I was pretending to be praying, when I was in class, when I
went to bed that night. I had visions of Fausto's hands caressing my breasts, the two of us lying in each other's arms for
hours, kissing, murmuring passionate words to each other.

I began to dream of becoming his wife, that is, if he really
was serious about marrying me. Still, I held off answering his
letters. I knew once I took that step the innocent affair would
no longer be a flirtatious game. It continued to puzzle me that
Fausto's daily letters did not add anything new to my understanding of his character. The monotony of his declarations of
love was deflating, but—and it pained me to admit this—his
constancy was weakening my defenses.

I COULD NO longer keep the secret from Rosita. In my room
late at night, sharing my bed, I read Fausto's letter of that day
aloud to her. "Should I start answering him, Rosita? What do
you think?"

"Not yet," Rosita said. "If he really loves you, he must suffer
for you first. That's the way it is in love. Then, when he wins
you, he'll appreciate you even more."

We had lost all interest in the nocturnal life in the convent—we had my own drama to entertain us. We would stay
up, well past midnight, reading Fausto's letters and talking
about love. We believed that our main purpose in life was to
find true love.

"I don't think my father will consent to Fausto courting
me. It would break Clemencia's heart. My stepmother is really

keen on getting her married off before she becomes a spinster. I cannot afford to alienate my father so. I need my father's good will. Otherwise, I'll end up in a convent just like
this one."

"Manuela, it sounds like you have no choice but to elope. It
would be so romantic to run away with a dashing lieutenant."
Rosita sighed.

I said nothing. I was thinking of how my mother's mistake
had ruined her life and created so much unhappiness. But
what if Fausto *was* the great love of my life and I let him go?
Another chance might never come. What if I said no to love
and I became a withered, sour spinster like Aunt Ignacia?

"I always thought that I would take control of Catahuango
and then live my life the way I chose to live it, Rosita. But Father has informed me that I will not be able to collect my right-
ful inheritance until my aunt dies.... That could be decades
from now." I was getting upset. "My greatest fear is that my
father will marry me off to a man I can neither love nor respect. Or that he will take me to Spain to live with his family.
He talks often about returning to Spain to live the last years of
his life. I'd rather die than live in that country, surrounded by
the enemy."

Rosita took my hand. "Manuela, there's a big drawback to
Fausto," she said in a kindly way, not wanting to upset me
further.

"You mean that he is a soldier in the Royal Army?"

"Yes. Politically, he's the enemy."

"I have thought about it, Rosita. And, if he really loves
me, he will change for me. Maybe someday we'll both go into
battle, fighting against the Spaniards. After all, he's a *criollo*
like us."

"Maybe after you marry Fausto, he can help you take Cata-huango away from your aunt. Then you can exile her...to the Amazon jungle."

I laughed. "That's too close. Now, Patagonia...even better, Tierra del Fuego—that's where she belongs!"

"Mongolia. Or how about...Siberia?" chuckled Rosita. We started laughing and rolling on the bed, reciting the names of faraway places. When we ran out of names, I lay on my back, staring at the ceiling.

"What is it?" Rosita asked. "Why are you so serious all of a sudden?"

"Rosita, I've never kissed a man before," I confessed. "What will I do when he tries to kiss me?"

"First of all, you have to let him kiss you. In the meantime, you need to practice. He'll be horribly disappointed if you don't know how to kiss. Let me show you how it's done." Rosita moved closer to me under the blanket, put her arm around my shoulders, and placed her open lips against mine.

ROSITA WAS RIGHT. I had no choice but to elope. My father would never consent to my marriage with Fausto. I determined I could not implicate anyone else in my plans. Jonotás, for the obvious reasons; Rosita, because she would be expelled from school and sent back to her family in disgrace. I also determined that it would be as hard to elope from school as it would be from a prison. Thus I would have to do it from my father's house, on a Monday at dawn before it was time for me to return to Santa Catalina.

I sat down to write my first letter to Fausto.

My dear Fausto,

Your constancy over these months is sufficient proof of the pure nature of your love. Since I know that my father will oppose our marriage, our only option is to elope and then get married. If you agree with me, meet me next Monday at four in the morning at the corner of Calle de Las Aguas and Carrera Montarraz.

Yours,

Manuela

I handed the envelope containing the letter to Jonotás, making sure my intentions were hidden from her. She gave me a quizzical look when she took the thick envelope. "He keeps asking for a token from me," I lied. "So I'm sending him a perfumed handkerchief. Maybe now he'll leave me alone."

She frowned as she placed the envelope under her turban.

THE HARDEST PART about planning the elopement was keeping it from my dearest friends. But once Jonotás took the letter, there was no turning back. I had to trust that Fausto's intentions were honorable. It did trouble me that we had never even had a conversation. But in the novels I read, this was how if often happened. The characters loved each other at first sight, a sign of true and everlasting faithfulness, and with great secrecy found a way to be together. Whatever problems arose, we could overcome them, relying on the glory of our love.

That Sunday, after saying good-night to Jonotás and snuffing my candle, I got up. I opened my window. In the silvery moonlight, I packed in a little trunk just the essentials for a day's travel, and nothing else. As the hours passed, my agitation grew. What if I was making a grave mistake and my life, like my mother's, was ruined? Yet the future my father painted for me was unacceptable, as was one more day in that asphyxiating school.

When the bells of the cathedral struck four times, I was fully dressed and ready. A shawl covering my head, I took my chest and, in inky darkness, crept down the stairs at the back of the house that led to the servants' entrance. I removed the crossbar, opened the door slowly, so it would not creak, then closed it just as slowly behind me. I walked on tiptoes until I saw, at the corner of Carrera Montarraz, Fausto and two horses waiting for me. I broke into a run. We kissed passionately but briefly. "Later," Fausto said. "Later, Manuela. Now we must get away from here as fast as possible."

I mounted my horse, secured my trunk, and we took off at a gallop. By the time the sun came up, we were miles from Quito, heading for the slopes of the volcano Imbabura, to a farm that belonged to one of Fausto's friends. The plan was to hide there until we could get married.

5

Natán

We found out she had eloped when Jonotás went to her bedroom on Monday morning to fetch her for school. Manuela was gone. She vanished without leaving a note, without a word to anyone. Jonotás figured out that she had taken her little trunk with some toiletries and the jewels she had inherited from her mother. This was the only evidence she had eloped. Jonotás later swore to me she had no knowledge of Manuela's plan to elope. She was as surprised as I was. I believed her.

Don Simón was not one to start wailing and carrying on about his misfortune. Instead, he immediately took steps to find out what had happened and summoned Jonotás and me to his office.

He addressed me first. "Natán, do you know where Señorita Manuela is?"

"No, sir," I replied, "I do not."

"You have worked here long enough for me to get a sense of your character. I believe you. I sense you are incapable of getting involved in any conspiracies."

When he turned to Jonotás, I felt weak in the knees. If anyone knew anything it was Jonotás.

"Jonotás," he said in his cold inquisitor manner, "do you know where she is?"

"No, I don't, sir," she said quickly.

"I believe you knew nothing about Manuela's plans to run away, Jonotás. But you know her better than anyone. Where could she have gone? What do you think could have happened to her?"

Jonotás looked down at her clasped hands, and I feared for both of us. I knew that Don Simón could not sell Jonotás, because she belonged to Manuela, but she could be hired away to another family in Quito, or—worse—sent to a town far away. I had known Jonotás all my life; the idea that we might be separated terrified me. But why didn't she have a ready answer for Don Simón? It was not like Jonotás. She always had a quick retort to everything.

Before too long, Don Simón got the information he wanted out of Jonotás. She told him that Lieutenant Fausto D'Elhuyar had been writing to Manuela for a while, and that Manuela had fallen in love with him. I was as stunned as Don Simón.

Don Simón blanched, and immediately sent us away. Perhaps he thought that history was being repeated, and that he was being punished, all these years later, for ruining Manuela's mother's life.

IT WAS AS though Manuela had died. Worse, it was as though she had never existed. No one dared mention her name in the house, not even the servants. They spoke in whispers, and lowered their heads when dealing with the family. All the servants—under the threat of being fired—were ordered not to breathe a word of Manuela's disappearance to anyone outside the house. The slaves, of course, were threatened with a lashing and with being sold.

At night, on the cot we shared in our room, Jonotás and I wondered where Manuela was, and when she would send for us. We were certain that she would not abandon us in her father's house.

When people ask me now why Manuela did something so stupid and risked ruining her life, just as her mother had, all I can offer by way of an answer is that Manuela gave herself to the lieutenant to hurt her father, and to get away from him and his family. When she returned, she talked to me and Jonotás briefly about her elopement, without going into details. After that, for as long as I lived with her, she never spoke about it, at least not in my presence. I have no doubt that she believed the lieutenant when he told her he would marry her. But I'm not surprised she ran away. I blame it on the romantic novels she devoured, which she often read to us. She had run off with the dashing officer the way heroines did in those books. I am sure it never entered her mind that after the lovemaking was no longer new, the lieutenant would lose interest in her and send her back to her father's house, a ruined girl, the same way it regularly happened in those books.

THE AFFAIR WITH Fausto D'Elhuyar was short-lived. Almost a month to the day after she ran off, shortly after dawn, when the sky was still dark, there was a knock on the servants' door. I opened it thinking it was the milkman, who came every morning at that time. Manuela stood there holding her wooden trunk. In the dark she looked like an apparition. "Manuela," I exclaimed. "Thank God you're back."

We embraced, then Manuela asked if anyone was up yet. I replied that only we servants were awake.

"I'm going to my room," she said. "Go get Jonotás and meet me there. Don't tell anyone else I've returned."

At that moment there was another knock on the door. This time it actually was the milkman. I took the day's milk from him, carried it to the kitchen, and then went to wake Jonotás up. I had to put my hand to her mouth to muffle the scream of joy when I gave her the news. On tiptoe, not wanting anyone to hear us, we went to Manuela's room and locked the door behind us. Jonotás and Manuela embraced and cried, kissing each other's faces, and I cried, too, seeing the two of them so happy to be reunited.

When Manuela had calmed down, she said, "I'm sorry for running away without telling you where I was going. I didn't want to make you my accomplices. My plan was to send for you as soon as I got married," she paused. "That wretch took me to a friend's hacienda, a day's ride from Quito. At first," she continued, anger rising in her voice, "like the idiot I am, I believed the rascal's promises, and we were happy. Barely three weeks after we eloped, Fausto told me he had received orders from Quito. Then he added (as if I couldn't see through his transparent lie) that it would be too risky to take me along with him to his new post before the promotion came through."

Fausto arranged for a party coming to Quito to bring Manuela home, and he promised to send for her as soon as he was promoted, which would be in a matter of months. "I won't be surprised if I never hear from him again," Manuela sneered. She was through shedding tears over Fausto. "Natán," she said, "be an angel and bring me a cup of chocolate and a slice of buttered bread?" She turned to Jonotás. "Bring me a jar of water so I can wash myself. Don't let anyone see you." To the both of us she said, "When I'm ready, I will send for my father."

The Manuela who had fled the house just a month ago, her head and heart so full of romantic notions, no longer existed. She did not seem meek or repentant, but defiant. She had left an innocent girl and returned a hardened woman burned by love.

6

␣

Fausto's promised letters never arrived, as I suspected they would not. But even if he had written, asking me to return and marry him, I would have rejected his proposal. Before Fausto departed for Guayaquil, as the blindfold of passion was removed from my eyes, I saw him for what he was: a frivolous Don Juan, a coward who preyed on romantic girls and was, worst of all, one of the enemy—a Royalist who would never cross over to the cause of independence.

The situation in my father's house now became untenable. Though the family had done everything they could to maintain secrecy, the news of my elopement became common knowledge in Quito. The nuns would not accept me back in Santa Catalina, and my father was averse to sending me to Catahuango, where he could not supervise my every move.

My bedroom became a jail cell. My stepmother and sisters looked past me as if I were not there. Whenever the family went to church or social events, I was not included. During the Sunday *tertulias* I was told to stay in my room until all the guests had left. The one exception was my brother. When José María came home on one of his weekend passes, he visited me in my room. His first words to me were: "What happened with Fausto doesn't change the love I have for you, my sister. But I better not run into that scoundrel again, because—I promise you, Manuela—I'll kill him."

"If you've really forgiven me, you'll do no such a thing," I told him. "Don't ruin your life over that worthless dog."

Knowing that Joche had forgiven me made my humiliation bearable. Yet, for all practical purposes, my life was over. No man would marry me in Quito, where, like my mother, I had been disgraced. I would grow old and decay inside the four walls of my bedroom. My other option was to immure myself in a convent, the emotional equivalent of being buried alive. My one desperate hope was that my aunt and ailing uncle would die soon and I would come into my inheritance. That could be years from now, I knew; years in which I would have to live under my father's roof, feeling his scorn, and that of his wife and my sisters.

I wrote letters to Rosita at Santa Catalina and got Jonotás to deliver them. There was no reply. Obviously my letters had either been confiscated by the nuns, or Rosita's replies had been intercepted by my family.

I spent my time reading history books, because my father had removed all the novels from my bedroom and burned them on the patio. When not reading, I sat by the window of my room embroidering. From it, there was a view of Cotopaxi. I looked forward to the late afternoons, when, catching the reflection of the setting sun, the volcano's snowy summit seemed to catch on fire. It was thrilling to see it discharge its great plumes of smoke. A part of me hoped the volcano would erupt and bury Quito in lava and that would be the end of everything.

I WAS BY THE WINDOW, reading, when a servant entered to relay that my father wanted me to meet him in his study. This was unusual. When I came in, he asked me to sit down.

"As you know, Manuela," he commenced, "for some time your stepmother and I have been thinking about returning to Spain. I have lived in Ecuador for almost thirty years. I am getting old, I miss my relatives, and I want to end my days back home. I see nothing but trouble brewing in the nations of the Andes. In the next years there could be bloody wars. I want to spare my family the bloodshed. I'd like your stepmother and sisters to live in peace and tranquility. However, before we can return to Spain, I need to travel to Panama to settle my affairs there. Juana and I think it would be advisable for you to accompany me. Away from Quito you might be able put everything that has happened behind you."

How much I resented him planning my life for me! Still, I decided it would be wise to overlook this. I was in no position to argue. And, after all, one of my dreams had been to travel and see more of the world. Furthermore, at that point I would've agreed to go to hell, that's how desperate I was to get away from Quito, where I was suffocating.

"How long will you stay in Panama?" I asked.

"You can plan to be away for at least a year."

"What happens to me when you go to Spain?"

"You're welcome to come with us. But if you prefer to stay

in Ecuador, you'll have to go back to Catahuango. You cannot live alone in the city."

"*Papá*, I'll go with you to Panama, but on one condition."

He frowned. "And what would that be?"

"That Jonotás and Natán come with us."

He became pensive for a moment. "I hadn't thought about it, but it's not a bad idea. They can help me in the store and keep you company."

For an instant I felt gratitude and tenderness toward him. I got up from my chair, put my arms around his neck, and pecked him on the cheek. "Oh, *Papá*, thank you, thank you! When are we leaving?"

"We leave for Guayaquil two weeks from today. We'll be there a few days, and then sail for Panama." He paused, regarding me. "I hope, Manuela, that this will be a good opportunity for you to forget the lieutenant and start anew."

"Yes, yes, *Papá*," I said. He had no idea that I had already forgotten Fausto. "May I go tell Jonotás and Natán?"

"Yes, you may. Tell them they should begin to prepare as of today for our departure."

I left the room feeling I was rushing toward a new life. How could I have known then that this journey, crossing the mountains and seas, would dominate my life for the next twenty years? Or that I would end up living my last years on earth in a godforsaken town between a pitiless desert and an indifferent sea?

7

PANAMA CITY
1815

As our ship entered the Port of Panama, I could not wait to set foot on land. I had already made up my mind not to go to Spain with my father. I would do anything to stay behind in South America.

I immediately fell under the spell of Panama, with its lush tropical vegetation, the scented breezes that wafted in from the Atlantic, and the variety of peoples of all colors and nationalities who inhabited it. My father's trading business was located on the ground floor of a two-story building in the old part of the city. He dealt in European imports: olives, hams, cheeses, wines, furniture, fabrics, the latest inventions. And he exported to the Old World silver and gold objects, mirrors from Cuzco, jewels, cocoa, rare woods, leathers, and exotic animals.

We lived in a spacious apartment on the upper floor of the building. The sea breezes wafted through the rooms of our home, whose doors and windows faced the courtyard. Purple and white bougainvillea draped the walls of the courtyard, which had a drinking well, a few tall coconut trees, and a garden in the shape of a rectangle, overgrown with crepe myrtle, cannonball flowers in many colors, and red and yellow hibiscus.

The apartment, with its high ceilings and tile floors of Moorish design, was furnished with the finest objects, thanks to Father's business. In the corridor connecting the living and dining rooms to the back of the house hung cages filled with parrots, parakeets, macaws, and brilliantly colored songbirds. Natán was put in charge of the kitchen, Jonotás in charge of the housecleaning, and I of cleaning the birds' cages, changing their water every day, and feeding them the seeds and fruit they ate. This new world was so enthralling, Fausto's betrayal began to lose its sting. Many mornings I woke up feeling my days in Quito were a bad dream that had no power to haunt me in this place so filled with sun and surrounded by a warm sea.

English was the language most commonly heard in Panama, and it was there that my girls and I learned it. I was kept busy as a bookkeeper, and receiving Father's clients. Many of the merchants who did business with his firm were Englishmen who spoke no Spanish. Father decided I should learn the language, and I was tutored every day in the late afternoon. My teacher was a humorless Englishman, so I insisted that Natán and Jonotás sit with me during the lessons.

Before, I had only been happy for short periods—while on horseback in Catahuango; during the first few days with Fausto. In Panama I knew contentment for an extended period of time. On the isthmus, everything conspired to make me thrive. D'Elhuyar had at least allowed me to discover my body. When I walked down the street, the ripeness of my breasts, my unblemished skin, my full, smiling cerise lips and black eyes drove men crazy. Suitors started to appear regularly to ask for my hand in marriage, but there was no one who caught my fancy or met my father's approval.

We had been living in Panama for over a year, thinking that, before Father left with his family for Spain, I would have to marry one of the wealthy suitors he brought home, many of them European. As a Spaniard, my father had a rather low opinion of all *criollos*, except for his wife and children, of course.

Then I met James Thorne. I didn't even notice him at first. Father often gave dinner parties for his business associates. James was the owner of a fleet of cargo ships based in Lima. He had the confident and attractive manner of a man who had made his own fortune. James was a tall, and slender beanpole of a man, with large steely-blue eyes and ash-blond hair. He certainly wasn't a hero out of my novels.

It was not unusual for one of Father's acquaintances to come to dinner more than once, especially if his stay in Panama was prolonged because merchandise was not ready, or ships needed repair, or the weather was bad for sailing, as it often was between December and March, when the strong and chilly trade winds made the sea roil with huge, furious waves that endangered many vessels. So when James Thorne became a frequent guest at the house, and I found him seated next to me at the dinner table, I never gave it a second thought. Certainly, I gave no indication that I was interested in him, except as someone with whom I could practice English and improve my pronunciation.

James asked my father if I might accompany him to a ball at the British consulate. Father granted him permission, without consulting me, of course. James and I looked like father and daughter, but I humored him to please Father. I was interested in the people we might meet there, certainly not in being with James, a lap dog I could dismiss or summon at will.

Thus I was flabbergasted when James Thorne asked my father for my hand in marriage, and even more flabbergasted when Father accepted and presented James with my dowry of eight thousand pesos. When I was informed of this transaction, I ran into my bedroom and locked the door. I cried and screamed and took scissors to the expensive dresses, fans, and shawls Father had lavished on me. I broke every glass object on my dressing table and swore that I would rather kill myself than consent to an arranged marriage to a man I did not love. I let Jonotás and Natán come in, and they spent hours picking up the mess my rage had made.

For days I refused to emerge from my room, refused all food, and refused to open the door to let Father in. James came to call on me, but he ended up in Father's office, where, I imagine, they discussed my situation. Two weeks went by in this way and I did not relent and see Father or "my intended." My girls listened to my ravings, without trying to calm me. They knew that eventually, unless I ran away again, I would have no choice but to give in. I could not remain locked up inside those four walls the rest of my life—and even if I ran away, where would I go? And with what money? And how far would I get before I needed help? My hope was for Thorne to give up and sail back to Lima. He could not stay in Panama forever. But I misjudged James's tenacity; he was ready to wait in Panama for as long as it took. It wouldn't be the last time James surprised me.

Weeks went by. Then one day Father came to my door, and though he was not the kind of man who was given to shouting, he did just that as he banged on the door. "Manuela, I have reached the limit of my patience. If you don't open the door, I'll have it torn down." Father did not make idle threats. I made him wait by the door a few minutes before I let him in.

Father sank wearily into an armchair and sighed. "You have made my life an ordeal," he said.

"Please, *Papá*, don't make me marry against my wishes," I pleaded, kneeling in front of him. "I want to be able to love my husband. Please don't make me enter a marriage that will make me unhappy for the rest of my life."

"Listen to me, *hija*," he said, holding my chin in his hand and staring into my wet eyes. "You may not believe it, but I've arranged a wonderful future for you. Mr. Thorne is a man of quality; he's rich, you'll live like a queen in Lima, you'll be received by the best society. He's well liked by the viceroy, and you'll be welcomed at court. Any girl in her right mind would give anything to have all that."

"I don't care about those things, *Papá*. Those are your ideals, not mine. Why don't you marry one of my sisters to James? I was not made for that kind of life."

"Manuela," Father said sternly, "Mr. Thorne does not want to marry your sisters. He wants to marry *you*."

"But I don't love him, *Papá*."

"What is this love, *hija*? Love," he scoffed, "like in one of those stories in the silly novels you read? You *loved* D'Elhuyar—and look what happened! Let me tell you a story: When I married my wife I wasn't in love with her. I chose her because I admired her moral qualities. With the passage of time, I have grown to love her, and I can say now that I have a most happy marriage."

How dare he compare me to my stepmother! "Father, I could never love James Thorne. I don't care how wonderful he is. He's not the kind of man I could ever admire, let alone love."

"It appears you don't understand your situation, Manuela. In Quito society, your reputation has been ruined. Ruined."

"If that's what worries you, I'll stay here in Panama."

"And do what, Manuela? Don't be ridiculous. You can't stay here, an unmarried woman, when I go to Spain. Anyway, all that is beside the point. You don't seem to understand that I have given my word to Mr. Thorne. Once I give my word, I never retract it. If you don't marry him, I want you to know you will not be welcomed back in my house in Quito. Your step-mother and your siblings will not live under the same roof with you after you disgraced the name of our family." He paused to let me absorb his words, then added, "If you're think-ing of going to live in Catahuango, I've been informed by the Aispurus that you're not welcome there, either."

I got off my knees. "You hypocrite!" I exploded. "How dare you accuse me of dishonoring your family name? You seduced my mother even though she was a girl and you were a married man, and then you abandoned her. Yes, don't make that face. You dishonored her name. Sir, if there is a hell, you will burn there forever."

"Don't make me strike you, Manuela."

Anger blinded me. "I swear to you, if you strike me, if you..." The words caught in my throat. I wanted to say that I would kill him, but I could not. Our anger hung in the air be-tween us.

"I don't like the turn this conversation has taken," he said, rising abruptly. "I'm going to leave you alone to think things over. Please don't lock your door again, because I will have it torn down. You will marry Mr. Thorne, and in years to come you'll be grateful to me. And that's the last word I'll say on this subject."

He walked out of the room. I slammed the door after him.

A FEW DAYS LATER, I informed my girls that one of the conditions to be met in marrying Thorne was that they would come to live with me in Lima. I resigned myself to my fate and began to look forward to moving to the City of the Kings, the greatest capital in South America, the city where it was said golden coaches traversed the streets.

I had no idea then that this loveless arranged marriage would set me on the road to crossing paths with Simón Bolívar. Had I stayed in Panama, I would most likely have never known passion, or what it was to live for an ideal.

Years later, in Paita, when Jonotás and I spent many evenings reminiscing, I admitted to her, "The truth is, Jonotás, I was relieved to marry James, just to get away from my family." What I kept to myself was that I was never able to forgive Father for betraying me. I never would forgive him for pushing me into marriage with a man I could never love. Until his death, Father wrote to me from Spain with some regularity. I burned each letter without opening it, but not before cursing his name.

8

LIMA
1817

Lima was neither the exuberant, lush tropics, like Panama, nor the green, snowcapped Andes, like Quito. Sailing down the Peruvian coast, I saw a gray desert and a melancholy range of small mountains between it and the Andes. The colorless country looked eerily barren, uninhabited. The leaden stillness of the Pacific mirrored the monotonous desert, except when schools of flying fish broke its flat motionless surface, or when we ran into pods of sperm whales, shooting tall plumes of white spray.

When our ship docked in the port of Callao and I breathed the scent of honeysuckle in the air, and I saw Lima's many cupolas and minarets in the distance, reminding me of pictures I had seen of Arabian cities, I sensed the city might hold mysterious possibilities.

As our coach passed through La Portada de Callao, one of the eleven gates of the adobe wall that surrounded Lima, I wanted to jump off the coach and immediately start exploring the streets and alleys of the city. The two pleasant years spent in Panama now felt merely a stopover on the way to the future. Something told me that Lima would be a defining place for me.

Built on the left bank of the Rimac River, Lima's green parks and public walks were like cool water on the eyes after the desolate coastline that spread for thousands of miles. The city's cobblestone streets were crossed by shallow rivulets of clear water that ran from springs in the mountains and were lined with promenades shaded by poplars and weeping willows, where, late in the afternoons and on Sundays, people strolled or sat to take the breezes from the sierra and gossip on the stone benches. The Plaza de Armas was larger than any square I'd ever seen. In it was the imposing baroque cathedral, the Palace of the Archbishop, the grand Palace of Government, and any number of fashionable establishments patronized by women of means. I would soon learn that the homes of wealthy families, with their neo-baroque façades, were more palatial than any I had seen in Quito or Panama. Lima's public buildings were imperial-looking, appropriate to the capital of a viceroyalty that at one point had spread from Guatemala to Tierra del Fuego.

The city had a bullfighting ring visited by famous toreadors from Spain, and the Teatro de la Comedia, where zarzuelas and dramas played continuously, and where the legendary actress La Perricholi was queen. Its great University of San Marcos was the oldest in South America, and students from all over the continent came to attend it. Most thrilling of all—there was a bookstore, where I could buy the latest English and Spanish novels.

I married James Thorne in the Church of San Sebastián in
Lima. Though James had wanted to throw a lavish wedding, I
insisted on a private ceremony. The excuse I gave James was
that I was not religious and a religious ceremony would have
felt like a farce to me. But the truth was I could not pretend
the occasion gave me the slightest joy. My brother, who was
stationed in Lima with the Royal Army, gave me away. Jonotás
and Natán were also in attendance.

My father's prediction that by virtue of my marriage I would
become a woman of consequence was correct. Whatever faults
the Englishman had—his devotion to the Anglican Church, his
prickly English reserve, his reactionary political views—he
was magnanimous toward me. As a wedding present, James
provided me with one of the finest coaches in the city. He had
chosen one of Lima's loveliest houses for us. Finely crafted furniture imported from England and France filled the rooms of
the house, which was situated on the Calle del Progreso, near
the home of the Marqués Torre Tagle. Marquises, counts, and
other titled and august members of the Peruvian nobility were
our neighbors. My house was staffed with many servants, and I
had Jonotás and Natán as my personal maids.

I was determined to get along with James and accommodate
his wishes. I wanted to be a good wife. Most women who met
James Thorne considered him attractive. Yet, when his ruddy,
bony hands and his lukewarm and freckled milk-white skin
made contact with mine, my body grew tense and cold. James
seemed content with having me as his ornamental wife, parading me in public as the beautiful mistress of his house. Despite my indifference to him in bed, when he was emboldened
by a few drinks after supper, he came into my bedroom and assumed that I must be eager to fulfill my wifely obligations. A

crafty, ardent lover, he tried to awaken my passion with all the tricks he must have learned visiting the bordellos of the world. But when he touched me, I didn't come close to feeling the thrill I had felt with Fausto.

I stopped feeling guilty about my lack of passion when I discovered that James, as was the custom of married gentlemen in Lima, kept a mistress. With Jonotás's help, who agreed to follow James one day, I learned she lived in a small farm on the outskirts of the city and that they had a daughter.

Right from the beginning, there was tension in the house: we argued about my smoking. He had tolerated my love of tobacco in Panama, where many women smoked. As soon as we landed in Lima, he informed me he disapproved of his wife smoking cigars in public because limeñas of good breeding did not indulge in that dirty habit. I continued to enjoy my cigars at home when he wasn't around.

A more serious disagreement arose when I refused to accompany him to Sunday mass. The agony of my years with the Concepta had soured me once and for all on the subject of religion. I had no desire to become an observant Anglican. Finally, James accepted the fact that I was not going to relent, and he began to attend mass by himself. Yet the resentment was clear on his face each Sunday when he left for church, and did not lift for several hours after he returned.

Lima's tapadas were famous in South America—women never ventured out in public without a shawl covering their hair and faces, only one eye allowed to remain uncovered. Though I deplored this antediluvian custom, the city was the most exciting place I'd lived in.

By far the happiest part of being in Lima was that my brother was stationed there as captain of the Numancia Regiment. To be reunited with José María, after not seeing him during the years in Panama, brought some joy into my life. Though I strongly disapproved of my brother's Royalist politics, my love for him overcame our political differences. He often came to the house for dinner, and I was pleased to see that José María and James got along well.

IT BECAME CLEAR to me that I would never grow to love my husband. To my relief, he was often away, either in the countryside visiting his mistress, or tending to the affairs of the hacienda, or at sea, looking after his shipping concerns. I did make an effort to become his friend. However, James's past was a mystery to me, as well as to most people who knew him. He told me he was born in Aylesbury, a town in Buckinghamshire County in England, yet he was reluctant to talk about his family, whom he referred to as "landed gentry." Why he came to South America, and how he came to acquire his fleet of commercial ships and amass great expanses of land, were a subject he chose not to discuss. Perhaps it was his discretion that helped him thrive in Lima, where Englishmen were generally not welcomed by the Spanish authorities. But the Spanish Empire was in such disarray by the early 1800s that its once formidable maritime powers were reduced to a small fleet of outdated ships. Thus James, with his fine commercial English vessels, provided a valuable service to the government by importing goods from Europe and exporting Peruvian products.

I SPENT MOST mornings with Natán and Jonotás, embroidering and gossiping on the balcony of my sitting room overlook-

ing the street. The balconies of Lima's great houses were closed
in, so that people could sit in them without being seen. If you
wished to call to someone from your balcony, all you had to do
was open a window and show your head. Balconies were an
excellent vantage point from which to keep up with the lives
of limeños.

Well into the evening, Lima's streets were populated by people selling their wares. It was a lively entertainment. By nine
in the morning, when the sun was out in full force, the Indian
ice cream vendors appeared, singing, "Ice cream, *dulce de
leche*..." Next came the sellers of pastries and breads, crying,
"Mouth-watering Guatemaaaaala bread!" They were followed
by the high-pitched song of the *tisaneras* publicizing their
juices: "The *tisanera* has delicious and cold pineapple juice!"
Around ten came Negro women who marched down the streets
balancing baskets on their heads. In these baskets they carried
pots heaped with rice and beans, and they sang: "Rice and
beans, white rice and black beans!" On weekends and during
religious holidays, old African women transited the streets on
burros loaded with huge baskets full of *tamales*. Their singsong
voices always brought a smile to my lips: "*Tamales, tamales* from
the sierra, steaming-hot!"

The sellers of fruits, offering oranges, tangerines, apples,
chirimoyas, and melons, came at noon, along with the for-
tune-tellers, who claimed they could read your future, interpret your past, and decipher your present. Cries of "Needles,"
"Thimbles," "Little buttons of mother-of-pearl" rang out all
day long. The salesmen of silver objects and china went from
door to door, offering Cuzco's beautiful gold-leafed mirrors. In
the early afternoon the streets belonged to the candy men, and
to the women selling spicy *ajíaco* and sweet *humitas*.

As evening fell, families sat on their balconies to take in the fragrant breezes that blew down from the sierra. The air was suffused with the aromas of steaming maize cakes, buttery biscuits fresh from the oven, and the sensuous scents of the flower-sellers offering their bouquets of violets and jasmine. All day long the street under my balcony was alive with a chorus of voices and songs. Some days it was enough to make me forget I was the wife of a man I did not love and remember that I could delight in a city where people seemed bent upon enjoying the pleasures of life.

I LEAPED WITH delight when I found out that my good friend Rosita Campusano was living in Lima. We had been out of touch since I ran away with D'Elhuyar.

We had our joyful reunion after the *audiencia* in which I was formally introduced at court to the viceroy and vicereine. I immediately invited her to my home the following day for an afternoon cup of chocolate. I sent my coach to pick her up and ran to the door to greet her when she arrived. Rosita had blossomed into a great beauty, though still diminutive in stature.

"You can show me the house later," Rosita said as we exchanged kisses and embraced. "Let's go where we can be by ourselves and talk."

We went directly to a small sitting room and sat in a corner overlooking the garden. After chocolate and pastries were served, I asked Jonotás to close the door and not to interrupt us until I called for her.

Rosita's father had secured a place for her at the court of Viceroy Pezuela y la Serna, where she had been lady-in-waiting for over two years. "It's an exciting place to be. There's never a dull moment," she said. "But tell me about you. I'm eager to know everything about your life since you left the convent in...well...such a hurry."

We both laughed. Although she wanted every detail, I gave her a brief account of the fiasco with D'Elhuyar. It simply was not something I wanted to think about anymore. "And you?" I asked. "Is there a love interest in your life?"

"No, there's no room for love in my life right now," she replied, without any trace of regret.

It was hard to believe my romantic friend had changed that much. "Being a lady-in-waiting keeps you too busy for love?"

"That, and other things," she said mysteriously.

"I envy you, Rosita," I said sincerely. "As you can see, I lack for nothing. But you know me, I can't be content just being a society woman. I long for—" I halted, not quite sure what it was I longed for. "Sometimes," I admitted, "I am bored."

"That will change when you have children, Manuela."

"I'm going to tell you something I have told no one. After I eloped with D'Elhuyar, my father had me examined to see if I was pregnant. The doctor told him I would never have children." I paused, remembering that painful day. "In Panama, I was examined again by eminent doctors who corroborated the opinion of the doctor in Quito." I sighed. "Maybe it's a blessing in disguise. I don't know why, but I've never desired to have children."

Rosita took both my hands in hers. "You seem to have made a good marriage. Señor Thorne is handsome. The viceroy is so fond of him."

"My father arranged the marriage, Rosita. And James is content with the child he has with his mistress."

"Oh, I see," she sighed, and we left it at that.

LATER THAT AFTERNOON, as she was leaving, Rosita pulled from her purse an envelope and handed it to me. "Read this when you have a free minute."

"Love letters?" I asked in jest.

"Nothing of the sort. Read it, and then we'll talk about it. Just make sure," she added, lowering her voice to a whisper, "that the contents of the envelope fall into no other hands."

I was excited. This surely broke the predictable routine of my days. I took the envelope and we made plans to see each other the coming Sunday at the bullfight. After Rosita left, I eagerly opened the envelope. To my surprise, it contained a proclamation by Simón Bolívar. Years had gone by since my days at the convent school when I was obsessed with Bolívar and the wars of independence. Now I lived in a world full of Royalists, and although revolution was in the air and I read about repressive measures in the controlled press, I didn't have anyone to discuss new political developments with. Yet I had never forgotten Bolívar. He was now in Nueva Granada, where he had dealt crushing losses to the Spanish forces in a series of recent battles. It was just a matter of time before that country was liberated. Lima's Royalists feared that after Nueva Granada Bolívar would next turn his attention to Ecuador and Peru.

I held in my hands the Liberator's announcement of the creation of the Republic of Gran Colombia. I memorized the words of his conclusion: "I contemplate with inexpressible joy this glorious period in which the shadows of oppression will be dispersed so that we may enjoy the splendors of liberty!" Bolívar's words filled me with hope for the future. Perhaps there was something I could do, after all, to lend meaning to my life.

THE FOLLOWING SUNDAY, Rosita and I went to the Circo de Acho, where, bedecked in our finest *mantillas* and combs, we sat in the first row of one of the eighty-four balconies reserved by subscription for the notables of Lima. Shortly after our wedding, James had said to me, "I'll go with you anywhere, dear, but never ask me to witness one of those barbaric bullfights." Sitting next to Rosita, waiting for the first *corrida* to begin, memories of my childhood flooded back to me—when Jonotás, Natán, and I would enact bullfights with the tame milk cows in the corral at Catahuango. One day Aunt Ignacia caught us in this game, and she forbade me to play it ever again, because it was for boys, not girls. "Someday you won't be able to stop me," I replied. "I will be the first *toreadora* the world has ever seen."

I fell in love that day with Lima's bullfights: the trumpet blaring at half past three, when the sun was warmest and brightest, to announce the start of the bullfight; the military marches and festive music of the orchestra; the trilled cries of the *aguardienteros* selling their potent firewater; the cheers and applause of the drunken populace; the fierce light in the bulls' black eyes; the bulls' brute strength; the reckless lancers; the balletic twirls and leaps of the long-limbed *banderilleros*; the valor of the matadors in their suit of lights woven with threads of silver and gold; the tragic but thrilling ending, when the noble dead bulls were dragged from the ring by horses, leaving behind a trail of scarlet liquid in the steaming sand, which moved me to tears.

I WAS STILL feeling giddy from the bullfight when my coach stopped to drop off Rosita at the entrance of the viceroy's palace. Before she stepped down, she took my hand. "Did you get an opportunity to read what I gave you?"

"Yes, and I don't know how to thank you, Rosita. It brought back the days when Bolívar was our hero. His proclamation made me wish I could do something to further the cause of independence."

"That proclamation is banned in Peru," Rosita said, dropping her voice to a whisper. "Please destroy it as soon as you can. You could get in trouble just for owning a copy of it."

All thoughts of the bullfight vanished. "I had no idea..."

"Manuela, are you really serious about wanting to do something for the cause of independence?"

"If there were a way," I said, surprised at the conviction in my voice.

She leaned close and put her lips to my ear. "There's a way, Manuela. And we need women like you."

Rosita gathered her things and covered her head and face with her *mantilla*. "I'll come to see you later this week. We'll talk more then. In the meantime, you must not breathe a word about our conversation to anyone. Not even to your girls."

THE NEXT TIME Rosita came to visit, we talked about politics and nothing else. I hadn't realized how starved I was for meaningful conversation. In Panama, a city of merchants with the mentality of pirates, every conversation was about commerce. Since my arrival in Lima, the world in which I lived was populated by Royalists and enemies of independence.

Rosita informed me that she was working as a spy for the *independentistas*. "Bolívar is a long way from Peru right now. It'll be a couple of years, at least, before he gets here." Then she added, "The information I gather, mostly by eavesdropping, or by just plain playing stupid, I send to General San Martín's contacts here in Lima. San Martín will arrive here long before Bolívar does. He will march from Argentina, over the Andes, to liberate Peru."

This was indeed news to me. Rosita's revelations made my head spin. "Isn't it dangerous, what you're doing?"

"Of course it is," she said, giving me a quizzical look. "But somebody has to do it. What's the worst they can do to me?"

"They can shoot you."

"Exactly," Rosita said. "What a small price to pay for the freedom of our nations. Countless people have already given their lives for the struggle. "I'd be honored to join their numbers."

The light in her eyes frightened, and excited, me.

"Listen, Manuela. Our current viceroy and his officials—a pack of wild donkeys would do a better job governing Peru."

I laughed.

"And from what I hear about the Spanish court," she continued, "King Ferdinand sounds as degenerate as Caligula. He's surrounded by greedy, brutal, corrupt, and ignorant men. Are these the people you want to decide how we should live our lives? Look at the chaos they've created in Spain. The country is bankrupt, the masses are starving and wracked with illness, the Inquisition is back." She paused. "We missed a great opportunity to achieve our independence when Bonaparte sent his brother to rule Spain. We must not do that again. This is the time to overthrow the Spaniards. If not now, we'll have to wait God know's how long before another propitious moment comes along. They are so weakened, their army so demoralized, that it won't take much of an effort to get rid of them once and for all."

That day I pledged my total allegiance to the cause. My old dreams of a free South America returned as if they had never left. I became immersed in conspiracy.

It had an extraordinary effect. I well knew that by collaborating with the patriots I was risking my position and my life. Anyone who was accused of helping the rebels was incarcerated, hanged, or shot, his severed head impaled on tall poles in Lima's plazas and on the main roads into the city, his eyes plucked by black turkey buzzards and other birds of carrion. The extremities of the conspirators, rotting and crawling with maggots, hung from the trees in the squares and from the balconies of government buildings.

I realized I had lived all my life in a world where turmoil and revolution and bloodshed was the norm, yet as a woman I had been a mere spectator of history. Events taking place around me were but a faint echo by the time they reached the confines of my inane and cosseted life. The emptiness of my marriage somehow emboldened me. The atrocities committed by the Spaniards to suppress the revolution were not enough of a deterrent to stop me from acting as my reawakened conscience demanded. Liberation would not be achieved unless patriots were willing to risk everything, living the way General Bolívar lived, risking his fortune and his life to achieve a higher goal. The way Simón Bolívar had spent the last twenty years—fighting innumerable battles; never giving up, even when he was incarcerated, exiled, or handed crushing defeats; never giving up, despite the attempts on his life, despite the hardships and illnesses brought about by incessant campaigning. I told myself I would rather die young, for a cause I believed in, than to live to old age as a Spanish subject, bound to James Thorne.

I BECAME A CONSPIRATOR. My main role, as defined by my fellow revolutionaries was to raise funds to help finance the patriot armies. To this end, I set out to cultivate the wealthy in Lima. I made social calls, gave dinner parties, and invited prominent citizens to tea to find out who supported the idea of liberation from Spain. Whenever I discerned that they sympathized with the cause of the patriots, I asked for financial support.

My brother was in the habit of coming to dine with us on Tuesday nights. I looked forward to his visits all the more when James was at home. José María's presence saved me from the tedium of dining alone with James. One evening after dinner, in the library, warmed by the French brandy that James favored, I saw a propitious moment to introduce the subject of the political unrest so palpable on the streets of Lima.

I asked my brother, "Is it true, José María, that San Martín is on his way to Peru?"

"If he is, we are ready for him. His troops will be exhausted after marching for thousands of miles. They wouldn't stand a chance against us."

"But his army has a reputation for ferociousness."

"They're nothing but a rabble of cowards," James interjected.

"You can call them anything you like, James, but cowards they are not. They're idealistic soldiers fighting for a cause they believe in."

"Mark my words, Manuela," James said. "If that mob ever overthrows the monarchy, the bloodbath that follows will make the French Revolution look like a drawing-room comedy. And if they ever succeed, remember you will be among the first people whose heads will roll."

"Maybe *your* head will roll, James. You're the Englishman. I'm a *criolla*. They're fighting for people like me."

"What about José María? Don't you think as an officer in the Royal Army he'll be one of the first targets of the revolutionaries?"

"Your husband is right, Manuela," my brother concurred. "You have very romantic notions about the rebels. They're a bloodthirsty mob."

The brandy had gone to my head. "Nothing we do will stop our countries from becoming independent from Spain. We cannot hold back the unfolding of history." The shrillness in my voice startled me.

James slammed his glass down on the mahogany table. "Listen to your brother, Manuela. Those romantic novels you read all the time have corrupted your judgment."

"I'm sure Manuela means no harm to us, James," my brother said, coming to my defense. "You just have to accept you married a passionate woman."

"From now on, Manuela," James continued undeterred, "I forbid you to ever again express in this house any sentiments of sympathy for those savages. What's more, as your husband, I forbid you to have any contact whatsoever with anyone associated with that cause."

After that evening, I only broached the subject to my brother when James was not around. I knew the day would come when José María would see the cause of independence the way I saw it. As for James, he would die a staunch Royalist. And the sooner I got away from him, the better.

Every chance I got, I tried to convince my brother to reconsider his allegiance. "The time has come," I would repeat tirelessly, "to rebel against Spain and side with justice and freedom." At first, José María looked at me as if I had lost my mind. Little by little, I noticed a change in him.

I COULD NOT COUNT on James's money to fatten the coffers of the patriots, so I began to sell my jewels, gold candleholders and other gold objects, as well as china and silverware we never used—he would never notice they were gone. I knew that if James found out about my involvement with the rebels he would repudiate me as his wife. He depended on the goodwill of the government for the prosperity of his business, and nothing mattered more to him than his business. James was a man without ideals, while for me death had become preferable to a life without them. Only money mattered to James—money and his Church of England.

I became extremely cautious where James was concerned to make sure he did not suspect anything about my secret activities. Once or twice a week after supper, I would announce that I had plans to visit a sick friend or to attend a *tertulia* for women organizing charity events. "Make sure your servants accompany you and that you're driven in the coach," he would say before he returned to his study to work on his accounts. As long as I promised to take the necessary precautions for my safety, James held no objection to my nocturnal out-ings.

I attended meetings at the homes of the conspirators, where Rosita was often present with the latest news gathered at the viceroy's court. At these meetings I felt an authenticity in my life, as if I finally mattered. I had found a cause to which I could give myself. At that moment in South American history, it was the only cause worth fighting for.

9

Jonotás

I took a bullet for Manuela Sáenz—that's how much I loved that woman. Neither the Liberator, not James Thorne—and certainly not Natán—would have done as much. How could I not love Manuela? She was the only white woman I knew who despised slavery. I knew she would never sell me. As long as she protected me, no white man would rape me, and no master would brand my face with a hot iron, like so many pitifully deformed slave women I saw throughout the Andes.

As Manuela's involvement with the revolutionaries grew, so did mine. She recruited Natán and me as her accomplices. Natán was unhappy about it. "If she wants to get beheaded, that's her problem," she said one night from her cot in our bedroom. "But why involve us? That's not how I want to end up. Don't you see the danger we're in, Jonotás?"

"I don't care what happens to me," I replied, "so long as General Bolívar frees the slaves when he defeats the Spanish."

"Free the slaves?" Natán sneered. "It will take more than one Simón Bolívar to get white people to abandon their prejudices about Negroes."

Natán kept her resentment toward Manuela well hidden. But she became a conspirator, too. Manuela started to write proclamations. She took advantage of the Englishman's business journeys to go out with us at night. We plastered Lima's walls with broadsides inciting Peruvians to revolt against the Spanish authorities. My favorite broadsides included salacious gossip from the viceroy's court, like the affair the vicereine was having with the Archbishop of Lima. All this intimate information came from Rosita.

We started to dress as men when we went out at night, not out of perversion, as many have accused us, but because in men's clothes we moved more freely than when we wore dresses. Under the cover of darkness, we armed ourselves with sabers and guns.

I knew that if Manuela was caught, she would be imprisoned, then exiled, out of courtesy to her brother's service to the crown, and also Thorne's wealth. Natán and I, on the other hand, surely faced hanging or the firing squad. Natán wanted no part of it, as I said. But she had no choice. Saying no to your mistress was unthinkable. As for me, I believed in the cause. I knew we Negroes would be liberated much sooner if the Spaniards were defeated. And I wanted to see the Spaniards crushed and pay for what they had done to my family.

When Manuela sent me to do errands for her, I would join the people gathered in front of the broadsides. Most of the poor people could not read, so they would gather around and wait for someone who could read the broadsides to them. I read them out loud every chance I got, pretending I was reading them for the first time. With a lookout posted to make sure there were no soldiers in the vicinity, I read to them. The people would mutter angrily in response and then quickly disperse. Often, by morning, the broadsides were scraped off the walls or whitewashed over. Still, when I passed in front of one, I felt proud, knowing that I had had something to do with it by helping Manuela and Natán to fasten that broadside to the wall. It made me feel like I, too, was working for independence.

We usually left the house around two in the morning, one at a time, in different directions. We decided on a meeting place beforehand. That way if one of us was caught coming or going, the other two would not be accused of treason. We carried the broadsides, the pots of glue, and the glue brushes in potato sacks slung on our backs. We wore Indian hats, to give the appearance of the peasant men who came to Lima from the sierra before daylight to sell produce. We stayed in our neighborhood, never venturing beyond the side streets leading to the Plaza de Armas. We kept away from the square itself because even at that hour it was heavily guarded. The walls of the great houses were our targets, as well as the doors of the convents and churches and public buildings.

One night we were pasting up a broadside on Calle del Carmen, just one street away from our house, when we heard footsteps approaching. Manuela turned to me and whispered, "Jonotás, it's the watchman." If the man got close enough and saw what we were doing, he'd blow his whistle to alert the soldiers in the Plaza de Armas. I had to do something. "Run," I said to Manuela and Natán. "I'll deal with him."

Before Manuela or Natán could stop me, I dashed toward the watchman who was carrying a lantern. He hesitated, seeing what must have looked like a dangerous Indian running toward him. "Stop or I'll shoot," he yelled. As the man cocked his pistol, I lunged at him, aiming my saber at his heart. As he fell back, his pistol discharged. My shoulder felt like it was burning. I had killed him. But the gunshot had alerted people who lived on the street, as well as the soldiers in the plaza. Manuela and Natán rushed to my side. I fell into Manuela's arms, too weak to stand. Natán tore off her shirt and bunched it under mine where the blood was seeping through. Then she lifted me on her back. I had no idea she was so strong. She carried me all the way to our house, which luckily was quite close. We got inside just before we heard the sound of soldiers on horses and people throwing open their shutters and calling into the night.

"In your condition, you can't go to the servants' quarters. I don't trust them," Manuela said. "Natán, help me take her to my rooms."

In the back of Manuela's bedroom was a small room where she kept her trunks. There they improvised a cot for me, undressed me, washed and cleaned my wound. I was still bleeding.

"She's going to bleed to death," Natán said.

"Don't talk about death," Manuela said. "Rosita will know a doctor. But we cannot send a message to her at this hour. Not to the palace. We need someone to come sooner. We cannot wait till morning."

Manuela did not know any doctor sympathetic to the revolution. So there was nothing to do but wait until she could send word to Rosita. I didn't want to die, though I began to think there was a strong possibility I would. I knew I had a chance to live, if I remained calm.

Sometime later, a servant knocked on Manuela's bedroom door to tell her that José María was downstairs. When I heard this, I thought that I had been found out. He had come for me, and I would be dead within days. Was it possible I had traveled so far from my *palenque* just to die in this way? While I lay there bleeding, and waiting to be arrested, I felt as lost and scared as on the day the white people arrived in San Basilio and destroyed it. How much would Manuela be willing to fight to save me?

I was feverish, in pain, yet fully conscious. I had never seen Manuela so agitated and nervous. "Tell José María to come to my room," she told the servant.

As soon as the door was closed, Natán said, "What are you doing, Manuela? He'll take Jonotás away. Manuela, please!"

"No, Natán," Manuela said. "José María is our only hope. Trust me—he doesn't want to see me ruined."

Manuela brought José María directly into the small alcove where I was hidden. I didn't know what to expect from him. He had always been respectful toward us, but he didn't love us as Manuela did. And I had never heard him express his sympathy for the emancipation of the slaves. "José María," she said, "Jonotás was shot and you have to help me."

He took a look at me and his face reddened with anger. "Do you know why I am here, Manuela?"

She shook her head no. "Our agents suspect the person who murdered the night watchman lives in this area, since he disappeared so quickly. The soldiers are conducting a house-to-house search. Tell me the truth, did Jonotás kill this man?" Before Manuela could speak, he exploded. "Manuela, you cannot shelter a slave who's a murderer and an enemy of the crown! You have to turn her in, or you'll be accused of treason."

"José María, please, listen to me," Manuela said, grabbing his hand in desperation. "I am responsible. I got Jonotás involved in this. If they take her, they must take me as well. I'll say I killed the man. I cannot live with myself if anything happens to Jonotás. You know me—you know I mean every word I'm saying."

I could hardly breathe from fear.

José María pulled his hand away from hers and started pacing the room. "I could strangle you, Manuela. Your recklessness is appalling." There was a long pause. I heard my heartbeats marking the time. "Still, you're my sister. Against everything I believe in, I'll give orders not to search the house."

"I never doubted you'd do anything else, Joche. We love each other too much," Manuela said, taking his hand and kissing it. Then she added, "There's something else you must do for me."

"What is it?" he asked, unable to look at her.

"I want you to go to the palace and ask to see Rosita Campusano. She'll know a doctor to send here. I fear that Jonotás's wound will become infected and she'll die, so there's no time to waste."

"You're insane," José María grumbled. "You're asking me, an officer of His Majesty's Army, to become a conspirator? If I'm found out I'll be shot."

"You won't be shot, my brother. As I have told you, General San Martín will be here soon and Lima will be liberated. I promise you that he will learn how you helped the patriots when they needed protection."

The argument continued, back and forth, and during it I must have passed out. But Manuela prevailed, and a few hours later a doctor arrived. He removed the bullet, cleansed the wound, dressed it, and left some opium for the pain.

Perhaps you now understand why I would have died for Manuela. Who besides her in Gran Colombia would have done what she did to save the life of a slave? If I had ever doubted Manuela loved me, that day sealed my loyalty to her. I would never leave her, no matter what. Only death would have the power to separate us.

10

Rosita sent word that General San Martín's troops, *las montoneras*, famous and feared for their fierceness in battle, were approaching Lima from the south. Riots broke out daily. Public buildings were defaced, looting and burning of stores was widespread. In daylight Spanish troops were shot at by snipers on roofs of houses. In response, the government declared martial law. Rich Spaniards became afraid to be seen in their opulent coaches, venturing out disguised as laborers.

As soon as I heard the long-awaited news that San Martín's troops had launched an assault on the walls of the city, I rode to the barracks of the Numancia Regiment. Without waiting to be announced, I burst into José María's office. Other military officers were present. "Gentlemen," I said, "please leave us alone. I have to talk to my brother about urgent family matters."

After they left, I locked the door and turned to José María. I said, "Have you heard the news about San Martín?" He nodded. "What do you plan to do?" José María turned away and began shuffling papers on his desk.

"Joche, I implore you. If you are a patriot, you have only one choice—to join the rebels. Aren't you tired of being treated as a second-rate citizen just because you are a *criollo*, while those Spanish leeches are entitled to money, the best occupations, to everything, just because they were born in Spain? Aren't you tired of deferring to the Spaniards and addressing them as our betters? Aren't you tired of their corrupt viceroys and their bloodthirsty generals, and their ungodly bishops? Aren't you tired of never being able to make our own decisions about what's good for our motherland? I will tell you—I am tired of it," I said, "and I am a woman. I can imagine how humiliating it must be for men to have to lick their boots, whether they're right or not."

"Manuela, have you forgotten that our father is a Spaniard?"

"Our father is back in Spain, Joche. He returned home. But South America—all of it—is our home. This is where you and I were born. It's our duty to rid our nations of their oppressors."

"I swore allegiance to our king."

"Their king, Joche. Not ours. How can a person of conscience swear allegiance to that degenerate? I'd rather swear allegiance to the devil!" I sensed Joche's opposition was weakening. I pressed on. "We have no kings in South America. We're fighting to establish republics, to end a world in which monarchies rule, no matter how depraved they may be. My brother, you are dearer to me than anyone in the world. This is your moment to prove yourself as a man, to enter history, to help achieve something great for the ages."

By the time I left headquarters, he had changed his mind. Later that day José María and his regiment deserted the Spanish army and attacked the viceroy's troops that guarded the palace. Panic spread among the Royalist forces when they saw their own men turning against them. The viceroy and his court fled the city and headed for the sierra. His disarrayed army followed him.

General José de San Martín entered Lima without any Spanish opposition. His first act was to declare Peru's capital a free territory. All limeños, with the exception of the reactionary aristocracy, welcomed him as the liberator of Lima. The old order had been dethroned and something new and exciting was about to begin. People danced in the streets, showing a spirit of brotherhood: perfect strangers embraced and cried in unison, "Long live General San Martín and his heroes. Death to the Royalists! *Viva* free Peru!"

WHILE THE SPANISH monarchy fell in Peru, James Thorne was in Chile on business. He returned to Lima not only to discover my role in the revolution but also to learn I had been awarded the Order of Knight of the Sun for my efforts to gain independence for my adopted country. The same man who had forbidden me to associate with the cause of independence was now beaming with pride over my role in it. I had become an asset under San Martín's government, and with his wife a heroine of Peruvian independence, his business would continue to prosper.

The day I was knighted, Thorne rode with me in an open carriage to the palace, where I would receive my medal. *Limeños* lined the streets to cheer their heroes as they passed. Humble people ran to my carriage to hand me bouquets of violets and crowns of laurel.

The ceremony took place in the grand salon of the former viceregal palace. All the important people in Lima, even those who mere weeks before had been open enemies of the patriots, were in attendance. When my name was announced, and my modest contribution to the fight for independence and justice described and praised by San Martín, I looked around the room to engrave that moment on my mind. Rosita was there, of course, on the dais with San Martín. My gratitude toward her was immense—if fate had not brought us together again, I might not have achieved this destiny. José María was also present, and it made me happy to see how proud he seemed of me. Though perhaps prouder of me than anyone else, Jonotás and Natán were not allowed in the grand salon. I would have loved to see their faces at the moment when I received the black sash with the gold medal pinned to it. Jonotás and Natán had risked their lives to help me. It was unfair that only the descendants of Spaniards were being recognized as heroes.

For entirely different reasons, I would have wanted to see my father, my stepmother and my half sisters, as well as Aunt Ignacia, my uncle, and grandmother in the salon. Despite their dire predictions for me, I had become a woman to be reckoned with.

The last two years had only increased my appetite for working to liberate my people. I would continue to work for the cause until all of South America was free. And the first step in that direction was to free myself of James Thorne.

book

TWO

An Adulterous Woman

II

QUITO

1822

Bolívar made love like he made war—obsessively, with an intensity and energy that at times made me fear I was on the verge of dying from his passion. On my first night with the general, it was almost dawn when we succumbed to exhaustion. We lay for hours, bodies entwined, both of us silent, just breathing.

I woke up around noon, lightheaded, my blood pumping fast in my veins, my heartbeats so loud I could hear them. I was alone in the bed. Where was he? I splashed some water on my face and dressed. As I was preparing to leave, one of the general's aides tapped on the door. He informed me the Liberator had gone off to take care of some business. He had left instructions that I was to be driven home in his official carriage. On the way to my father's house, the air that came in through the window of the carriage invigorated me—as if I were hiking high in the Andes.

From that day on, I counted the hours of the day till evening, anticipating that moment when I would lie again in bed with him. Our hunger for each other was insatiable. Because of my disappointing experiences with sex, I was afraid that if I gave myself to him without reservation, he would abandon me. Sensing that, Bolívar set out to conquer my body and soul. Whatever he touched, a country or a woman, he vanquished, and he would not rest until he succeeded. For the first time I understood religious fervor, how the mystics turned themselves over completely to God: in their surrender they found a deliverance that superseded all the aches of the body and the desires of the soul. By giving myself to him I found solace in my existence. All my life I had been tormented, wanting to escape the present, wherever I found myself, even when I helped in my small way to liberate Peru. Finally I could say I was happy where I was, even if it turned out to be only for a brief period.

Bolívar spent the days taking care of affairs of state, but the nights belonged to me. We would meet at his headquarters, and before we had finished our first drink, we would be tearing at each other's clothes, so desperate to unite that sometimes we made love on a couch or on the floor.

By comparison to his life—he was almost fifteen years older than I—my own life seemed negligible, as if it had just barely begun. As the days passed, I told him everything that was worth knowing about me. In particular, he wanted to know what it had been like growing up in Catahuango. When the subject of my husband came up, I explained it was a marriage arranged by my father. "I see," Bolívar said, and he never asked me another question about James Thorne.

I wanted Bolívar to re-create for me with a luxury of detail his military triumphs, his heroic campaigns crossing the *llanos* and the Andes, his defeat of General Morillo, the Spaniard sent by the monarchy to pacify Venezuela and Colombia, and who had committed unspeakable atrocities. I wanted to hear in the Liberator's own words how he had crushed Morillo's forces at Boyacá. My questions seemed to irritate him. "Battles are horrible things, Manuela. The taking of human life is nothing to boast about." All my illusions about the splendor of conquest were crushed with that comment. Next I tried to make him talk about his marriage. He grew cold and silent, refusing to talk about his wife and her tragic death. Nor did I dare ask him about the countless women he was rumored to have had as lovers.

Yet he warmed to the many similarities in our stories of childhood. Both his parents died when he was a boy. First his father; a few years later his mother. All he remembered of her was that she played Mozart on a clavichord, and that the house was always filled with music. Like me, he, too, had been raised in the country, in the custody of unaffectionate relatives. The warmth and affection he received in childhood came from the slaves to whom he had been entrusted. His slave José Palacios had been with him as long as he could remember, just as Natán and Jonotás had been with me. He talked about his nanny, the slave Hipólita, as if she had been his true mother.

In one of these nightly conversations, he told me about his beloved tutor, Simón Rodríguez. "One day, a man came to the door of our house in Caracas. He had heard that my family was looking for someone to tutor me. I was seven years old. Many teachers had given up tutoring me because of my insolence and lack of discipline. Hipólita led me to the living room, where my mother and grandfather were in the company of a stranger. 'Simón,' my grandfather said, 'meet Professor Simón Rodríguez, your new teacher.' I had to stop myself from laughing. There stood a tall, sinewy man dressed in old clothes that were too big for him and wearing battered, dusty shoes. His black eyes, though, showed a ravening light new to me. Many years later, when I read *Don Quixote*, I realized that if Don Quixote had walked the earth, he would have looked like Professor Rodríguez."

His head propped on pillows, lying beside me, Bolívar seemed completely relaxed telling me the story of someone who was precious to him.

He continued: "I was trying not to laugh at the ungainly appearance of this man, when I saw he was accompanied by a little dog. I tore free from Hipólita's grip and ran to pet the dog. I was about to pick her up when Professor Rodríguez said, 'Stand up, Lulu, and greet your new friend.' To my utter delight, the dog stood on her hind legs and gave me her right paw. I shook her hand gingerly. Professor Rodríguez said, 'Her name's Lulu, and she's a mammal, like you. Which means she grew in her mother's belly, like you, and after she was born she was fed from her mother's teats, like you.' He'd given me my first lesson . . . can you believe it, Manuela? I had been told by everyone, including the many teachers who never lasted more than a few days, that I had been brought into the world by the stork. Nobody had bothered to tell me I was a mammal." Bolívar broke into a free, joyous laughter.

"I envy you such a teacher," I said.

"It was sheer chance that he came to our house. I doubt I would have become the person I am if I hadn't met him." He paused. "This must be boring for you."

"General, nothing you say or do bores me. I meant what I

said about envying you such a teacher. The Concepta nuns made learning a torture for me."

"My poor Manuela. Luckily that wasn't Professor Rodríguez's method. After he had been a few days at the house he said to my mother and grandfather, 'What this boy needs is to learn from the only book worth studying—the Book of Nature. I need permission from your graces to take Simoncito to your country home to start teaching him everything he needs to learn.' They were glad to grant him permission, because until that point I had refused to learn anything from anyone.

"In the country, he woke me up at dawn to start the day doing gymnastics, which we did practically naked. The slaves were scandalized. Hipólita was convinced I had fallen into the hands of a madman. She grew to tolerate him when she saw that I had stopped throwing tantrums about every silly thing. Swimming in the lake, fencing, horseback riding, climbing mango and coconut trees, taking long, strenuous walks—that was, at first, the extent of my education. For an anatomy lesson, he took me to see the slaughtering of a cow. When the entrails were ripped out, Professor Rodríguez took the organs in his hands, still bleeding and warm, and he explained to me what they were and what function they had in the human body. To teach me astronomy, we slept under the stars and he'd point out the different constellations until I fell asleep."

Remembering these events from the past, Bolívar's smile was wistful, far away, lost in a happier time.

"As time passed, Professor Rodríguez began to pay more attention to my intellectual development. First of all, there was Jean-Jacques Rousseau. He had many great ideas, Professor Rodríguez told me during one of our walks, but the most important was that the day was at hand when government by the aristocracy would be replaced by government by the people. That meant, he explained, that one day soon people like Hipólita, not aristocratic people like my family, would run the world. He said, 'Listen to me, Simoncito, and listen good. Here's where the American man is different from the European one: on our continent, revolutions will be started by the aristocracy.' Then he added the most astonishing thing, the words that marked me for the rest of my life."

Bolívar bolted upright on the bed. "'What that means is that the liberation of the slaves, the liberation of Venezuela, will be carried out by you. Yes, you!' He put his hand on my shoulder. 'I'm afraid that you are the chosen one. You've been put in this world to liberate Venezuela and to end Spanish tyranny in the New World. You will be the one to liberate our beloved motherland from the misgovernment of His Majesty the King of Spain.'"

By the light of the candle, it was the first and only time I ever saw Bolívar's eyes moisten. I was so moved by his emotion, I had to look away to hide my tears.

"I believed everything he told me," Bolívar continued. "But as you can imagine, Manuela, this news, though thrilling, also frightened me. How would I—a mere boy—ever go about accomplishing such a mighty task? As if he had read my mind, the professor said, 'Take care of your body, and read Rousseau, and cultivate a good heart, and the rest will take care of itself. Remember, the only riches worth having are the ones of the mind and spirit. That's the wealth that no one can take away from you. Everything else in this world is transitory—*sic transit gloria mundi.*'"

Bolívar lay down again beside me. He remained still for a

moment, then turned, took me in his arms, closed his eyes, and fell asleep.

That night, I felt as if he had given me the key to the secrets in his heart.

DURING THOSE MAGICAL NIGHTS in Quito, we often fell asleep in the middle of a long kiss. As dawn approached, I would get up and dress, and arrive back at my father's house before light broke. I knew all of Quito was watching me, and I tried to maintain a modicum of propriety regarding this love affair.

It wasn't long before I understood Bolívar would never entirely belong to me. He lived and breathed solely for the cause of independence from Spain. His true mistress was the battlefield. Bolívar probably saw me as no more than an oasis, a rest stop on the way to greater conquests. It was hard for me to accept that love was but a tiny portion of what he wanted. I had to ask myself if this was enough. Sometimes I lied and said yes, and sometimes I knew I would do anything, no matter how foolish, to keep him.

Although I saw no evidence of other women pursuing him, I could not be sure I didn't have rivals in other cities with claims on his affections. I had heard many stories about the women he had left behind as he moved on to the next military campaign, to liberate the next country, fight the next battle. My only hope was that he would come to see how I was *different*. I determined not to be one of those women he left behind. Wherever he went from now on, I'd follow him. I'd follow him until I captured his heart. Then it would not matter where he was or how long I would have to wait until he returned to me.

AS PREPARATIONS BEGAN for Bolívar's journey to Guayaquil, I fully expected that he would ask me to go with him. After all, I was personally acquainted with General San Martín. One night after we made love, I broached the subject.

"Ask me anything, but not that, *mi cielo*." He drew me close. "It wouldn't look good. Besides, this expedition could turn out to be dangerous."

"I don't care about danger," I said, pulling away. "I'd rather die than be separated from you."

"Please, Manuela," his tone betraying slight annoyance, "it will be hard for me to say good-bye to you. This will be a short separation. I'll return to Quito very soon, I promise you."

Once I was out of his sight, how long would it be before I became a pleasant memory? And what if he did return soon? Sooner or later he would march off again, and I would be left behind. I decided not to plead with him anymore. The only way to gain his respect was to behave with dignity.

He interrupted my brooding to say, "There is something you can do for me, Manuelita." It was the first time he called me Manuelita, the first time any man had ever called me by my diminutive. It was because of him that later I became "Manuelita" to those who admired me and "*la Sáenz*" to those who hated me.

"You know I will do anything for you," I gushed, forgetting my dignity. "Nothing would make me happier than to be of use to you, my general."

"Then, stay here and be my eyes in Quito. If there's anything you think I ought to know, write to me immediately. With you here, it will be like I am here, too. It will give me peace of mind in Guayaquil knowing you're here looking out for our interests."

The way he said "*our* interests" made me catch my breath. He considered us a couple. "I'll do as you say, my general."

"That's my Manuelita. Come," he coaxed me, getting out of bed and stepping on the cold wooden floor in his bare feet, "let's dance."

He started humming a waltz as we spinned naked around the room, our bodies illuminated by a single candle burning on the nightstand. Feeling his swelling press against me, I said, "Simón Bolívar, you listen to me, *señor*. Liberator or not, if I find out you're making love to other women, I will get to Guayaquil before you know it and"—I squeezed his member— "I will cut this off, pickle it, and send it as a present to King Ferdinand."

He laughed. "That's how I want you to talk to me, Manuelita. I like a woman with a dirty mouth. Talk to me like that when we're making love."

I laughed, too, though beneath my mirth was fear of what was to come. Soon the volcanoes of the Andes, the freezing wastelands of the cordilleras, the tumultuous rivers of Ecuador, the Amazon jungle, the fate of millions of people and thousands of soldiers of Peru and of Gran Colombia would stand between us.

12

Bolívar left for Guayaquil. I felt vulnerable and restless. In Lima, I had Rosita with whom I could talk about politics and books, attend the bullfights and theater, and gossip shamelessly. But Quito hadn't changed in the years I was away, it was still an extended convent, and its small-minded citizens measured all human conduct by the teachings of the Roman Catholic Church. The only excitement in town was provided by the rumbling volcanoes nearby, frequent tremors, and the chance these could turn into cataclysmic earthquakes.

Social invitations stopped arriving. To *quiteños* I was Bolívar's abandoned mistress. They assumed that he had tossed me aside and already replaced me with the first woman he met on the road. To while away the hours of the day, I returned to embroidering on my balcony with Jonotás and Natán. The concentration required for embroidering always soothed my nerves. I certainly was not about to start attending mass every day, which was how most women of my class socialized. When I went out walking or riding with my girls, I could hear people snickering behind our backs. Often I saw them pointing at us, as if we were curiosities. If upon my return to Quito, as a heroine of Peruvian independence, *quiteños* had begun to forgive me my peccadilloes, now they were once more unfriendly toward me.

Though I wrote to Bolívar daily, no reply came. I consoled myself by thinking that he had more important things to do than write to me. The future of Peru was at stake. But with each day of silence, my uncertainty grew. Was there another woman lying with him at night? I knew he hadn't forgotten me completely, because an officer stopped by each day to bring news of his march on Guayaquil. This visit provided some solace.

One afternoon I was on the balcony embroidering, Jonotás at my side, chattering the gossip of the city she had picked up shopping in the market, when I pricked my finger. "Damn it," I blurted, flinging the embroidering hoop to the floor. I placed the finger in my mouth as tears streamed down my face.

"Let me see," Jonotás said. She grabbed my wrist and gently pulled the finger away from my lips. She inspected the finger. "You're not bleeding, Manuela. Why are you crying?"

I looked away, ashamed of my outburst. Jonotás got up, picked up the embroidery hoop, and tossed it in the sewing basket.

"Manuela, you got to stop this," she chided me. "You can't waste your life waiting to hear from the Liberator. Have you forgotten you came to Quito to get your money? When are you going to do that?"

I had not forgotten my dream of selling the hacienda and

moving to Europe, away from Thorne, away from Ecuador, away from everything that had stifled my growth all my life. Bolívar had distracted me from thinking about anything else.

"You're not going to feel better sitting there embroidering and eating sweets all day long. You'll get so plump that when the general sees you again he won't recognize you. You need to get out of town for a day or two, Manuela. A long ride in the open air will do you some good."

My aunt had not responded to the notes I had sent her. She was trying to stop me from asking for what was rightfully mine. "Tell them to saddle three horses tomorrow morning," I said. I had not finished saying these words when I started to feel better; it was the first time since Bolívar left that I had a thought that was not about him.

ALL MY LIFE, Catahuango had loomed large, the repository of so many dreams. As a child, my relatives often began sentences with, "As the heiress of Catahuango," or "When you inherit Catahuango." Once I was old enough to understand what this meant, Catahuango, my legacy, began to symbolize my freedom. The hacienda had been in my mother's family for two hundred years. All its land lay within the confines of the Avenue of the Volcanoes, in the heart of the Andes. It was land that held magical powers for the Indians who had lived there before the Spaniards arrived and enslaved them. It was a place shrouded in ghosts and danger because of its proximity to active volcanoes. It was also one of the most valuable pieces of cultivated land in Ecuador, rich in grains, fruit, and livestock.

My plan to sell the hacienda and move to France or England

with Natán and Jonotás would allow me to meet great men, travel in societies where I did not feel imprisoned. Even though I had read novels and history and had learned English, I felt insecure in the company of educated men. How I wanted to hear the great minds of our time discuss the works of Voltaire, the ideas of Rousseau, and the philosophers of the Enlightenment; how I wished to learn French, to see the great ruins of antiquity, to speak with Baron Alexander von Humboldt about his travels in South America; to participate in the salons of dazzling Parisian women. How wonderful it would be to see the plays of Racine and Molière on the Parisian stage, to attend the opera in Italy, to listen to concerts by the masters of the fortepiano, the clavichord, the cello, the violin. If I had been born Manuel instead of Manuela, all these things would have been a part of my education. The only way I would ever make these dreams come to fruition was with my own money.

Cunning would be required to get Aunt Ignacia to surrender control of Catahuango. I knew open confrontation with her would get me nowhere. I had written her a letter from Lima offering Ignacia a generous financial settlement to renounce her legal claim as my mother's executor. It went unanswered. So I had arrived in Quito prepared—but only as a last resort— to do battle with that tedious old crone. Like all the women in the Aispuru family, she was hard-headed and formidable when cornered. After living in Catahuango for over a quarter of a century, Ignacia thought of the hacienda as her exclusive property. To sell the land and the animals, as I proposed, meant she would no longer have a home.

From Quito, it was half a day's journey by horse to Catahuango. My girls and I were on the main road of the Avenue of the Volcanoes as the sun began to rise. I spurred my horse and put some distance between myself and them. By mid-morning the volcanoes were in plain view, save for the peaks of the highest ones, which were swathed in a white shroud. In the distance, to the left, towered the massive Cotopaxi, its plume of smoke sinister in the morning light. Between the top of Cotopaxi and the flawless cerulean sky there was not a cloud, nothing but blue.

I rode on a prairie flanked by fique plants, their stems crowned with yellow flowers as tall as the weeping willows. The willows were all bent by the wind that blew in the direction of Quito. We passed Indians carrying their wares to the city, the red-skirted, black-hatted women with their babies on their backs. The men wore white pants, short purple ponchos, and white hats.

The sun was high in the sky, its white light almost blinding, when we left the main road and entered a lane of black volcanic soil flanked by purple wildflowers. This *camino* led to the family house. We passed low huts made of straw and mud where the field hands lived. From the orchards of pear and peach trees came the songs of blackbirds and mourning doves. Memories flooded my mind of the time I was old enough to ride horses far from the house and the three of us began to explore on horseback Catahuango's woods of cedar and palm, its apple and peach orchards, its lush meadows where cattle and sheep grazed, and the fields of lustrous obsidian soil, crossed by transparent streams, planted with corn, wheat, sweet-peas, barley, potatoes, scallions, and arracachas. Despite the stories we'd heard of the pumas that came down from the mountains to kill livestock, and sometimes people, I could not resist riding to the foothills of the mountains to look for herds of the enchanting but haughty llamas. On clear days, it was possible to spot in the ridges of the cordilleras timid vicuña families, and, lording it above them—and this was the greatest thrill of all—the majestic condors, their shadows gliding across the landscape.

My aunt and grandmother always protested loudly against my excursions. One afternoon I returned from one of my forays on the hacienda perspiring profusely, my dress splashed with mud. "Manuela," Aunt Ignacia said when she saw the state I was in, and the condition of Jonotás and Natán, "riding the way you do is not proper conduct for a young lady from a good family. If you persist in behaving like a boy, I'm going to forbid those black wenches to accompany you. I'm tired of their arrogance. They only take orders from you. One of these days I'm going to punish them, and maybe that will put some sense in their heads."

How I despised Ignacia when she insulted my girls. Jonotás and Natán were my sisters, the only people I loved in the world.

"I forbid you to raise a hand to them," I replied. "Do I have to remind you once again that Mother left them to me? They are not your property."

"I warn you, Manuela," Ignacia went on, "no man in his right mind is going to marry a girl who runs around with Negroes and behaves like an Amazon. At least no decent man I know of."

"I will never get married. I will take many lovers, but never a husband," I said, delighting in her scandalized expression. I grabbed the girls by their hands and ran from the room, laughing.

My relatives, both male and female, would cross themselves at such displays. Surely they prayed I would not grow up to em-

barrass them like my late mother. My aunt and uncle threatened to take away my riding privileges, but I scoffed at their
threats. I would return from my rides smelly, ravenous, sun-
burned. It was so exhilarating to race the horses in the invigo-
rating thin mountain air and see the wild animals that it would
take me hours to calm down. I would stay up until late at night
with Jonotás and Natán, planning the day when we would live
under the same roof, far from my mother's hideous family. Sitting in bed together, we exchanged stories. I would tell them
about convent school and what I learned there, about the other
girls, their pettiness and silly concerns, and about the cruel
nuns who were my teachers. The girls, in turn, would tell me
what happened at the farm while I was away at school. I read to
them from history books and taught them to read and write.

When Aunt Ignacia discovered me giving lessons to my
girls, she of course disapproved. But my grandmother said one
night at dinner, "You shouldn't object to Manuela teaching her
slaves. Giving lessons is the first ladylike thing I've ever seen
her do. Leave her alone. Maybe she will become a nun and
teach at a convent in Quito."

"That would be a great miracle indeed. There is a better
chance of all the volcanoes in Ecuador becoming inactive than
of Manuela becoming a nun," Ignacia sneered, as if I were not
there. "I just hope you're right, *Mamá*, and we don't live to regret the day those Negro wenches learned to read and write."

I wanted to grab my aunt by the neck and push her ugly face
in my bowl of steaming soup.

IN GIRLHOOD, I was only happy on my horse, roaming the
land. When the weather was warm and sunny, my girls and I

would tie our horses to the blackberry briers, undress, and bathe in the pools of diaphanous water created by the mountain streams. Afterward, we would dry each other off with our baby alpaca ponchos, spread them on the grass, and lay down naked to let the sun dry our hair. Often, we played my favorite game. We improvised makeshift swords and imagined ourselves to be soldiers in the revolutionary armies. Then we attacked the trees with our swords and hacked at them, pretending they were Spanish soldiers we were beheading. No one ever saw us enacting our battles in which we cavorted naked, else my family would have put a permanent end to my jaunts.

At dinner one night I refused to pray before starting the meal. When my grandmother chastised me, I reminded my relatives I was an atheist.

My grandmother crossed herself. "People were burnt by the Inquisition for saying less than that, Manuela."

"When South America is free of the Spanish Crown," I said, "we will give all the priests and nuns a taste of their own medicine and burn *them* at the stake."

"Manuela, *hija*," my grandmother said, "who puts these ideas in your head? In our family we don't talk like that. It must be those Negro witches you're always with. You had better come down from that cloud before you hurt yourself. Insolent women like you end up badly."

"I thought it was women who knew Greek who ended up badly," I said, reaching for the tray of roasted corn.

I WAS SMILING at the recollection of these scenes when we passed through the gates that led to the main house. A man I did not recognize, leading a burro loaded with potato sacks, approached us. I stopped him. "Good morning," I said. "Does the *señor* know if Doña Ignacia is at home?" I asked.

"*Sí, señora*, she is," the man said, his gaze full of curiosity to find out who was this lady accompanied by two Negro women wearing turbans.

Streams coursed through the eucalyptus groves, their scent filling my lungs. Sheep, donkeys, and llamas grazed in the corrals. Although many painful memories resided here, I could not deny the enchantment of the place. The land was greener than anywhere I had ever been, and the sky above the volcanoes in the distance, their snowcapped summits gleaming in the sun, was bluer than the purest aquamarine.

Barking dogs rushed to meet us as we drew near the house. The handsome building looked well kept, but it was cloaked in an aura of sorrow. Not until Estelita, the Indian cook, appeared on the front porch in her apron, to call the dogs, did I stop feeling like a stranger.

"*La niña Manuela* is home," Estelita cried and hurried down the steps to greet us as fast as her old limbs allowed. We dismounted and exchanged embraces with her.

Leaving the girls behind to chat with Estelita, I walked up to the house. The dogs had alerted Aunt Ignacia to our arrival. She appeared on the front porch, clothed in black, as if she were mourning not her loved ones but her ever having been born. Ignacia didn't seem to have aged so much as to have withered, dried up, like a stalk of corn left unpicked at the end of the harvest.

"Welcome, Manuela," she said and offered a wrinkled cheek for me to kiss. The glacial tone of her greeting told me I was anything but welcome. Still, Catahuango was my property and

I would not allow my aunt's coldness to make me feel as if it had been a mistake to make the journey.

"Thank you, *Tía*," I said. The affectionate epithet left a sour taste in my mouth.

"I hope you are planning to stay for a while."

"I just came for the day with Natán and Jonotás." She could not disguise her wince at my mention of the girls' names. "I'd like to spend a few hours on the farm before I return to Quito this afternoon."

"It's *your house*, Manuela," Ignacia said. "You can stay here for as long as you like. You must be tired after such a long ride. Would you like to join me for refreshments?"

We entered the gloomy drawing room, as cold as a mausoleum, to wait for the chocolate to be served. Nothing seemed to have changed since my last visit. All my fond memories of Catahuango were of the outdoors; the dark interior of the house had always made me feel ill at ease.

While we waited for the servant to bring our food, I made no mention of my unanswered letters, and Ignacia asked not one question about my life. She behaved as if she had last seen me just the day before. I wondered if news had reached her at the farm of my intimacy with the Liberator. To break the awkwardness created by her silence, I said, "You look well, *Tía*."

"I'm as healthy as I can hope to be at my age," she replied with a finality that closed the door on that subject.

When I asked about the old servants, Ignacia said dryly, "They either died or left Catahuango. Only Estelita remains."

I waited, as was the custom in Ecuador, until the chocolate, pastries with blackberry jelly, guava paste, and cheese were served. Then I broached the reason for my visit.

"*Tía*, I'm in Quito for only a short time. I don't know when I'll return to Ecuador again." My aunt's impassive stare did not indicate the least interest in my present or future life, so I continued. "There was a time when I thought I might end up living in Catahuango, but that seems unlikely now. What do you think about selling the farm? I'll give you half the proceeds, and you can move to Quito, where you could live comfortably and be closer to other people."

"If that's the reason for your visit, you've wasted your time coming here, Manuela."

I had promised myself that no matter how unpleasant she was toward me, I would not lose my temper. By law I was supposed to receive dividends from the farm upon coming of age. It had been years since I had received a cent. Was it possible the harvests had failed year after year, that the herds of livestock had been decimated by disease? Or could it be that my aunt's overseers were cheating her? What was the situation? "If Catahuango is no longer profitable, why not sell it before it's too late?" I said.

Ignacia straightened her back and wrang her hands. The thick, knotted veins in her neck looked alarmingly taut, as if they might burst. "Manuela, I will never sell Catahuango as long as I live. You will never see a cent from it until after I am dead. And if you persist in trying to gain control of the hacienda, I am prepared to declare in court that you are not my sister's daughter." As if to drive a stiletto in my heart, she added, "May I remind you that on your birth certificate, the identity of your parents was marked as 'unknown.' Furthermore, I swore to myself when you ran away with that lieutenant that I would only leave the land upon my death."

Though I did not respond to her insults she had more to say. "You and your so-called revolutionary *compadres* are responsible for ruining all the haciendas around here. Before all this rubbish about independence, the decent families worked hard and made an honest living. But these ridiculous wars have ruined the countryside, and all trade. Every time a battle is fought nearby, the soldiers requisition our grain, and our animals are slaughtered to feed them. You and your kind are responsible for ruining this land your mother left you. Ecuador was the armpit of the universe when the Spaniards ran it; but now that it's run by half-breeds and Indians, it will never, ever become a civilized nation—ever. Nothing good has come out of your so-called war of independence, and it never will. Mark my words. These mongrel nations of Indians and Negroes and mulattos will never amount to anything."

"Aunt Ignacia, please," I said. "I ask you to respect my beliefs. I didn't come here to be insulted."

"I always knew you would come to no good, Manuela," Ignacia continued, her voice rising. "From the day of your bastard birth, you have brought nothing but shame to our family. Look at you, look at what you've become—a woman of the streets, servicing generals. Thank God my mother died before she could see you become an army whore." She rose, indicating our visit was over. "I will repeat it in case you didn't hear me—until the day I die, you will not see a cent from Catahuango. Until the day I die, I will damn you. And even after I'm dead, I'll continue damning you for the shame you and your mother have brought to the Aispuru name."

I, too, rose to my feet, my knees shaking. Although Ignacia was old and feeble—and I had been taught to respect my elders—I could not control myself. I unleashed my open palm on Ignacia's cheeks once, twice, three times until she collapsed on her chair, a heap of seething hatred. I ran away from the room, knocking vases and bric-a-brac from their stands and tables in my desperation to get away from her.

13

1 8 2 3

I returned to Lima hoping I would become Bolívar's official mistress. Bolívar ruled without any significant opposition in Gran Colombia and was still loved by the people he had freed from Spain. Never again would the Liberator be so honored and respected as he was at that moment.

An emissary of the general met me in the Port of Callao with instructions that I should proceed directly to my house, that Bolívar would contact me later. This cool reception was unexpected, and I had no choice but to return to playing the role of Señora de Thorne.

James received me as if he were not aware of my romance with Bolívar in Quito. He seemed delighted to have me back in Lima. The time was not propitious for a confrontation. I myself was not sure what role, if any, I would play in Bolívar's current life. So I spoke to James only about how Ignacia had refused to relinquish her control of Catahuango.

"I'm sorry you had to make such a long trip for nothing, Manuela," he said. "I'm happy to see you home again, my dear. I'll make sure from now on you get a larger household allowance, to make up for your aunt's selfishness." Then he presented me with the dresses and jewels he had bought for me while I was away. I feigned pleasure as I unwrapped his expensive gifts.

THE WORD IN Lima was that Bolívar was planning to move from the Palace of the Viceroy into La Casona, which had been the viceroy's country house and was located in the nearby town of La Magdalena. As the days went by, with still no sign from him, my anger grew. One morning after James had left the house, a messenger arrived with an unsigned note that said, "Come to La Casona this afternoon."

Accompanied by Jonotás and Natán, I traveled by coach to the general's new home. Three months had gone by since Bolívar and I had parted. My hopes about us had survived, fed largely by my imagination and the few little gestures he had made in my direction. I had no idea what to expect from this meeting.

I was led directly to his office, where I found him pondering papers on his massive desk. His aide-de-camp closed the door and left us alone. In his presence all I wanted to do was run across the room and throw myself into his arms, but I stood still.

"Manuelita," he said, getting up from his chair and rushing toward me, smiling, "thank you for coming to see me."

I extended my hand. Bolívar took it, kissed it, and then put his arms around my waist and pulled me toward him. He kissed me on the lips, but I did not part mine to receive his kiss. I could not control my tears. I turned away—not wanting him to see me like this.

"Why are you crying, Manuelita?" he said quietly. "Aren't you happy we are together again?"

I pressed my open hands on his chest and backed away from his embrace. "Of course I'm happy to see Your Excellency again. It's just that..." My words trailed off. I did not want to explode with ire at the careless manner in which he had treated me. I sat down on a chair, opened my purse, pulled out a lace handkerchief James had brought me from Chile, and dabbed my cheeks. Next I pulled out a cigar and lit it. He had allowed me to smoke in his presence in Quito. I wondered if he would allow it now. My hand shook. The general sat on the chair opposite mine and regarded me tenderly. "I know I haven't been the most attentive lover, Manuelita," he said, "but you have never been out of my thoughts all this time."

"May I remind Your Excellency that I am not a mind reader," I said, not caring if I sounded too harsh. "If you had taken a few moments to write me a note since I arrived in Lima, or to dictate one to your secretaries, that would have been sufficient."

"Manuelita, I moved out of the palace so we might have privacy. If you came to see me there, the scandal would be too great. Here, if we are discreet, we can meet without creating an uproar."

I kept on smoking my cigar, staring at the ceiling.

"Manuelita," he said softly, "I'm no different from other men: I long for the intimacy and comfort of the woman I love in my bed. More than that, it is clear to me that you're not just another woman passing through my life. Until I met you,

Manuelita, I had never met a woman who could satisfy me in so many ways."

D'Elhuyar had taught me put no credence in the words of men when it came to love. But I recognized that caution was hopeless. I would do *anything* to keep Bolívar interested in me.

IT WAS CONVENIENT that James's business demanded frequent travel to other ports and other countries. During his absences, I spent the nights with Bolívar at La Casona. Often we would stay up until well past midnight, talking, dissecting the character of the men in his circle whose allegiance he was uncertain of. When James was in Lima, I became accomplished at creating plausible excuses to be away from the house all day so I could spend time with the general.

Daily, Jonotás and Natán went out to the market, the public plazas, the parks, and returned home with the rumors that went unreported in the newspapers. I instructed them to befriend the servants and slaves of those Bolívar did not trust to find out what they were saying about him. Providing him with useful information was a way of making myself indispensable. As Señora de Thorne I had come to know the most important families in Lima, and I understood a thing or two about limeños.

Despite the precautions I took, our love affair soon became common knowledge in Lima. As I became more confident of my place in the general's affections, I grew more indifferent toward James. He never acknowledged the change in our relationship, perhaps hoping that I would eventually come to my senses. Our marriage became that of two barely civil strangers bound to each other by convention. James and I stopped dining together, and communicated mainly through the servants. When his business associates came to the house for dinner, I excused myself, pleading illness. Ultimately, I left my husband no option but to confront me.

One night I was getting ready to visit the general when James burst into my bedroom without knocking. "Is it true what people are saying about your intimacy with the general? Is it true, Manuela?"

He had never before raised his voice to me. I was amazed at how little I cared. "It's true, James. The general and I are lovers."

"Are you aware how you're publicly humiliating me, Manuela? As your husband, I have the right to demand you stop seeing him at once," he said, calmer, his voice barely above its normal register.

"My dear friend," I replied in English, the language in which we sometimes communicated, "I don't see His Excellency in order to hurt you. I see him because life without him is inconceivable to me. I'd rather die than not be with Bolívar."

"Very well, then. If you persist in your insensate behavior, I'll have to send you to your father's house in Spain."

I took a step toward him. "James, when I was a girl I was ordered around by my mother's family, by the nuns, by my father. I am a woman now, and I will not take any orders from anyone. Not even from you, husband or not." All the frustration of this enforced marriage was about to erupt.

"Many women accept marriage as another kind of slavery," I said steadily. "I am not one of them. I am a free woman. You did buy me from my father once, but you cannot buy me from Bolívar. There's not enough money in the world to buy me away from him."

"If you think that Don Si-món Bo-lí-var is above the law, you're mistaken, Manuela," he said, scornfully enunciating the syllables of the Liberator's name. "I can make a great deal of trouble for him. He will come to regret this foolish affair. Just because he liberated this nation from Spain doesn't give him the right to claim the wives of the men of Peru."

"Don't be ridiculous, James. What can you do to harm the general? Hire an assassin? You'd never do anything that might jeopardize the status of your business. You seem to forget that Bolívar *is* the government. As for making you a public cuckold, so far, out of consideration for your position in the city, I've made every effort to be discreet. But if you persist in tormenting me, I will write a proclamation about my love for the general and paper the walls of Lima with it." Sensing by his silence that I had gained the upper hand in the discussion, I added, "Please leave my room; I am preparing to see His Excellency."

The Englishman stood frozen, his face red, his lips pressed into a thin line the color of ice, his clenched fists pressed against the side of his legs. I sat in front of the mirror and resumed brushing my hair. A few moments later James left, softly closing the door behind him.

JAMES BEGAN TO spend more time with his mistress. Why was it acceptable—indeed a badge of honor—for a man to have a lover, while it was forbidden to a woman?

No, I would not stop seeing Bolívar as long as he wanted to see me. I would not be forced out of my house, either, not until I was ready to leave it for good. After all, I came with a handsome dowry. Besides, I was still a valuable asset to James—I remained the heroine of Peruvian independence he could parade on his arm at society functions; the English-speaking hostess who could entertain his business associates.

WHAT I HAD been dreading finally happened. The Liberator marched off to create Bolivia, the new country that would complete his vision of Gran Colombia. This was another test of endurance for me, the second time he was leaving me behind. This time, however, Bolívar made sure I heard from him, if not in his own hand then in that of Santana, his secretary. No word came from him, though, about when he might return.

Everything in my luxurious home reflected the Liberator's absence and my loveless marriage. The rooms with high ceilings and many-paned windows where I displayed beautiful objects from all over the world became oppressive and stifling; the tiled corridors as glacial as the wind of the highlands; my bedroom a gold cage where I was indentured to the Englishman.

I spent many hours of the day reading Spanish love poetry. I memorized verses of Francisco de Quevedo, his definition of love: "It's an embracing ice, a cold fire...it's a coward with a hero's courage, it's walking lonely in a crowd..." In a rocking chair in the library I read love poems aloud, until I was hoarse. Other nights I locked myself with my girls in my bedroom and we drank wine and sang sad romantic ballads, until I fell into a stupor.

Only Rosita could understand my predicament. Though Bolívar and San Martín had not parted as friends after their meeting in Quito, Rosita and I shared the deep bond of being in love with the men who had given Peru its independence. It had been over a year since San Martín had left for Europe with a promise that he would send for Rosita. But even after San Martín's wife died, he had not asked Rosita to join him. She lived in an apartment on the top floor of the National Library, spurned by her family and by society for her affair with a married man. Thorne considered Rosita a ruined woman and forbade me to invite her into our home. So I met with her elsewhere.

One morning we rode in my coach to the seashore, to picnic on the esplanade that overlooked the ocean. After our luncheon, Rosita and I strolled along the esplanade, the vast grayness of the still Pacific beside us. Our black lace mantillas were draped over our shoulders. We had uncovered our heads because there were no other people on the promenade. We were both so alike: our Quito past, the convent, our illegitimacy, our looks, though Rosita had a darker complexion—her features betrayed a distant African ancestry—and now we shared the pain of absent lovers.

"Before I met Bolívar, I could bear living with the Englishman. Now he's repulsive to me, Rosita. With every passing day, I blame my father more for my unhappiness."

"I don't like to see you sad," Rosita said, regarding me with affection.

From where we stood, we could see a whaling vessel entering the Port of Callao, flying the American flag. Hundreds of feet below us, flocks of shrieking seabirds fed off the still waters.

"At least you will have your own money when you sell your hacienda," Rosita said. "You can survive without Thorne."

Of course what she meant to say was; "If Bolívar ever tires of you, you won't be destitute like me."

"True. Someday I'll be a rich woman, if my aunt doesn't outlive me. When I sell Catahuango, you can come live with me. We'll open a hat shop. And on the side a little candy story. We'll make the most delicious sweets in the Andes."

She laughed. "Knowing you, Manuela, you'll eat every sweet before the first customer comes. But if San Martín doesn't send for me, I like the idea."

"Of course he will send for you," I said with conviction, to reassure her. Rosita so desperately wanted to join him in England.

"It's been over a year since he became a widower, Manuela. I thought once he settled in Europe he'd send for me. Don't feel too sorry for me, though. Even if I never see San Martín again, I don't regret—have never regretted—having been his mistress. To welcome him to a liberated Lima, in that intoxicating period after the defeat of the Spaniards—my life *was* glorious. Even if I've lost the support of my family and my place in society, it was worth it for those fourteen months of glory."

I took Rosita by the arm and we walked back toward my coach. When the driver held my hand to help me climb inside, I turned around to look at the pallid sky over the ashen ocean and thought, "Rosita's past could be my own future."

As we approached the National Library, I reached for Rosita's silk purse, untied it and poured into it all the gold coins in my own purse. I retied the ribbons of her purse and placed it in her lap. She leaned her head on my shoulder. "I was a woman who once had my own carriage," she said. "Now I live on the charity of my friends."

"Rosita, don't think of my help as charity. You're the sister I wish I'd had. Whatever I have is *ours*."

The coachman stopped in front of the steps of the National Library. We embraced and kissed. As the driver opened the door, Rosita covered her head and face with her mantilla, leaving one eye exposed, in which I read fear, the fear of a woman who saw a bleak future ahead of her.

BOLÍVAR RETURNED IN triumph from Bolivia. One evening, wanting to see him, I had my horse saddled and rode the city's unlit streets to La Casona. I had not sent word ahead, and I sensed by the awkwardness of the guards at the door, that perhaps I had come at an inconvenient moment. I hurried past them, shoved the sentry posted at the general's door out of my way, and entered his bedroom.

Bolívar and a woman were naked in bed. The woman hid her face in a pillow.

"Manuela! Please wait outside," Bolívar yelled, as he scrambled to get out of bed.

I dashed toward the woman, whom I recognized as Doña Teresa de Herrera y Alba, a high-born *limeña* prominent in her devotion to the Catholic Church. She had made a point of snubbing me in society since I had become Bolívar's lover.

"Hypocritical whore," I lashed out at her, striking her back with my riding crop. "You whisper behind my back for doing openly what you do in secret!"

Doña Teresa covered herself with the bed linens, screaming hysterically. Bolívar tried to restrain my punishing arm. I pushed him away, scratching his cheek. "Traitor," I shouted at him. "I see I'm no more to you than another whore. A free ride to satisfy your insatiable lechery. That's all I am to you."

Doña Teresa grabbed her garments and shoes and fled the room.

Bolívar let go of my arm and sat down, blood trickling down

his cheek. The sight of his blood made me pause. I took a towel and dipped it in the jar of water on the nightstand and handed it to him. He sat in silence, his face covered by the towel.

I did not regret what I had done—his betrayal was crushing. I had risked so much for a man who treated me as another spoil of war. He was no better than Fausto D'Elhuyar. I headed for the door.

Bolívar removed the towel from his face and said, "Manuela, please close the door. Come here and hold the towel until the bleeding stops."

LATER THAT SAME NIGHT Bolívar asked me to leave the Englishman and move into La Casona. I decided to end my marriage in order to save my life. Married to Thorne I had almost been buried alive in a life of shallow concerns. My involvement in the revolution had given me a chance to play a part in the creation of history. I would pay *any* price to help the Liberator solidify his dream of a Gran Colombia. If Bolívar loved me only while he was in Lima, I would return his love without thinking of the consequences. I consoled myself with the thought that just to have his love for now was more than most women could ever hope to have.

THUS BEGAN THE DAYS of our greatest passion. Never again would we know the luxury of so much time together, nor would Bolívar ever again be so healthy and vigorous. Finally, I gave myself to him as I could not before. I let him possess me in many new ways, the way he preferred, with me on my hands and knees and him exploding in me from behind. We did not

tire of each other in bed. We would postpone that moment
when we became fully satisfied, eager to explore our limits as
lovers. I walked about during the day feeling sore between my
legs. I bore the discomfort proudly. Those nights contained the
happiest moments of my life. It was then that I came to realize
that the body and the soul were one single entity, that true
love could only be experienced in the body if it resided first in
the heart. D'Elhuyar and the Englishman had created a frozen
place in my heart for men. I only allowed Bolívar to know me
in my deepest intimacy when I saw him sacrifice something
for me. During those days of sexual exaltation at La Casona, I
came into my own as a woman, I became Manuela Sáenz, and I
felt the glory and the beauty of being this woman. It had nothing to do with the fact that I had become Bolívar's official mistress, that all of Peru knew I had moved into La Casona, with
my girls, to be the lady of the house. Instead, I was the most
powerful woman in Peru, because no other woman was loved
with more intensity. Later there would be other happy days,
but these would be intermittent. At La Casona it never oc-
curred to me our happiness would one day come to an end.

THERE WAS ONLY one last step to be taken before I freed myself from my past—my unfinished business with James
Thorne. One day when I got word he was traveling on business,
I went back to his house for the very last time, to collect the
valuables that were mine.

The Englishman had lavished upon me all the accoutre-
ments of rich limeñas. My bedroom overflowed with riches.
Gold opera glasses from Cuzco, silver brushes and combs from
Potosí, pearls from Japan and Panama, emerald necklaces from

Muzo, watches set with rubies and pearls, gold and mother-of-pearl vanity cases encrusted with diamonds and emeralds; fans made of feathers from exotic and rare birds; handbags embroidered in gold and silver; Chinese silk gloves; a gold cigar case, my initials inscribed in diamonds; ivory cigar holders; an emerald and diamond tiara boasting stones fit for a vicereine.

Each ring, necklace, brooch, or bracelet had a story—a birthday, an anniversary. There was no question that I would take the pieces I had inherited from my mother. As for James's gifts, my father had provided him with a lavish dowry, so I had no qualms about taking back what rightly belonged to me.

I knew at that moment I might well be saying good-bye to my life of privilege and wealth. The mistress of el Libertador would lack for nothing, that was so. Yet leaving Thorne for a future of uncertainty was a gamble. But there was no going back to feeling dead in my body and soul. All my life I had enjoyed riches and felt dissatisfied, empty. Simón Bolívar made me the free woman I had always wanted to be. If there were consequences to be paid for my rashness, so be it.

14

Natán

I was happy to be back in Lima. For the first time since I could
remember I had a life that was my own, not Manuela's. Before we left for Quito, I had fallen in love with a freed slave
named Mariano who wanted to marry me. We had met in the
market. One day I passed by his stand where he sold nails,
hammers, saws, knives. He had just looked up after receiving
money from a customer and our eyes caught each other's, both
of us surprised. I had been attracted to other men before and a
few had even proposed marriage, but I was determined to wait
until a man I wanted came along. When our eyes met I blushed
and kept walking. "Hey, pretty lady," I heard behind my back.
I knew it was him calling me. I turned around. "Did you say
something?"

"You have a name?"

"Silly Negro," I said, taking a good look at him. He was
dark-skinned, rather on the short side, with a little round

belly and huge hands. "Of course I have a name. Why? You don't?"

"My name's Mariano," he said, leaning on the counter of his stand. "What's yours? Come and talk to me."

"I don't go around telling my name to just any man who speaks to me," I said. "And I have better things to do than talk to you. I have work to do." As I walked away, swaying my hips, I heard him say, "I know you'll be coming back, mystery woman. I'll be waiting for you tomorrow."

Usually, such forwardness would have put me off. But there was something about this Mariano. The mischievous sparkle in his eyes attracted me. I like men who make me laugh. Funny men are always intelligent. And I was thirty years old. If I waited much longer to get married, I might never have a family—my most cherished dream.

The next day, even though there was no need for me to go to the market, I strolled by Mariano's stand with my shopping basket. When he saw me he greeted me again with "pretty lady," displaying two rows of strong teeth. I didn't smile back. "Do you have this kind of nail?" I said, pulling a nail from my basket.

Instead of taking the nail, Mariano touched my wrist. "I knew I'd see you today," he said. "You're just the prettiest thing since they invented silk."

I didn't pull my wrist away. "You insolent Negro!" I said, putting on a serious face. "Do you have this kind of nail or not? Because if you don't..."

Mariano took the nail from my hand, and then took my hand in his and planted his lips on it. And that was that. I had never met a Negro with that kind of confidence.

✧⊃✧

FROM THAT DAY ON, not a day passed that I did not find an excuse to go to the market. I kept our romance a secret, even from Jonotás. The idea began to form that I should ask Manuela for my freedom. Mariano said he wanted to marry me. "Natán, tell your mistress I'm ready to buy your freedom, if that's what it takes."

I was about to ask Manuela for the freedom she had always promised me when she announced we were going to Quito to sell Catahuango. Since she said it would be a short trip, I decided to wait to tell her about Mariano and his marriage proposal until we got back.

Mariano was unhappy at this news. "If you really love me," I said, "you'll wait for me. Manuela promised us we'll be back in a few months. She'll be so happy when she sells her farm, she'll not think twice about letting me go."

THE NEXT DAY AFTER we returned to Lima, I went to see Mariano. From the way his eyes lit up when he saw me, I knew his feelings for me had not been diminished by my absence.

"Now that you are here, let's get married as soon as possible, *negrita adorada*," Mariano said, kissing me. "Tell your mistress I am ready to buy your freedom."

"Mariano," I protested, "you won't have to do that. Manuela's not like other white people. Manuela cares for me. She's like a sister to us. She wants my happiness."

"I know she's been a good mistress to you, Natán. But kind or not, white masters do not easily give up their slaves."

He was wrong, I was certain. I had known Manuela all her life. She always insisted that I called her Manuela, not *doña* or *señora*, even when there were white people present. She always said we could have our freedom any time we wanted it, and I believed her. The right moment to ask for my freedom would come soon. Then I would settle down with my Mariano to have a family.

Manuela was always full of surprises. No sooner had I gotten up the nerve to talk to her about my plans, she moved out of Mr. Thorne's house and went to live at La Casona, taking Jonotás and me with her. Again I would have to wait until things settled a bit. Another month passed before the situation at La Casona presented a moment to speak with Manuela.

She was never more relaxed than when she sat down to embroider. One afternoon, when Jonotás was off on an errand and we were sitting together in her sewing room, choosing patterns and colors for a tablecloth, the moment seemed favorable.

"Manuela, there is something I've been wanting to tell you for a long time." She smiled, her face full of curiosity, as I told her the story of how I had met Mariano.

"Well!" she exclaimed. "You could have fooled me. I had no idea. Oh, Natán," she said, embracing me, "you deserve all the happiness in the world."

"That's not all, Manuela," I continued, now that I had her undivided attention. "He's a free man and he wants to marry me."

"My felicitations, my dear. This is the best news." Her joy for me was genuine—I could see that. "He will be the luckiest man in the world. When can I meet Mariano? You have to bring him here as soon as possible. I'm so eager to meet him.... But if I don't think he's worthy of you, I'll tell you so."

Manuela was full of questions about Mariano. What did he do for a living? Where was he from? How old was he? Had he been married before? How long had he been a free man? Was he handsome? And (a question that almost made me shudder) would he like to join the general's army? When I had answered her questions, Manuela took my hand and said, "Come with me, Natán."

Manuela asked me to take the seat in front of her dressing table. She opened the chest that contained her jewels and pulled out a pearl necklace, a diamond brooch, and a gold chain with a crucifix made of emeralds. She laid them out on the table for me to admire. I knew the pieces. They were beautiful and very costly ornaments. "These will be part of your dowry," Manuela said. She took the pearl necklace and roped it around my neck. I looked at myself in the mirror, not believing it was me. The exquisite pearls from Japan made me forget I was a slave.

"Look at you," Manuela clapped her hands in delight. "You look like an African princess. Oh, Natán, you will look so regal on your wedding day."

Her generosity was overwhelming, yet she had not uttered the words I longed to hear. Sensing my disappointment, Manuela said, "Of course you're free to marry Mariano. You didn't even have to ask. However, I must ask you to delay your happiness for a little while until my own situation with Señor Thorne and the general is resolved. The general has decided to go after the renegade Royalists troops hiding in the Andes. The liberation of Peru will not be secure until these forces are defeated. The Liberator has vowed to persecute and destroy them. After the Royalists are crushed, that will be the best time for you to get married. As the patriot you are, I'm asking you to make this great sacrifice for our cause, Natán."

It was hard to mask my disappointment. I wanted her to free me right then and there. I was sick of following her from place to place. I was sure that the Liberator and the battles for independence would be fine without me. And probably without her. Manuela was asking me to drop the subject of my freedom and to postpone my marriage. I had given this woman almost every waking moment and every hour of my life, and the first time I asked her for anything she was asking me to wait. The battle I wanted to fight was for an end to slavery, for an end to my enslavement, not for the liberation of the descendants of the Spaniards in South America, whose egotism knew no bounds.

Perhaps Mariano had been right after all, that I would not achieve my freedom unless I fought for it.

LIFE AROUND THE LIBERATOR was lived moment to moment, and eventful. Preparations were under way for the new campaign. This time, Manuela was determined to join the general and his troops. Without room for doubt, he let her know this was impossible. A kind of war started between the two of them. Manuela mounted a campaign of her own to get the general to change his mind. She moved out of their bedroom in La Casona and refused to eat meals with him. She was playing a dangerous game. It was clear to me then that he must have loved her very much to put up with her haughtiness.

A few days before the general was set to depart for his campaign, Manuela sent for Jonotás and me. We found her in her bedroom in a state of delirious excitement. *"Mis niñas,"* she said, running toward us, her arms open to embrace us. "I have the best news." What crossed my mind at that moment was that she was going to say her Aunt Ignacia had died. Which would have made me happy for Manuela. Instead, she said, "The general has given us permission to follow his troops. We will not be marching with the main regiment, but in the rear guard. We will be a day or so behind them, taking care of the wounded. At all times we must be ready to send reinforcements to his regiment in case they're needed."

It was good news for her, because the women who followed their lovers in the army, or who disguised themselves as men to join the troops, were punished with fifty lashes if they were caught. Obviously, special dispensations would be made for Manuela.

Jonotás and Manuela jumped up and down with joy, but I was seething. I already dreaded trekking across frigid mountains, crawling up slippery cliffs, being perpetually drenched, infested with chiggers and fleas, maybe eating rodents to stay alive. I had heard about all these things from slaves who helped the officers fight their wars. Not to mention the unpredictable attacks of the Indians—rock slingers whose aim was much more accurate than any weapon in use in the army of the patriots.

Manuela was content to give up her life for the cause of liberation; and Jonotás, of course, would give up her own life to protect Manuela's. I, on the other hand, resented more and more the war of liberation from Spain. It's true that the general and many of his followers were abolitionists, and one of the promises he made was that slavery would end once South

America was free from Spain. Yet I could see quite plainly what
the end of slavery had meant to the Indians. They were no longer owned body and soul by white people, but the Spaniards
treated their dogs better. The Indians' lot had improved little
in the three hundred years that had passed since their so-
called liberation. All I wanted was to be with Mariano. Yet I
could not breathe a word of these thoughts to Manuela, or even
to Jonotás.

Manuela had more to say. "*Mis niñas*, I've decided that if we
want to be treated with respect by the troops, we need to dress
as soldiers."

To me, putting on a soldier's costume was just a silly game
left over from childhood. Jonotás and Manuela, however, were
deadly serious about it. Dressed as soldiers, they felt as if they
had the power of men. Like so much of what I did when I lived
with them, I also dressed as a soldier, though I much preferred
wearing a dress. I enjoyed the way men looked at me when I
wore a dress, and their compliments made me feel good.

I HAD LIVED my entire life in a world at war, where violence
and cruelty were the norm. Yet I had never seen combat first-
hand until this Peruvian campaign. In the remote Andes,
where we were going, there were Indians who had never even
heard of the Wars of Independence. They were used to the idea
of having a king. It was here that the last Spanish regiments in
Peru were hiding from Bolívar. The high cordilleras were a
perfect place from which to launch surprise attacks and then
flee.

Everybody knows the names of the great generals who led
the people against the Spaniards and liberated South America.

But what of the men they commanded? Who were they? The slaves fought because their masters ordered them to fight, the way Jonotás and I followed Manuela wherever she went. The rest of the soldiers—Indians and *criollos*—were mercenaries who fought for a change of clothes, tobacco, and food. Few of the soldiers in the patriot armies believed their lot would actually improve after the defeat of the Spaniards. Often, when they got tired of fighting—underclothed, shoeless, hungry, and sick with scurvy—many deserted, fleeing to hide in the forbidding jungles, or the woods of the cordilleras, or the frozen wastelands of the high Andes, where they could blend in with the permanent fog—if they did not freeze to death first. I believe many of these soldiers fought because the taking of human life was one of the few pleasures left to them.

FOR THE NEXT year, we followed the Liberator's troops across the baking deserts of the coast and up the icy peaks of the cordilleras. Often, the Indians mounted surprise attacks on us, provoking avalanches or raining stones upon us with their slings. When our troops entered an Indian village, looking for recruits, all the able-bodied men had run away to hide in caves in the snowy reaches of inaccessible mountains, where no one dared go after them. That's how much Indians feared what the Spaniards would do to them if they were suspected of collaborating with the revolutionary army. On our march, we heard accounts of Indians who refused to feed the Spaniards and were burned alive in their huts. Those Indians were the lucky ones. Others were drawn and quartered—tied to four horses heading in separate directions. The corpses of the men were dismembered: their heads and limbs hung in the trees, their intestines festooning the branches, and the trunks of their bodies cubed and cooked in soups that the villagers were forced to eat. The leftovers were tossed to the dogs and pigs. Pregnant women were forced to gather in the plaza where the Spanish soldiers tore out their fetuses and presented them to the fathers. Afterward, the men were flayed alive, their testicles and penises cut off and inserted in the vaginas of their wives and daughters. The rest of the women of the village were raped. Their lives were spared so that they could teach their children to fear what would happen to anyone who rebelled against the crown. When I heard about these things, I wished all the Spaniards dead. After all, it was the Spaniards who had kidnaped my people in Africa, and the Spaniards who had destroyed my family. For that I would loath them until I took my last breath.

As a slave I had been taught that we Negroes were superior and more valuable than the smaller, reserved Indians, who never adapted to white society. Africans eventually lost their languages, whereas the Indians still spoke among themselves in Quechua and Aymará. Maybe we Africans thought there was no chance of ever returning to Africa, while the Indians, knowing they were the majority of the population, secretly clung to the hope that one day they would drive off the invaders from their ancestral lands.

We Negroes made exotic house servants, the white man thought, whereas Indians were valued only for their knowledge of farming. After the king freed them, Indians became invisible. The people fighting the Wars of Independence, and this included Manuela and Bolívar, couldn't care less about the Indians. At least when the Indians were slaves, their masters had to feed them to keep them working. Now most of the

Indian men in the cities lived in an alcoholic stupor, while their wives and children died of hunger.

That's why it was no surprise to me that most of the Indians were mercenaries fighting for the Royalists. They must have understood, after centuries of Spanish rule, that the Wars of Independence—whether they were won by the Spaniards or the patriots—were not being fought on their behalf.

It was during this campaign that Manuela learned to shoot a musket, wield a sword, and use a lance. For the first time she seemed fulfilled. She had been waiting all her life to become a soldier. She won the admiration of the general's troops as a woman who, in a soldier's uniform, could fight like a warrior on the battlefield, and, in a dress, transform herself into a lady. As part of the rear guard, she won the soldiers' love by succoring the wounded.

The campaign was to become one of the Liberator's great successes. Before he could claim victory, however, he had to defeat a large and well-armed Spanish regiment garrisoned near Cuzco. The Liberator's bravest soldiers marched ahead to engage and battle the renegades. We in the rear camped on the shores of Lake Tumaca, to wait for news of victory so we could bring the troops provisions and assist the wounded. We were waiting to receive word of another success when a messenger arrived—the Royalists had cornered our troops on a plateau at the edge of a precipice. From the slopes of a mountain they were decimating our regiment with rocks, cannon, and mortar fire. Our soldiers had no cover on the open plateau, where their only defense was to dig trenches.

Manuela, hearing this news, said to Colonel Herrán, who was in charge of our division, "There's not a moment to lose, Colonel. If the Liberator is defeated, everything we've fought for will have been wasted. We must all go at once to the defense of our men."

Colonel Herrán immediately gave orders to prepare for a march on the enemy. Anyone who could ride and use a weapon left the camp at a gallop. Only the sick and wounded remained behind. They were given arms to defend themselves in case they were attacked by unfriendly Indians.

Riding at full speed without stopping, we reached the area where the battle was being fought late that afternoon. Colonel Herrán and Manuela decided that the attack on the Spaniards could not wait till morning. After studying a map of the area, Manuela came up with a plan that was as bold as it was mad. She proposed that we climb the back of the mountain where the Royalist troops were lodged and attack them from behind. It amounted to a suicide dash to take horses down that sheer slope. We might all die from broken necks before the Spaniards had a chance to fire a shot at us. But if by some miracle we succeeded, we might create a great deal of confusion and give the general's troops a chance to regroup and counterattack.

When we reached the top of the mountain, our meager and exhausted troops began to lose their spirit. We needed horses with wings to roll down that incline. Manuela grabbed the Colombian flag and addressed the men, "We have two choices now, my brothers. To live as heroes or to die as cowards. If we must die, let's do it with dignity." Next she hoisted the flag against the darkening sky and, crying "Death to tyranny," spurred her horse and plunged toward the Spaniards, firing her pistol in the air. Without hesitation, Jonotás followed, firing her pistol, too. Seeing Manuela flying into that precipice, she transformed from a flesh-and-bone woman into a figure larger than life. In that moment I forgave her for her reckless-

ness, for everything—I could not deny the heroism and the
fire of Manuela Sáenz. I spurred my horse after her. Not to be
outdone by three women, our soldiers followed. I was terrified
sliding down that slope, firing my gun, but I can honestly say I
had never felt so intensely alive.

As the Royalists tried to thwart our descent, General Bolívar,
seeing the Colombian flag flying down the incline, took advantage of the distraction and led his men up the mountain to
engage the Spaniards in hand-to-hand combat. The Royalists
had relied on their superior artillery to weaken the Liberator's
forces. Caught between two flanks, they became confused.

By sunset, the enemy had been slaughtered. Rills of blood
ran down the mountain. Condors hovered in the sky like ravenous angels of death, waiting to feast on mountains of
corpses.

Later that night, we collected buckets of blood from the
prisoners as they were beheaded so that the Liberator's staff,
who had run out of ink, could use it to write letters to Lima announcing our victory.

That day I thought of a book Manuela read to us so long ago.
The story flowed from her lips in a way that made Don Quixote
more demented, Sancho Panza funnier, more pathetic, and
wiser; the people they met on the road larger and more vivid
than anyone we would ever encounter in real life; the roads of
Castille, the towns of Spain, the caves, inns, mills, rivers, and
forests more enchanted than any place in a fairy tale. Don
Quixote's and Sancho's wisdom was filtered through Manuela,
so that she squeezed out its essence, its very truth. I understood that day that Don Quixote was her ideal, and Jonotás and
I were her Sancho Panza.

After this victory, Bolívar's troops dubbed Manuela "La Coro-

nela." She became, in effect, the most admired woman in Peru. Bolívar was acclaimed, even worshiped, in the Americas and in Europe. He became the most celebrated man in the world, the South American Napoleon, and Manuela, empress.

GRAN COLOMBIA was a restless hornets' nest. Late in 1826, it became imperative that the Liberator return to Bogotá where his vice-president, General Santander, was plotting against him. Manuela pleaded to accompany him, but the Liberator reminded her that the march to Bogotá would be grueling. Manuela, being Manuela, did not give in easily: had she not proven she could keep up with him in the Andes? He reminded her that she had become a controversial figure, and he wanted to put out the fires of discontent along the way, not stoke them. The Liberator prevailed. He left Manuela settled in La Casona, with promises he would send for her as soon as he reached Bogotá. He knew that without him to protect her, she, too, was at risk from his political enemies. She was relieved, then, that he left some of his most trusted men behind to look after her.

The general had made many new enemies by dividing Peru to create Bolívia. Soon after he left Lima, on the night of January 25, 1827, the troops in Lima, led by Colonel José Bustamante, led a coup that overthrew Bolívar's government. Manuela's protectors fled or were incarcerated. Her life was in danger. There were many in Lima who would have loved to see her hanged. All mail going in and out of the city was censored; there was no way to send word to Bolívar of the danger she was in.

Manuela chose to act rather than wait for Bustamante to strike first. Many soldiers in Lima, still loyal to Bolívar, had not forgotten how she had fought alongside them, dressed their wounds, and raised money to make them uniforms. So Manuela donned her colonel's uniform, and pinned the Order of the Sun medal on her breast. Jonotás and I also dressed in military garb and followed Manuela on horseback to the Lima barracks. Addressing the soldiers from her horse, she incited them to start an insurrection and get rid of the usurper Busta-mante. The soldiers cheered her and the Liberator and swore they would fight to protect his legacy. That night, around mid-night, Bustamante's cadre burst into La Casona, dragged Ma-nuela from the house, and locked her up in a cell at the Convent of the Nazarenas. The nuns received orders to withhold pen and paper from her.

Jonotás was taken to Casa Matas, a prison for female crimi-nals, where she was surrounded by murderers and women who tried to pass themselves off as men. I was so afraid for her. And for myself, too. The only reason I escaped the same fate was that the night they were arrested I was staying at Mariano's.

I had to do something to help Manuela. Although Mariano tried to dissuade me, I told him I had to act as my heart de-manded. I could not abandon Jonotás and Manuela when they needed me. I acquired a nun's habit and disguised myself as a sister of charity of Santa Rosa of Lima. Then I went to the con-vent where Manuela was being held. I guess I had not lived with Jonotás and Manuela in vain—their recklessness was contagious.

I found Manuela in a small cell, with just a cot, a chair, and a bucket to relieve herself. She was dirty and smelled bad, her face was puffy, her eyes red, as if she had not slept for days. She smiled when she saw me. Her first question was about Jonotás. Did I have any news about her? Manuela became enraged when I told her Jonotás was locked up in Casa Matas. She wanted to know what people in the streets were saying about the Liberator—had he made it to Bogotá?

"I don't live for myself anymore, but for Bolívar," she said. "Natán, he needs me. I must escape and go to him."

We discussed schemes to help her do this. I suggested that I could come back with a nun's habit hidden under my skirt and she could leave with me wearing that disguise.

"Natán, I can't let you do that," Manuela said. "If you're caught helping me, they will hang you without mercy." It was true. Slaves were forgiven little in Gran Colombia.

"No," she said, "we must wait. If you can come to see me again, bring me pen and paper to write letters. In the meantime, get word to Jonotás not to despair. Tell her I will not abandon her. We will leave Peru together. I promise you. We'll get out of this land of swine and never return."

I did not want to leave Peru. I was tired of following Manuela from country to country, and I was sick of war. What I wanted was to marry Mariano, and live in one place, under one roof. And yet, in the last two years I had come to see Manuela as a great woman, one who would be remembered in South American history. This was not the time to tell her how I really felt. Manuela had been a kind mistress, a sister, a friend, and now she needed me. I would not desert her, even if that meant I would have to postpone my own life with Mariano. After all, this was not the first time I had asked Mariano to wait for me.

15

The door of my cell opened and James Thorne walked in. I was stunned. I rose from my cot, smoothed my hair and my dress, and offered him my hand. When his lips brushed my skin I did not feel the usual revulsion. In the time I'd been living with Bolívar, my resentment toward James had begun to wane. I pointed to the only chair in the cell. He took it and I sat on the edge of the cot.

"How are they treating you, Manuela?" His tone of concern, not reproach, was unexpected.

"At least the nuns can't make me get on my knees and say the rosary in this convent."

James smiled and his face relaxed. He had always enjoyed my sense of humor, and apparently still did. It was admirable of him to come see me when I was so helpless and friendless. I suspected that Rosita had tried to visit and the nuns had turned her away.

"Manuela, I have come to offer you help," he whispered.

It was clear to me how difficult it must be for him to do this. I had made him a cuckold, a laughingstock. There was probably no other man in the Andes who would come to the aid of an adulterous wife. "James, I am sorry for—"

"That's the past," he said, stopping me. "I came to talk about the present, Manuela. Perhaps you know that the talk in Lima is that you will be hanged. I am here to say that this will not happen." He placed his chair closer to me until our knees almost touched, then leaned forward. "As you know, I am held in high regard by the Church, even though it is not my own. I have been extremely generous with the bishopric of Lima for many years. I can manage your escape. I am confident that I can negotiate with the new government. They need my ships. I can bribe government officials. I promise you I won't give up until I succeed."

I was trembling with the effort not to cry. "And what do you want in return?"

"I was wounded when you left me for Bolívar, I won't deny it. But over the years, as my admiration for you has grown, so has my love. With you gone, that big house is the loneliest place on earth. If you wish, we could settle in Panama or Chile. I—"

"I've underestimated the kind of man you are, James. And I am grateful," I said. "But I can't return to you. I don't love you. Nothing has changed in that respect in the years we've been apart. Even if I were never to see Bolívar again..."

"Fine," he said, briskly. "Fine. So let's get back to the matter at hand. We must move quickly to arrange your release and book passage for you for Ecuador."

"I can't leave without my girls, James," I said, even though

I knew he disliked them. "I made a promise I would never abandon them. They must accompany me."

James gathered his hat and walking stick. "As you wish. I will arrange that, too. Now I must go. We must move quickly."

I rose from my cot to say good-bye, offering my hand. "Thank you, James."

"I made a pledge to be your husband in sickness and in health, Manuela. As long as I live, I will do everything in my power to protect you. Never forget this."

Two days later, accompanied by Jonotás and Natán, I sailed from Callao in an English frigate. Guayaquil was my destination. As the arid mountains behind Lima began to fade in the distance, I said a silent good-bye to Peru. I was of two minds about leaving Lima. The city represented my unhappy marriage, but it was also the place where I became a heroine of independence and the soldier I had longed to be since my schooldays in Quito. Most important, I became one with Bolívar in Lima, happy for the first time. In Lima my love for Bolívar had ripened, and he had become more than a lover—a true husband. My destiny was to share his life. In Ecuador, I would be closer to Colombia, where, I hoped, I would join Bolívar as soon as he wrote to me asking me to meet him in Bogotá.

I was twenty-eight years old and I had seen much of the treachery and cruelty of men and become acquainted with the arbitrary nature of life. In the eight years since I arrived in Lima to wed James Thorne, I had become another woman: weary, hardened, but not disillusioned. I had Bolívar and the future glory of Gran Colombia to live for.

book
THREE

Bolívar's Liberator

16

SANTA FE DE BOGOTÁ,
COLOMBIA
1828–1834

I had little to do in Quito except daydream about Bolívar and about what our life would be like when we would be reunited. To keep my mind from going dormant, I read aloud to Jonotás and Natán the same books I'd read to Bolívar at night in Lima— the Roman historians he loved, and *Don Quixote*. The adventures of the mad knight and Sancho made us laugh hard, leaving us breathless, teary-eyed. I began to think of Bolívar as the Knight of the Sorrowful Countenance, and of myself as his Sancho Panza. Since meeting Bolívar, I, like Sancho, had spent most of my life on the road. From each expedition on which we sallied forth, I returned battered, like Sancho. But Sancho dreamed of a high rank for himself and his children, and to govern a rich island, a kingdom that he could place in the hands of his minions so he could loll about. What did I want? I followed Bolívar because I loved him, and I loved him because by following him, I could live for an ideal, something greater than myself. After I had tasted a measure of the Liberator's greatness, I could not go back to living the aimless life of a wealthy woman. My desire to be at his side was my chief reason for living. Apart from *el Libertador*, I felt useless, like a limb severed from a body. When I was with him, he made me feel I was at the center of his world. I loved the way he called my name. When he said "Manuelita," I felt as though he were not only naming me, but listing all my attributes, and even my foolishness. I loved the way he lingered on each vowel, prolonging the sounds, as though naming me were a kind of foreplay and my name was a charm used to cast a spell. When he said my name with so much feeling, I was certain of the powerful bond of our intimacy. I recognized it as the true language of lovers, a language understood only by the two of us, and from which everyone else was excluded. Almost two years had gone by since I had heard his voice calling me across the room, or across the bed, or whispering in my ear. It was his voice, with the warmth and sonority of the way people spoke in Caracas, that I missed most of all. What gave me the fortitude to wait for him was the knowledge that no matter how many women threw themselves at him, they were not part of his destiny. I was. I alone had captured Bolívar's heart.

IN THE BEGINNING I waited patiently, trusting that we'd be reunited soon. But as the months passed, I became angry. Had I fallen in love with a man whose true mistress was war? I sat down and wrote:

Sir,

How can you claim to still love me and be so oblivious to my predicament? I am starting to believe that you have forgotten your Manuelita, that another woman has replaced her in your affections.

I did not want to appear pathetic: I wanted the general's passion, not his pity. I could not in seriousness allow myself to contemplate the possibility that he had fallen in love with someone else and no longer wanted me as his lover. I did not want Bolívar to call me to his side because he felt guilty, but I had no choice.

"I left my husband," I continued, "to follow you, to fight by your side in battles. Need I remind you, with all the respect that you deserve, that I did not end my marriage to spend the rest of my life waiting for you. My general, I am not a woman made for waiting." If this letter sounded like an ultimatum, I had to risk it. I signed it, "Your loving Manuelita."

The world seemed to be running out of air for two months, when, at last, I received his reply.

> Your kindness and your charms awaken my frozen heart, Manuela. Your love returns to life one who was close to death. I cannot be without you, I cannot of my free will deprive myself of my Manuela. I am not as strong as you; I need to see you: the distance that lies between us is unbearably cruel. You are with me, even though you're far away. Come to me, come soon, come sooner.

I SLIPPED OUT of Quito late one night. As Bolívar's enemies were watching my every move and might try to assassinate me once I was on the road, I took every precaution to elude them. A few days earlier, a cadre of loyal lancers from Bolívar's army left for a farm in the vicinity of Cotopaxi to wait for me. Then, late one night, Natán left in a carriage with my trunks to join the lancers. The following night, dressed as laborers, donning hats, *ruanas*, and the woven sandals the Indians wore, Jonotás and I left my father's house by horse at midnight.

In Lima, I'd lived in mansions and palaces filled with beautiful things. Now my possessions were packed in half a dozen trunks, but they included what I prized most in the world—Bolívar's letters to me, as well as the letters his secretary and aides-de-camp wrote to me when Bolívar was too busy to answer my missives himself. These letters were the only tangible proof I had of his love.

After more than two months of traveling on roads bordering terrifying precipices, we arrived in Bogotá, the capital of Colombia. It was summer, a late afternoon in January of 1828; the air that welcomed us, wafting across the savanna, was dry and balmy. As we emerged from the woods of oak trees at the edge of the plateau, my excitement grew when I spotted, miles off, the spires of the city's churches. I spurred my exhausted horse, Jonotás and Natán close behind. I felt light-headed, both from the altitude and my proximity to Bolívar. As I rode toward him, my hair loose in the breeze, I forgot the hideous months of the trip, the hardships, the exhaustion that had overcome me so many times. Just the day before, my back and buttocks had ached so much I wondered whether I would arrive in Bogotá in one piece.

The Camino Real was lined with weeping willows, and the lower slopes of the mountains that ringed the city to the east were draped with alfalfa. We passed fields planted with corn, wheat, quenopio, fields carpeted by the turquoise flowers of the potatoes, where Indians labored knee-deep in what looked like lilac lakes in the dark-blue light of late afternoon.

The light was almost gone when we reached the city. Its streets were deserted and the windows of the houses shut. Bogotá's Moorish architecture reminded me of Quito's. But the natural setting was different. Crystal-clear streams raced into the streets from the cordillera. The gurgle of rushing water was everywhere, like the song of birds heard in the tropical cities of Ecuador.

I knew that La Quinta was situated directly below Mount Monserrate. When we came to a street that seemed to run through the city directly from the belly of the mountain, I brought my horse to a halt, yanked the reins to the left, and lashed him one, two, a dozen times and raced to the house in order to make it before night fell. Close to La Quinta, I slowed when my eye caught sight of slogans crudely scrawled on the walls of the buildings. The most incendiary one said: "Death to Bolívar, Tyrant of the Andes!" A shiver ran through me, and I decided there and then I would enlist Jonotás and Natán to help me whitewash those walls tomorrow.

SANTANA, BOLÍVAR'S SECRETARY, met me as I dismounted inside the gates of La Quinta. "The general is holding an important meeting, Señora Manuela," he explained. "He's left orders that you should be taken directly to your rooms."

I had finished bathing and put on a new gown I'd had made especially for our reunion when I heard a discreet knock on the door. "Enter," I said, thinking it was Santana returning to take me to Bolívar. The general came in; I rose. Before I had time to say a word of greeting, he took me in his arms, pressing his mouth to my lips. I was so overcome to be finally in his presence that I began to cry.

"Come, come, Manuelita, you don't want me to start crying, too," he said, kissing away the tears on my cheeks. He took my face in the palms of his hands and gazed at me with tenderness. But even as we sat on the bed and he inquired how my trip was, I sensed an impatience. Suddenly he took my hand and said, "Come with me. There are some friends I want you to meet. I want them to see how beautiful you are." He led me to the library, where a group of officers was gathered, drinking and talking around the fire.

After his officers left, Bolívar gave me a tour of the house: the petite salon, its walls decorated with gilded mirrors bedecked with candleholders, a room with a massive marble fireplace; the grand salon, painted dark olive, for official receptions; the red and gold room, where he played cards and distracted himself at the billiards table; and the long, narrow dining room where we would dine tonight. All the rooms of La Quinta had wooden floors carpeted with mats made of straw harvested in the lagoons of the *páramos*—it was a pleasing Indian touch amid furniture in the English style and imported European *objéts*.

As he showed me through the house, Bolívar peppered me with questions about his friends and acquaintances back in Ecuador, what news I had of Peru, the details of my journey. By the time we sat down to supper, it had become clear that the general was trying hard to appear spirited for me. He could not quite conceal his distraction. When the soup was served, he tasted it, then, abruptly, pushed the bowl away and snapped at the servant. "This soup is cold, damn it. Take it away."

He barely touched the rest of his food. The servants looked

uncomfortable, as if they were afraid something unpredictable would happen next. This irascibility over small things
was a side of his that I hadn't seen before.

His battles may have taken a toll on Bolívar. He had departed Lima a conqueror, full of vitality and confidence, and
now I found him frail, weary, uneasy, his hair ashen. Equally
alarming, he didn't laugh at my jokes.

His declining health was apparent; I did not dare introduce
the subject. As if he had read my mind, he said, "I haven't been
feeling well lately, Manuelita. I know your presence will help
restore my health. I'm happy to see you."

Later, sharing a bottle of champagne before the marble fireplace, enjoying the warmth of the fire in facing chairs, I saw,
his mood brightened as we toasted our reunion. I wanted nothing so much as for him to ravish me. I still desired him. I loved
both what I could see of him, pale, shrunken, and that which
was invisible to the eye.

For months, I had dreamed of making love to him again. Yet
tonight Bolívar did not seem anxious to become amorous despite his passionate greeting when I had arrived. *El Libertador*
was far away. Finally I discovered the reason for his remote-
ness: he was obsessed with an upcoming convention in the
town of Ocaña, near the border with Venezuela. I begged him
to tell me about the event.

"Manuelita," he said, "our future depends on the outcome
of Ocaña. I am convinced that if the new constitution my enemies propose is accepted and Gran Colombia is broken up into
several countries, it will be catastrophic. The great majority of
our people, as you know, are illiterate; they need a strong central government. Otherwise, anarchy and endless civil wars
that will last for hundreds of years will be the future of these

nations." As he spoke these words, his eyes shone, staring at something that was not in the room, perhaps not even in this world. "One thing I know for sure is that my enemies will oppose any position I take." He paused. "What they want most of all is to crush me. They care more about defeating me personally than about the future of the country."

I reached for his hand and held it tightly. He had worked for this all his life. "How can these men be so shortsighted?" I said, becoming angry.

"Manuelita, *mi cielo*, you have no idea how tired I am of dealing with them. The two main characteristics of the Colombians are their hubris and their disloyalty. This is a nation of uncivilized Indians. I finally understand why San Martín went to Europe and stayed there. But I have to make an effort to go to Ocaña. I'm not quite ready to give up."

I had just arrived, had not yet spent a night with him, and already he was talking about leaving me again. "I'll be happy to go with you to Ocaña," I said. "You need a comfortable bed to sleep in, clean linen, good meals. Also," I said cautiously, loathe to bring up the subject, "you'll be more vulnerable to your enemies when you're away, no matter how well protected you are. Besides," I added, unable to hold back, "when you left me in Lima you said you would return shortly. Well, two years went by before I saw you again."

Bolívar stiffened. Even if I risked alienating him, I had to give voice to the thoughts that had tortured me for two long years. This was not how I had imagined our first night back together. I wanted it to be romantic, not full of recriminations.

"It's not a good idea for you to come along, Manuelita," he said, shaking his head. "Vice-president Santander will use your presence in Ocaña against me with the undecided delegates. He's the one who instigates all this resentment. I know he's plotting against me. But I cannot remain in Bogotá because I'm afraid, damn it. What sort of a leader would I be if I let fear dictate my actions? A military leader must be fearless," he said, his voice rising. "Santander and his followers tell the people I want to become king. And the people believe them. I've fought all my life against the Spanish monarchy—isn't that proof enough that I would never seek such a title?"

"Of course it is," I said, gripping his hand once more.

Agitated, Bolívar continued, "I tell you, Manuelita, it wounds me that Colombians idolize Santander because he's drafted tomes of Byzantine laws, while they mock and ridicule me, who fought for their freedom and spilled my blood for them."

"Colombians prefer the mediocre dream of being citizens of an insignificant country over the worthy dream of being a mighty nation," I said, looking for a way to make him feel better. "It's the destiny of great leaders to be misunderstood. All I have to do is open any page of Plutarch to see that." He never tired of reading *Parallel Lives*. On so many nights at La Casona in Lima, during the time of our greatest happiness, he'd asked me to read Plutarch to him before he went to sleep. "Colombians cannot understand your greatness, my general," I continued. "Instead, they understand Santander because he's small and insignificant, like their own vision." I was so furious my hands were trembling. Though I had never met Santander, for years I had despised Colombia's vice-president. In the time I'd known Bolívar, most of his unhappiness had been caused by the actions of this man. Santander's power over Bolívar was great because he controlled the public funds of Colombia and could withhold them, and often did, when Bolívar was in the middle of a military campaign. "If I ever get close enough to that coward, I'll put my hands to his throat and strangle him."

It was the first time I had seen the general smile since my arrival.

"Manuelita," he said, "don't let anybody catch you talking like that. Besides, Colombians are not the only people who misunderstand me. Or the only ingrates. My Venezuelan compatriots don't like me, either. As for Santander, we have to respect him for his service to Colombia. His actions are misguided, but he believes he's working for the good of the people." He paused, searching for a way to explain it to me. "The tragedy is that the inflated code of laws he's written will create a nightmarish bureaucracy that will be the ruin of our nation—we'll never be able to shake it off. These nations are not ready for democracy, Manuelita. Santander forgets our people need to learn to read and write first, before they can think for themselves. This country is not the United States. Their model will not work for us."

He sipped his champagne, and then, without warning, threw the crystal glass in the fireplace, where it exploded into tiny shards. My hands flew to cover my eyes. I shivered, but Bolívar barely took notice. His mood was even bleaker. "I may not have much longer to live," he said, his voice becoming hoarse. Holding my gaze, he added, "I can't stop thinking for a minute about that damned convention. Trust me, Manuelita, I'd rather die than live to see my legacy, the ideal of a united Gran Colombia, repudiated."

I searched for words to assuage his pessimism but found none.

Bolívar convulsed into a fit of coughing. He was spitting

blood in his handkerchief. I started to get up from my chair to call for help, but he motioned me to stay where I was.

It was not just his graying hair that made him look older. Now I could see unmistakable signs of advanced tuberculosis imprinted on his features. When a log flared in the fireplace, his prominent cheekbones and sunken cheeks made him appear almost mummified.

In the past I had been forced to share the Liberator with other women, with his military campaigns, with his status as the most powerful man in the Andes. Now my rivals had metamorphosed into something more elusive and insidious. It was an abstraction, an idea, the uncertainty of his political future, the limited amount of time he might have left to live.

"Come, *amorcito*," I said, hoping to break the tension. "Shall we continue our conversation tomorrow? You need to rest; and I hurt all over after months on a horse. My behind is crying out for a good soft mattress. You should not worry about anything tonight—this is our reunion. You are no longer alone. I'm going to take excellent care of you. Tonight I need a little heat to take the chill out of my bones."

Later, when I blew out the flame of the candle, Bolívar turned to face me, embraced me, kissed my chin, rested his cheek on my breasts, and instantly fell asleep. My voracious lover had become a nursing child. At rest, the skin of his face had the unhealthy sheen of parchment. Listening to his labored breathing, I was glad I'd come to him before it was too late.

I WAS AWAKENED by rushing waters calling me in the air like fresh-winged voices. A song of water, a susurration of the streams that hastened from Monserrate, filled Bolívar's bed-room. He was still asleep, facing the wall. If I closed my eyes and listened, I could imagine we were on a boat, sailing down a swift-moving river.

Through the interstices of the door and windows, slivers of gray light filtered into the bedroom. Quietly I got up, combed back my hair, and drank a glass of water. The cold water soothed my throat, still parched from the dust of the road. I wrapped myself in a *ruana* and in my slippers left on tiptoe, closing the door behind me.

I sat on the low wall facing the patio, where noises reached me from the kitchen; the servants were already at work. The aroma of boiling chocolate and roasting *arepas* wafted in the morning chill. Right behind the house loomed Monserrate, a gigantic swollen breast, draped in verdant forest all the way to its summit, crowned by a chapel. The rising sun spread like a fan of golden light behind it. This house was so much more welcoming than La Casona, a severe building with high ceil-ings and a garden that was no more than a rectangle of dirt sprinkled with patches of grass and a few anemic-looking rose-bushes. Soon after I moved into La Casona, I suggested to Bolívar that we plant a fig tree as a symbol of our union, but also as the start of a real garden. La Quinta was intimate. Sur-rounded by gardens, it was a walled-in country home, secluded yet just outside the city.

The gardens had been cloaked in darkness when I arrived the night before, now I saw the beds of multicolored carna-tions that encircled the house. A veil of morning dew covered every tree, plant, and flower, and a frosty fog rose from the ground. Birds serenaded the new morning. I recognized the plaintive coo of the mourning doves; the rest of the birds' calls were new to me.

I stepped on a path made of what looked like fossils and pebbles. The garden was as compact as a forest, every inch of soil supporting vegetable life. Wild flowering plants sprang up untamed. From the heights of Monserrate streams ran down through the garden, where wooden bridges arched over translucent brooks. New paths opened in every direction, taking capricious turns through the terrain so that it was impossible to see where they led.

Tall walnuts, cedars, oaks, cypresses, cherries, and pines, their trunks and branches decorated with green moss, attested to the age of this garden. Hummingbirds were already feeding from flowering caper bushes, red camellias, purple and lavender fuchsia. The hummingbirds seemed unafraid of me, as if they knew they had no enemies in this garden. Orchids, of many colors and shapes, nestled in the branches and trunks of the trees. Papayuelos laden with ripe yellow fruit, and borracheros, with big bell-shaped ivory flowers, also grew in the garden. On my trip over the Andes, the Indian porters had pointed out the small trees growing on the side of the roads, explaining that these flowers could be used to put a person in a trance or, if too much of the flower was used, to poison them. The flower was also taken by Indian priests for special rituals.

I took a narrow uphill trail lined with hedges of wild roses and purple and white chrysanthemums. The vines of the curuba fruit wove a tangled canopy overhead, hiding the sky. At the top of the path, sheltered by tall walls, was a secluded pool fed by a stream. The walls encircling the pool were lined with lime-colored ferns.

From the hill I saw the city below. To the west, in the distance, the endless savanna was a placid green sea. To the south rose the red-tile roofs of the houses of Bogotá, over which towered the high steeples of the churches. I was horrified to see so many churches. I hoped Santa Fe de Bogotá was not another pious Quito. Anything but another Quito. Had I moved from the Rome of the Andes to the South American Vatican?

I leaned against the wall and took a deep breath. The cool morning air quickened the flow of blood in my veins. The weariness of the months of traveling was lifting. I was finally here with Bolívar. My mission was clear: I was in Bogotá to make his life easier, make him a home where he could find solace, restore him to wholeness. I would have to prove myself worthy of his trust. I was still unsure of my place in his affections. I knew he desired me—or had desired me, when he was well—by the passionate way he made love to me. I knew I alone made him happy, made him laugh. We danced for hours; he confided in me, and his ideals for Gran Colombia were also mine. I knew, too, that countless women would be thrilled to be his mistress.

I would have to make myself indispensable to him. I had become an outcast in Peru and Ecuador, and doubtless the same would happen in Bogotá. All for the privilege of being next to the man who had made my dreams of a free South America a reality. He had attained for me everything I had wanted to do myself but couldn't, because I was born a woman.

THE HAPPINESS I had dreamed of during the time I waited in Quito to join the general in Bogotá was a chimera. I had hoped we would be able to recapture the passionate nature of our love, but Bolívar's lust had waned. His appetite for the flesh had diminished. Now and then there were flashes of our old intimacy. So, instead of bemoaning what no longer could be, I treasured those rare blissful moments, although each time I feared it would be the last we would ever have.

In Lima, Bolívar had been at the pinnacle of his glory. True, he had many enemies; but his adversaries were fighting a losing battle, since the tide of history was with the general. By the time I arrived in Bogotá, Bolívar's power was slipping; he was fighting a battle that I was not sure he could win. In Lima, the Spaniards had been his enemies, but here he was fighting the Colombian *criollos*, his own people. Just two years ago, the majority of the people in Gran Colombia shared his ideal of unity, of a vast powerful nation the equal of any empire in Europe, or in the Americas. But in order to achieve the unity needed to form just one powerful nation, it was now necessary to fight and crush the many brutal *caudillos* who had risen all over the Andes and who wanted to rule over large expanses of land with the absolute power of feudal lords. Colombians no longer shared Bolívar's vision because it meant more warfare. Most of the people were ready to give up the great dream just so they could live in peace. The man who had done the most damage to undermine the general's authority was Vice-president Santander, who, with his promises of peace and prosperity, had captured the imagination and the hearts of the Colombian people and turned out to be a formidable foe.

ONE NIGHT at dinner with a small group of officers, after Bolívar had spent the whole day working on his speech for the Ocaña convention, with a nervous gesture he knocked over his wineglass. His face turned red. "These people will not rest until they've crushed my life's work," he roared at us at the table, although we had not been discussing politics. "Not until I'm dead, and not even after I'm gone. I gave them the sky over their heads, the water they drink, the plots in which they're buried. Yet every chance they get they remind me I'm a foreigner—they have nothing but contempt and scorn for my friends, my family, and me." He was trembling from the exertion of this outburst. I ran to his side, made our excuses, and took him for a stroll in the gardens. Our guests were left to finish dinner on their own.

NO MATTER HOW much I indulged him, patiently listened to him rail against Santander and his minions, tried to amuse him with clever remarks at the expense of his adversaries, I remained powerless over his growing pessimism. His unshakable confidence, grounded in the liberation of four countries, had been shattered by these Colombians, who vilified him, accused him of being a despot, of wanting a crown.

When he was accused in print of being an autocrat, or a dictator—no better than the most bloodthirsty viceroy of Spain—he flew into monumental rages, kicking the furniture, smashing vases and imported crystal to the floor, or against the walls, tearing up documents and feeding them to the flames. He would refuse to eat, or to see anyone—even me—and stayed locked up in his office until his fury passed. These outbursts would leave him feverish and weakened. With each tantrum, my hopes of bringing his health back lessened.

I asked Santana to show me all the newspapers that arrived at La Quinta before anyone else saw them. I read through them carefully; if I found any disparaging remarks about the general, I burned the newspaper before he saw it. I made a list of the writers' names and instructed Jonotás to find out who these men were and where they lived.

BOLÍVAR WAS SO obsessed with his Ocaña speech that he forgot to eat, locked up in his office with his aides. I decided to take the matter into my own hands, and made an appointment to talk to his doctor. He confirmed what I already knew about tuberculosis: the best treatment for anyone in the general's condition was rest, plenty of fresh air, and nutritious meals.

I began to plan Bolívar's menu with the cook, María Luisa. I insisted that he eat three regular meals. If the general was in his office, missing his noon meal, I sent José Palacios to inform him his food was getting cold. One day, Palacios brought back word that Bolívar was too busy to stop working. I hurried to the office and did not bother to knock.

"Manuela," Bolívar said, unable to mask his exasperation, "I don't have time for you right now."

"Gentlemen," I said to his aides and secretaries, as if I had not heard a word he said, "the general's food is getting cold. He needs to eat."

With a cutting gesture of his hand, Bolívar indicated that the others should leave. As they filed out of the room, one by one, their eyes showed their disapproval of my conduct. When we were alone, Bolívar got up from his chair. His pupils shone, his lips trembled. "I will not tolerate this kind of public behavior from you, Manuela." He only called me Manuela anymore when he was angry with me, otherwise it was always Manuelita. "You must never, ever, interrupt my work, much less give me orders in front of my men. Is that clear?"

"Señor," I said, "with all due respect, if you keep tiring yourself, if you fail to obey your doctors, you are not going to go to Ocaña, and you will not save Gran Colombia because you will be dead. May I remind you that we need you to stay alive in order to govern this country?"

After an unpleasant silence a smile insinuated itself on his lips. Bolívar said, "Let's go eat María Luisa's delicious cooking."

Soon I had him eating three meals regularly, and taking a siesta. Regardless of the weather, at five-thirty each afternoon, I came to Bolívar's office and reminded him it was time to conclude business for the day and to join me on the veranda for an aromatic water. Exhausted from receiving people, dictating letters, and working on his speech for Ocaña, the general sat with me on the terrace by the entrance of La Quinta, in front of the fountain, where wild ducks stopped to drink and splash merrily before making their way to their roosting places. As Bolívar and I sipped herbal teas, we listened to the whispering sounds of the fountain, inhaled the inebriating honeysuckle growing alongside the veranda, and admired the vivid colors of the sunset over the savanna of Bogotá. Dusk had a soothing effect on Bolívar's nerves, and he would inquire about my activities during the day, and we would talk, as comfortable with each other as an old married couple. Soon color returned to his cheeks, and he stopped coughing blood.

As Bolívar's health improved, on sunny afternoons we bathed in the secluded pool surrounded by tall ferns. Jonotás and Natán poured into it hot water infused with lavender and medicinal herbs they had gathered in the mountains, or which they bought in the markets from the Indian doctors. Alone in the pool, with Jonotás and Natán waiting outside its walls at a discreet distance, ready to bring in anything the general or I desired, Bolívar caressed me, kissed my breasts, drawing into his mouth my erect nipples, holding my aroused body against his emaciated frame while I rubbed his back with loofah. As the general lathered me in my most intimate parts, the lover in him returned and I would take his hardness and ride it like a mermaid at sea.

In my old age, during those sweltering Paita afternoons, during the long siestas when even the flies dozed, I would feel remnants of desire ripple through my aching bones and joints, and remember, after bathing in the pool, the walk to our bedroom, where a pot of hot creamy chocolate redolent of cinnamon and nutmeg awaited us. We drank the bracing brew and made love. Not the ardent lovemaking of our first years together, but a reposed kind of lovemaking that was a long, supple, intimate embrace, a kind of communion. Bolívar would explore my body without the hunger of unsatisfied desire; he would caress me, stroke me as if I were a delicate object whose every detail was known and cherished by him.

Years later, when I had nothing to do in Paita but to remember, I would recall those first months, living with Bolívar in Bogotá in La Quinta, as the happiest days of my life.

17

Jonotás

Over twenty years after my people and I were torn from our *palenque*, uprooted from our land—the saddest moment of my life—Natán and I were back in Nueva Granada, now known as Colombia. Though this was the country where we were born, I never thought of it as home. This was the country where my parents had been slaves, escaped, then were taken back into slavery. I could only hate such a land; arriving in its capital made me angry. Colombians were the people who had killed my parents. I could never forget that.

We were in Bogotá because Manuela was following the Liberator. Of the men in Manuela's life, I admired and respected only Simón Bolívar. He treated his slave, José Palacios, as if he were a member of his family. Palacios had been with the general since his childhood, just as we had taken care of Manuela. Natán and I never established any closeness with José Palacios, who dressed and behaved like a white man. I suspect he was jealous of Manuela's closeness to his master. But the Liberator was kind to us. He knew of our loyalty to Manuela. I admired him because he wanted to abolish slavery. In his Constitución Boliviana he had called the ownership of people "the greatest violation of human dignity." And he added that there could be no equality where slavery exists. Even an ignorant slave knew what that meant.

WE HAD BARELY settled in La Quinta when Manuela received a note from James Henderson, British consul in Bogotá. He requested an audience. Calling me to her rooms, letter in hand, her eyes shining, she said, "Great Britain is the mightiest nation on earth, Jonotás. A diplomatic overture from him means that other foreign dignitaries will follow his example. This," she added, relishing every word, "sends the message to the rest of the diplomatic corps that I am the First Lady of Colombia, not just another of Bolívar's mistresses." I was happy for her. Manuela deserved to be respected.

For days she thought about nothing else except the preparations required to receive the consul. She wanted to make a good impression, to be a credit to the Liberator. English tea would be served, accompanied by scones, plum cake, and cucumber sandwiches. These were foods that she had offered to James Thorne's English business associates when they visited their home in Lima.

"I want you there all the time, during the interview. So be sure you wear your nicest clothes," she said to me. I protested that this was never done.

"It's very important that you're there, Jonotás," she insisted, "I want him to understand that I'm not a woman bound by any conventions. What's more, I want to make clear to him that La Quinta is my home and that I make the rules here."

Eucalyptus logs burned in the fireplace as they greeted each other. Mr. Henderson complimented Manuela on her fluent English, on her elegance, on the beauty of Ecuadorian women, on the exquisite taste of the room in which they sat and the loveliness of the orchids on display.

Manuela apologized for General Bolívar not being able to receive the consul. "He's buried in work concerning the upcoming Ocaña convention," she said as she poured the tea and served Henderson a slice of plum cake. He made approving sounds when he tasted it. Then, after they chatted about Bogotá's weather—which Mr. Henderson liked, as it reminded him of London—Manuela inquired after the consul's family. Mr. Henderson made excuses for his wife, who was not feeling well enough to accompany him on this visit. But, he assured Manuela, she sent her warm regards. Then it was up to Manuela to wish the consul's wife a speedy recovery. She concluded by extending an open invitation to her through him to visit La Quinta whenever she felt so inclined. When they seemed to have run out of pleasantries to exchange, Manuela offered him a cigar, which the consul declined. This did not prevent Manuela from lighting a cigar herself. After she savored the inebriating aroma, the two sat there in silence, staring at the burning eucalyptus logs.

I was wondering about the true purpose of Mr. Henderson's visit to La Quinta when he cleared his throat. He took another sip of tea before he spoke. "As you know, Mrs. Thorne," he began, "as His Majesty's representative in Colombia I also look after the affairs of British subjects when they seek my help."

When he called Manuela that—Mrs. Thorne—I realized

why Henderson had come. Four years after she had left James
Thorne, he had not forgotten about her. She was of course
grateful to him for having rescued her when she was in jail
in Lima. At times, she said nice things about him. Even I had
begun to think of him better. After all, he had saved not
only her life, but mine. But why would he not leave Manuela
alone? Wasn't it enough that he had a mistress and his own
daughter?

"I've never met your husband," Mr. Henderson said, "but
we have many friends in common back in England." He stopped
to sip his tea. "In any case, Mr. Thorne has written to me, au-
thorizing me to arrange for your passage back to Lima."

Manuela placed her hands on the arms of her chair, straightened her back, threw back her shoulders, and pointed her chin
at him. It was as if I could see inside Manuela's head. Henderson was turning from the British consul, sipping tea before
her marble fireplace, paying homage to her important position, into everything that had ever made her miserable. He
had become the tyranny of Spain, her father, the despicable
Aispurus, the stupidity of Quito society, the nuns she despised.
Worst of all, Mr. Henderson had become the James Thorne to
whom she had been sold by her father which, she often pointed
out, "made me feel like less than a slave, because slaves do not
sell their own children."

Manuela dunked her cigar in her cup of tea. She rose as the
consul was helping himself to another portion of plum cake
and said, "I think you've had enough cake for this visit, Mr.
Henderson." She snatched the plate from his hand, knocking
over his teacup, spilling tea on his pants, and flinging, one by
one, the pieces of English china in the fireplace. "Jonotás, I
need you!" she cried. All the time, I had been standing by the

door, frozen, barely breathing, amused but worried by her recklessness. "My pistol, please," she said.

I ran, fetched it from the cabinet, and handed her the weapon. She took it, pulled back the hammer, and pointed it at Henderson's chest. "Sir," Manuela said, pale with a rage that lit her eyes like fire, "you have exactly five seconds to leave this room." I started counting along with her, "One, two . . ."

Henderson stumbled to his feet, his face as white as frosting on a cake, bowed to her and, in his confusion, to me also before hurrying out of the room. We followed him. I asked the butler to get his things. On the terrace, the consul put on his hat and signaled for his coach with his cane. He did not wait for the livery boy to open the door of the coach but opened it himself. As he clambered inside, Manuela fired in the direction of the garden. Shrieking wet birds flew in a dark cloud out of the trees. Henderson sank into the coach, as his startled horses stampeded toward the gates and disappeared down the street in the chilly rain.

Manuela turned to face me and we fell into each other's arms, shaking with laughter.

The next morning, while we were helping to dress her, Manuela said that the general, after hearing about the incident, remarked, "I don't think it means war between England and Colombia, Manuelita. But, my love, you have to try to be a little more diplomatic." Then he'd burst into roaring laughter. "It's been years since I've seen him laugh like that," she said.

18

James was not ready to concede defeat. He sent a threatening letter, a raging document reminding me that I was bound to him by law and, as his wife, had sworn always to obey him.

I was grateful to James for coming to my aid in Lima. And he was indeed my husband—but, oh, how I hated that word. Did that give him the right to be my master, to rule over my soul? I accepted only one man as my husband, and it was hell not being near him. In order to achieve a final break with James, I had once and for all to burn every bridge that led back to him.

For days I wrote and rewrote a letter that would make it unequivocally clear to James that he had lost me forever. I would start the letter, then tear it to pieces because it did not reflect my true thoughts, did not say what I wanted it to say.

My letter must be of such finality that he would never want to hear from me again.

One drizzly afternoon I sat by the fire in the library, poured myself a glass of port, lit a cigar, and decided I must finish it.

My dear and distinguished friend:

No more, sir, for God's sake! No! Why do you make me write to you, breaking my resolution never to do so again? What do you accomplish but put me in the painful position of saying no to you a thousand times?

Sir, you are excellent, inimitable. I will never deny your qualities. But, my friend, to have left you for General Bolívar is no reflection on your fine qualities.

Do you think that I, after being the favorite of the general for seven years, the one who owns his heart, would prefer to be the wife of the Father, the Son, and the Holy Spirit, or even of the Holy Trinity?

I know very well that nothing can bind me to him under the auspices of what you call Honor. Do you think I am any less honorable because he is my lover and not my husband? I do not care in the least for social conventions. They were created merely so that we could find new ways to torture each other.

Let me be, my dear Englishman.

I have an idea: in heaven we will marry again; but no more on this earth. What do you think of this proposal? In the celestial realm we will live an angelic life, exclusively spiritual. Everything will be done in the English style in heaven, where a perfectly monotonous life is reserved for the people of your nation (when it comes to love, at least, because who is more talented in commerce and the affairs of the sea?) You English seem to experience love without pleasure, conversation without charm; you walk slowly; you greet each other with reverence; you rise and sit down gingerly; you joke without laughter. These are divine qualities, but I, miserable mortal being that I am, make so much fun of myself, of you, and of all other English formalities, that I would have a difficult time in heaven. It would be as hard for me to live in heaven as in England, or in Constantinople, because although you are not tyrants with your women, you are more jealous than a Portuguese man. I want no part of that.

Enough of my humor. Seriously, without smiling, with all the seriousness, truth, and purity of an Englishwoman, I tell you I shall never come back to you. You are Anglican, I am atheist, and that is an insurmountable religious barrier. That I love someone else is an even greater barrier.

See how grave and serious I can be when I need to be?

Always your friend,
Manuela

That letter put an end to all contact with James for quite a while. But years later, when I was old and indigent in Paita, and when now and then the past vividly resurfaced in the guise of hearing from those who had played major roles in it, I heard again from James. Ten years or so after I settled in Paita, a couple of weeks before Christmas, a letter arrived from Lima. I immediately recognized James's handwriting and opened the pale-cream envelope without a second thought. As I unfolded the letter, a piece of paper fell into my lap. It was a cheque for 200 pesos, in my name. James's note was brief:

Dear Manuela,

A business acquaintance passing through Paita brought me the news that you have taken up residence there. I was glad to hear that you are in good health. Please accept, as a token of esteem from an old friend who wishes you well, this small Christmas present.

Ever yours,

James

I may have maligned James repeatedly over the years, but once again he had come to my rescue at a crucial moment: we were months behind in our rent and close to being evicted. Jonotás badly needed new shoes. I wore old, moth-eaten dresses. James's thoughtfulness helped to relieve the sadness that overtook me each December, the month of Bolívar's death. James would continue to send me a cheque for the same amount every Christmas until he died. At long last I began to think of him not as an unwanted husband who had bought me from my father, but as a considerate old friend. Our correspondence, however, remained reticent, more on his part than mine. I didn't ask about his personal life, and he offered no information about it. My hope was that James, who was by then over sixty years of age, had found a woman who cared for him.

19

The political atmosphere at La Quinta was febrile. Almost daily, news reached us of an uprising brewing somewhere in Gran Colombia; of conspiracies to overthrow the government; of the malicious lies spread about the Liberator and his intentions to become king. More troubling, we heard constant rumors of plots to assassinate him. The latter were taken so seriously that he ventured out on the streets only if he was accompanied by a personally picked regiment. I persuaded Bolívar to double the number of guards outside and inside La Quinta.

I had hardly left the grounds of La Quinta since my arrival in Bogotá. But as no threats had been received against my own life, to distract myself from the political intrigues, I decided to explore the savanna on horseback. In Bogotá I had a fine stable of horses to chose from. Bolívar suggested that soldiers accompany me on my jaunts. Feeling in no immediate danger, I declined his offer. As a precaution, Jonotás and Natán dressed in uniform. I wore patent leather boots, black velvet pants, a *ruana* over my blouse, and a Panama hat. We carried pistols and swords, just in case.

On those infrequent rainless afternoons when the air was warmed by stirring currents that flew up from the tropics, we rode to the open fields on the outskirts of the city. Sometimes we rode far north on the plateau until we came within sight of snow-peaked volcanoes. In these uninhabited areas of the countryside, we competed in our own horse races, the way we had done as girls in Catahuango. At other times, we stopped for a drink of water at the settlements, where the Indians lived in circular huts made of mud and bamboo, unchanged in their ways for hundreds of years, living as they did before the arrival of the Spaniards. I grew enamored of the endless verdure of the savanna, astonished by its variety of delicate and rare orchids, which I wore in my hair at the evening *tertulias*.

On our daily excursions, I noticed the commotion we caused among the men of the city when they saw the three of us on horseback, wearing men's trousers and carrying arms. Bogotá's women drew their shutters closed, or turned their backs to us. Only the boldest of the prostitutes, those who dared to come out during the day to solicit customers, seemed unshocked. I had learned to spot them by the fact that they went barefoot, their toes adorned with rings and baubles, ankles festooned with bangles, their feet immaculately clean. Unlike the rest of Bogotá's women, they did not hide their hair under absurd hats. When I caught their gaze, I saw none of the contempt I was met with everywhere else in this city. Sometimes I threw coins at them. Had I not been born the daughter of a rich woman, I could have been one of those women.

The city itself seemed to me a larger, more sepulchral Quito. The architecture of Colombia's capital had none of the Andalusian gaiety of the buildings in Lima. Unlike the friendly *limeños*, *bogotanos* spoke in hushed tones, dressed in somber colors, and walked with the tiny steps of frozen people born far from the sea. Quito, which was higher in altitude than Bogotá, was closer to the sun, so its people had a warmer disposition. Bogotá, with its large population of unemployed and wounded soldiers, was poorer than Lima, its citizens dirtier, smellier, its flea- and rat-infested streets crowded with beggars, cripples, and criminals, its side alleys reeking of urine and excrement. Its citizens proudly wore their unhappiness on their faces. One breathed this poisonous atmosphere in the streets.

The nights in Bogotá were spectral and morbidly silent. As soon as it was dark, *bogotanos* got on their knees to say the *Angelus*, and locked themselves in their homes to have supper and go to bed. Only in an emergency would anyone venture out, and then always accompanied by a servant leading the way with a lantern. The only places that remained open at night were the dusky cantinas where the Indians drank themselves into a *chicha* numbness. Prostitutes roamed the streets, finding anonymity in the darkness.

Late at night, I lay awake, wondering whether Bolívar's enemies would triumph, whether the man who had claimed my body and soul would ever again be the lover I had known. These thoughts were often interrupted by the eerie cries of the night watchman patrolling the deserted streets. The ringing produced by his bell, like the cries of shrill little night creatures in the air, was followed by the call of the hour— "It's eleven o'clock"—and then the weather—"It's drizzling, and there's no moon,"—and the final cry of "All's well in Bogotá. May God be with you at this hour!"

Lying in the warmth of our bed, I felt protected with Bolívar next to me. But outside the walls of La Quinta, I imagined a vast cemetery inhabited by vengeful spirits and criminals who took refuge in the frigid blackness.

I had nightmares. Nuns made me stand for days in the wet, freezing corridor of the school in Quito—my feet mired in blood, deprived of food and drink, mocked by the other girls as they passed me on their way to class. I dreamed of being tried by hooded Inquisitors who echoed the disapproving voices of my father, my aunt, my grandmother, and James Thorne. The Inquisitors condemned me to torture in contraptions that broke my bones and tore my flesh, then hanged or burned me at the stake, and sometimes both. I died surrounded by a cheering mob calling me a *bruja*, a bride of Satan. Other times, I saw myself encircled by statues of bleeding Christs on the cross, his blood soaking me, burning my skin.

I would awake from these nightmares shaking, gasping for breath, only to find Bolívar snoring beside me in our bed.

ONE MORNING AT BREAKFAST Bolívar said, "Manuela, we must make sure that *bogotanos* see us together in public. Otherwise, they will think I am trying to hide you. Tomorrow afternoon we will go for a ride through the streets of Bogotá in the open carriage."

On this outing, I wore a dress and hat and wrapped a shawl around my shoulders, allowing the population for the first time to see me dressed as a lady. As we entered the Plaza Mayor, I saw scrawled on the walls of the cathedral, a sign in huge

black letters: "Simón Bolívar was born in Caracas Eating Shit
Like a Pig." I did my best to keep Bolívar distracted by my chat-
ter. I did not want to see him humiliated in my presence.
Bolívar asked the coachman to stop.

"Bastards," I cried out, before he could say anything. "How
dare they? What disrespect! You were born a prince!"

"Manuelita, you must admit the Colombians have a mischievous sense of humor," he said.

"I will make sure that sign is painted over tomorrow."

"And then what? It'll be a waste of your time and energy. If
you do that, they'll write it over and over again. The best thing
to do is to ignore it, and all the other insults. The truth is,
nothing surprises me about Colombians. They are an ungenerous and malicious people. Have you heard what they say about
themselves? God made Colombia the most beautiful nation in
the world—and to correct his largesse, he populated it with
the worst people on earth."

I laughed, though I was still furious.

The following afternoon, I sat down with my girls to
embroider in a sunny spot of the garden behind the main
house. I could tell Jonotás was burning to tell me something.
"What is it, Jonotás?" I said.

"Manuela, you should have heard those women in the market this morning. While their servants were shopping, they
gathered like gaggles of geese to talk about your ride in the
coach with the general."

I secured the needle in the shawl I was making and looked
up. "What were they saying?"

"They were saying"—Jonotás pursed her lips, raised her

chin, and mimicked them in a babyish voice—'the general's conduct is a disgrace! His behavior is inexcusable, unfit for a head of state. Not only does he bring his adulterous mistress to live with him, but he has the nerve to go out with her in public. Did you see that carriage? Not even the viceroys had such a fine carriage. Soon they'll be riding in a golden coach!'"

I snorted. "What imbeciles. They forget that the general was born to the wealthiest family in South America. If he wants to ride in a golden coach, he was born to it. What else were they saying?"

Jonotás did not hesitate, imitating another lady: "'That woman is shameless! Did you know she's a bastard? She was run out of Quito for eloping with a soldier. She left her husband, a respectable Englishman, to be the general's whore.' Sorry, Manuela," Jonotás said, switching to her normal tone, "but that's what they were saying."

"Those stupid women, they can go to hell!" I said.

"First I'd quarter them, fry them in oil like pork rinds, and then feed them to the rats," Jonotás said, and spat.

Without looking up from her knitting, Natán said, "Why do you want to do that to the poor rats?"

I laughed. "Next time we go riding into town, remind me to wear a mustache. If those witches are scandalized, let's give them some reason for scandal."

"Can I wear a mustache, too?"

"You and Natán can wear beards if you like," I replied, and returned to my needlework.

BOLÍVAR DECIDED IT was time we had dinner parties to introduce me to the Bogotá families sympathetic to him. "If you are going to continue living here," he said, "we have to present you officially, so to speak. We must not give the impression we are hiding anything from the people. The best way to neutralize the tongue-wagging is to show we have nothing to hide. Colombians have to get used to the idea that you are here to stay."

I had never mentioned to the general the commotion my rides with Jonotás and Natán caused in the city, or the scornful looks we received. Yet I wanted to be an asset to him, not a liability. "I'll do it, if you wish," I said, then added, a bit timidly for me, "Sometimes I get the impression *bogotanos* disapprove of me."

He grinned. "Well, I'm sure they haven't seen many women like you around here. You do have an original way of presenting yourself. When you go riding dressed as a man you cut quite a figure." He paused. "Whether they like you or not, Manuelita, you are the First Lady of Colombia."

DINNER PARTIES BEGAN at La Quinta. I worked closely with María Luisa to prepare roast beef, suckling pig, duck cooked in red wine, rainbow trout—whose pink flesh tasted like salmon—caught in the streams of the savanna, boiled white potatoes, and fried yellow and purple ones, salads of beets, carrots, boiled quail eggs, petits pois, and corn, and dressed with olive oil from Villa de Leyva. Also pastries filled with *arequipe*, guava, and blackberry jam. For every meal I ordered a fresh supply of sweet corn *arepas*, which Bolívar loved.

Jonotás and Natán brightened every room of La Quinta with flowers—they were gifted at making exuberant floral arrangements. I pulled from my trunks gowns I had not worn since my days as James Thorne's wife.

Dinner party after dinner party, the men showed up alone, making excuses for their suddenly indisposed wives. Eventually, a few couples bestowed their presence on us. I tried hard to be a charming hostess, making our guests feel welcome and attending to their every need. If I sensed they were ambivalent to Bolívar's cause, I tried to build support. I was convinced that if I was welcoming, gracious, affable, I would make a favorable impression that my guests would talk about with their friends.

Yet, it was nearly impossible not to be repelled by the Bogotá women the men brought to my dinners. Most of them were fragile-looking, and so white that they did not seem made of flesh but of eggshell. The prettiest might remind me of snow-white orchids, yet the majority had the sickly pallor and the translucent skin of creatures that dwelled underground, never exposed to the sun. They all had lovely heads of hair that gleamed in the candlelight. I had been told that *bogotanas* washed their hair in urine, which they considered the best treatment for beautiful and healthy hair. Was that also, I wondered, why they reeked of perfume—to cover up the odor?

I tried hard to engage the women in conversation. They replied in girlish tones, giggled, and blushed when I asked them a direct question. Whenever I asked them about their political opinions, they would invariably respond that their husbands were the ones who had political opinions in their home. The fact that I had my own ideas was seen as a sign of bad manners and a lack of modesty. I swear these women did not care whether the Spaniards or the patriots ruled, so long as they were allowed to continue their privileged lives, the most exciting part of which involved going to mass and to daily confession.

More than once I had to restrain myself from grabbing one of these ladies by the shoulders and shaking her hard, screaming in her face, "Wake up! This is not medieval Spain. It's 1828!"

Though an atheist, every day I thanked God that I had been born with a skeptical mind. I knew these egg-white creatures were the product of the same miserable education I had been subjected to by the nuns in Quito. All of us had been taught to mistrust the senses: the eyes, ears, mouth, and tongue were instruments of the devil. We were taught by the nuns to close our eyes and pray to the Virgin Mary, clutching a rosary in our hands, as our husbands mounted us and entered us through a hole in a sheet that covered our bodies. The morning after, we were to run to our confessors and beg forgiveness for having succumbed to temptation.

I did not give up trying to win the favor of these women. After dinner I would sit and chat with them for a short while, until I announced a need for fresh air. I would then excuse myself and join the men—who were drinking and talking about subjects that excited me.

I have no doubt that most of Bogotá's men resented my brash behavior. On the other hand, Bolívar's officers, the Irish in particular, seemed to relish my company and considered me one of them. To them I was not the oddity I represented to most Colombian men—in Europe they must have seen many independent women like me.

20

Natán

In Bogotá, like everywhere else in the Andes, ladies of society met regularly in their sewing circles to socialize and make costumes for the statues of the saints in churches and convents.

Jonotás and I were in the library with Manuela, making floral arrangements, when an invitation addressed to Manuela—to attend the sewing circle of Doña Ana María Holguín—was delivered.

"You know how much I enjoy embroidering and knitting, but can you imagine *me*," Manuela said to us in a mocking tone, "making costumes for a *saint?*"

I could not and was about to agree with her when she said, "The general will want me to behave diplomatically and not slight Señora Holguín. I'll go—once—and then won't have to do it again."

MANUELA RETURNED FROM her outing in a bad mood. We had to wait till dinner to find out how it had gone at Señora Holguín's sewing circle. When the general and Manuela dined alone, Jonotás and I took care of serving dinner.

Often the general was tired, in bad humor, or ate very little. Manuela tried to cajole him into tasting the food, pointing out that she had made him the *ajiaco*—one of his favorite soups. She would chatter about rumors that reached her ears, usually things Jonotás or I had brought back from the market, or else she asked him questions about his day. Tonight it was she who was morose, not him. The general noticed her mood. "How was your visit to Señora Holguín's?" he asked.

Manuela shrugged off the question, at the same time beckoning me to refill her wineglass. The general insisted. She took a big drink from her wine before she answered: "Well, my general, after we drank our chocolate and ate pastries—which were delicious—the ladies began to discuss their ideas for new Easter costumes for the statues of the Virgin of Chiquinquirá and Our Lord of Monserrate in the cathedral. Suddenly I got the most marvelous inspiration. I said, 'We have many wounded soldiers roaming the streets of Bogotá, dressed in rags. Why not make clothes for them, instead?'"

Manuela speared a potato out of the plate of steaming *ajiaco* and began to chew it, taking her time.

I was dying to hear what had happened.

"A very good idea. So?" the general said, holding the spoon with his soup in midair, his eyes open wide.

"You won't believe what happened next, my general," Manuela said, after she washed down the rest of the potato with a sip of wine. "My proposal was met with silence. I elaborated, thinking that perhaps they needed more explanation. 'Why not make clothes for the poor? For the beggars? For the sick? For the children of our dead soldiers? There are so many in the streets going hungry and cold. Why can't we help clothe *them*? Why make costumes for statues that do not care whether they are dressed or undressed?'"

I had to put my hand to my mouth to repress a giggle. Bolívar continued to watch her with an amused expression.

"Well, Señora Holguín's sewing circle just looked at me, as if I had proposed copulating with the devil in public."

Bolívar let out a loud chuckle.

Manuela went on: "They went back to nibbling on the pastries and cheese, and sipping their chocolates from their gleaming silver cups, just as if I had never spoken a word."

"It offends me that Bogotá's women do not appreciate you," Bolívar said.

"I don't care what those women think of me, my general. The only approval I seek is yours. As long as you're happy with me, they can go to hell."

"Approve of you?" Bolívar said, his eyes shinning. "You're my greatest joy, Manuelita. I wouldn't want to change anything about you. You are perfect the way you are. I'm sorry I cannot provide you with women like Rosita Campusano here in Bogotá. There are a few brilliant women in the city, but unfortunately they are admirers of General Santander."

"They can't be too bright, if they prefer Santander to you," Manuela said.

The general laughed again. He did enjoy her jokes. She was the only person who could make him laugh.

TRUE, MANUELA HAD not made many friends in Bogotá, but that was nothing compared to how unpopular Bolívar and his government were.

It made Bolívar's blood boil that Santander had the support of the people and he did not. Bolívar was aristocratic, stiff, like an Englishman. He was simply not Colombian enough. He was uncomfortable in the presence of humble people. Colombians thought he was cold and ruthless, and he was. Once I heard Manuela saying to him, "*Señor*, you have to be more expressive with them. More tropical. More *caraqueño*. The people want from our politicians public displays, demagoguery. They interpret your reserve as arrogance. After all, they are sick and tired of the cold indifference of the Spanish viceroys."

Despite her prodding, the Liberator could not change his temperament. When a mother presented a baby to be kissed, Bolívar touched the infant as if he were afraid to get his hands dirty. He was baffled by the Colombians; he could never understand why, though he had given them their independence from Spain, they still saw him as a foreigner. The truth was that—at best—they respected him, but he never earned their love.

Colombians preferred Santander, a level-headed, modest man who did not seem arrogant. They liked him because he was one of them. He had come from the provinces and had made his own way in Bogotá, using his intelligence and charm. Bolívar, on the other hand, was proud and prone to violent tantrums when he did not get his way. He would always be seen as a spoiled rich boy who had been educated in Europe, like a future king. Colombians mistrusted their liberator because he was forever declaring "war to the death" to this one and that one. They longed for peace, of which Santander had given them a taste soon after independence. Even more, Colombians loved Santander because he was a devout Catholic.

If the *criollos* mistrusted Bolívar, the Indians were indifferent to him. To the heroes of independence the Indians were impenetrable people who spoke strange languages and often refused to learn Spanish. Santander, however, was interested in the Indian roots of the nation and in improving the Indian's lot, probably because he himself had Indian blood. Manuela, Bolívar, and his followers dismissed Santander because he was of Indian descent and not educated in Europe. It is true that Bolívar treated his slaves well, that he loved José Palacios and the slaves who reared him, and it's also true that he wanted to see an end to slavery. As Manuela never tired of reminding us, he had written, "Slavery is a gangrene that begins in one limb and, if the infected limb is not cut, it spreads until the entire body dies." But when he spoke about the "chains of slavery," he was thinking mostly of how the *criollos* felt enslaved by the Spaniards—the slavery of the Indians or the Africans was not his main concern.

After years of following Manuela and Simón Bolívar, I came to my own understanding of the political reality of the Andes. The way I saw it, both Bolívar and Santander won the Wars of Independence without making great changes. The Wars of Independence were about money and business—*criollos* were tired of paying heavy taxes and having the Spaniards control trade and reap all the profits. *Criollos* were fed up at having their children barred from the same schools as the children of the Spanish aristocracy. And *criollos* hated the fact that they were considered unfit for government and fit only for manual work, along with slaves and their descendants, whether Indians or Negroes. That's what offended *criollos* the most—to be lumped together with Negroes and Indians. Anybody who was not one hundred percent European they referred to as "the race of the earth."

If Bolívar and Santander had coexisted in one man, he would have been the ideal ruler. The tragedy of Colombia was that by choosing one man over the other, Colombians would never be able to see but half the truth.

21

A s Bolívar's departure for Ocaña became imminent, my
anger at Santander grew. The damned convention should
not even be taking place. It was putting Bolívar's health at
risk, and it was taking him away from me. He was overworked,
not sleeping in preparation for his departure. Still, he went on
with the demands of the state.

At a dinner for his officers who were staying in Bogotá,
straining for a note of levity, I said to the guests, "This fine
dining room, my friends, was built by orders of our Vice-president Santander. Take a good look at it, note the elegant design
of these beautiful windows and doors, because this dining
room is the vice-president's finest achievement. This dining
room—and this dining room alone—will be remembered long
after those ridiculous laws he's obsessed with have been abol-
ished as obsolete. Only this lovely room assures him a place in
the history of Colombia."

Some of the guests burst into laughter; others chuckled nervously. Bolívar frowned, but I hoped that my sarcasm secretly pleased him, that he was only pretending to disapprove of my lack of restraint.

We were no sooner alone at the end of the evening than he said: "Manuelita, it doesn't become you to needlessly provoke the vice-president and his allies. You must be careful of the things you say, especially when you've had too much to drink."

"Can't you see the dirty dog wants you dead so he can become president? It's better to expose him for the conniving traitor he is."

"That may be true, Manuelita," he conceded. "But if the vice-president hears about tonight—and in this city it is impossible to keep a secret—he may think I put you up to it. We must not give him any more ammunition to attack us."

It was no secret that my temper often got the best of me, especially when I had had one too many drinks. Even so, I was not yet ready to promise to stop criticizing Santander. I knew that if he could be removed from office, many of Bolívar's most pressing political problems would evaporate. The vice-president's poisonous intrigues were what stirred the den of vipers that was Bogotá.

"My general, I just want him to know that any enemy of yours is also my enemy. If he dismisses me as a foolish woman, then he doesn't know the first thing about me. He's making a grave mistake." As I said these words, I realized how absurd it was for me to be obsessed with a man I had never met. Santander was not welcome in La Quinta, and he and Bolívar met only in the presence of government officials. I had seen his likeness hanging on the walls of government buildings and drawings of

him that appeared in the newspapers. His presence had become so vivid for me that sometimes I even dreamed of him. I
was convinced that if I could meet him just once, he would lose
most, if not all, of the power he had over me.

Bolívar put his arm around my shoulder. "Manuelita," he
said softly, caressing me to stop my shaking, "you say these
things because you love me. But we must be careful. We have
too many enemies. We don't want my opponents accusing you
of interfering in the affairs of Colombia. Remember that to
them we are usurpers who are trying to control the destiny of
their nation." He paused. "I have an idea," he said, his mood
brightening. "I know what would cheer us both up. Why don't
you play your little piano for me? I would like that very much."

Though I was far from an accomplished pianist—practic-
ing bored me—my interpretations of Andean folk dances always put Bolívar in a good mood. Only at these times was I glad
I had been sentenced to the Conceptas' school, where girls
learned to play the piano or the harp as preparation for married life.

I played my usual repertoire of *pasillos, guabinas,* and *bambu-
cos.* After each tune, Bolívar clapped loudly. "Come here," he
said when I was finished, pulling me onto his lap. We kissed
and sat there for a while, not talking, just feeling our warm
bodies touching. I raised my head from his shoulder and said,
"*Señor,* there's something you can do for me if you want to make
me happy."

"Ask me anything, Manuelita. Go ahead."

"I'm going to miss you so much, my love," I said. "I don't
seem to be able to hold on to you for very long, do I?"

"It will be a short separation, I promise you." He smiled re-
assuringly. "I should be back in a matter of weeks."

"My general, please take me with you to Ocaña. I promise not to be a burden."

"Palacios will take good care of me," Bolívar said. "You know how strict he is with me."

José Palacios would look after his needs—that was true. I would have to use another argument. "You need a woman in your bed at the end of the day to be your confidante and to keep you warm at night. How can I be sure some woman won't throw herself at you?" I said. "I'd better not hear there's another woman taking my place, because, I swear to you, I will ride to Ocaña and pluck out her eyeballs with my fingernails."

Bolívar threw his head back and laughed. "I wouldn't want to expose anyone to your fingernails. I know what a formidable weapon they can be." He never tired of alluding to the night in Lima when I scratched his face after finding him in bed with another woman. "Seriously," he went on, "you needn't worry about that, Manuelita. Those days are over. Just take a look at me. I am a sick old man," he said, not without a measure of self-pity. "You're the only woman in my life, my sweet. Since you arrived here I've been happier than I've been since I was a young man. No other woman can compare with you. I'd be a fool not to realize that."

I prided myself in not being the kind of woman who resorted to tears to soften a man's heart, but tonight I violated my own rule.

"I promise to hurry back," he whispered, embracing me. "Really, Manuelita, why would I want to deprive myself of the joy of your company? If for some reason I'm delayed, I'll send for you. You believe me when I say that, don't you? You have my word of honor."

"That's what you said when you left me in Lima." I pulled

away from his embrace. "And then I was locked up as a criminal. I was lucky to have escaped with my life. I have valid reasons to be anxious about what may happen to me without your
protection in this city. This time I'm not going to wait two
years before I see you again. I'm as devoted to Gran Colombia
as you are, but you don't go to bed with Colombia at night. You
go to bed with me."

"I need your help *here*," he snapped, "not in Ocaña. I need
someone in Bogotá I can trust completely. If you want to be of
help to me, right here in La Quinta is where I need you. Will
you do that for me?"

Once more I had to accept that my services as an intelligence
gatherer overrode any concerns he might have about my safety.
It *was* selfish of me to keep insisting he take me with him, knowing that his enemies would use my presence at the convention
to incite the people against him. I understood all this. Still, I
was angry. I placed my hand on his cheek, brushed my lips
against his. "I will do as you say," I whispered. "I will not let
you down. But remember, I will be in this unfriendly city
counting the days and the nights until you're back in our bed."

"You know my greatest happiness is to hold you in my arms
all through the night." He paused. "There's something else I
want to ask you to do for me. I'm leaving behind Colonel Croftson and Pepe París to protect you. You know that if anything
happened to you, it would be too much for me to bear. Manuelita, promise me you will not be reckless."

His concern for me was touching. After I promised I would,
he kissed my face, my neck, my hair, and roared as if he were a
famished lion about to tear into my flesh.

EARLY ONE MORNING in March, two months after my arrival at La Quinta, the general and his regiment, in full regalia, left Bogotá.

Jonotás and Natán, María Luisa, the gardener, and the rest of the servants gathered with me outside the gates of La Quinta to bid him victory in Ocaña. A crowd of well-wishers in a festive mood, among them the families of the soldiers, their mothers and sisters and younger brothers, their sweethearts, and other supporters, cheered the general and his troops loudly and repeatedly.

I hid my apprehension and sadness behind a mask of optimism; I did not want Bolívar to go away worrying about me. He needed all his strength for Ocaña. I mingled with his officers and soldiers, wishing them good luck, giving last-minute instructions to José Palacios about medications and special foods for the general. As Bolívar rode off on Paloma Blanca, I joined the crowds chanting "To victory in Ocaña!" "*Qué viva el Libertador!*" "*Qué viva la Gran Colombia!*" I stood there waving good-bye, cheering and chanting slogans with his supporters, until Bolívar and his troops disappeared from view.

As I went back to the house, followed by my girls and the ministers of state who had remained in Bogotá, as the high gates closed behind me, I knew I could not afford to wallow in my feelings of helplessness. From this moment on, I would have to think about my safety.

22

The situation for me in Bogotá quickly turned ugly. The following morning after the Liberator had left for Ocaña, I was in the dining room, reading newspapers and having a cup of chocolate and *almojábanas* just out of the oven, when Jonotás came into the room, still carrying her market basket with the day's provisions. She dropped the basket on the table, then pulled from her pocket a torn piece of paper. Without saying a word, she handed it to me and stood there, her eyes red with anger, waiting for me to read it. It looked like a small broadside torn from a wall. It could not be just another pasquinade slandering the general. It had to be worse to get Jonotás so angry.

The sheet was about me. I read:

Bogotanos!

Since January of this year a foreign woman and her slaves, dressed as
soldiers, have been parading the streets of Bogotá, displaying for all to
see their degeneracy. Manuela Sáenz, an Ecuadorian subject, a scandalous woman of the most objectionable morals, who abandoned her
husband in Lima to become General Simón Bolívar's kept woman,
has been living in La Quinta, where she holds court in the manner of
the concubines of Louis XV. It is no secret that Bolívar is determined
to become King of Colombia, perhaps even Emperor, and he has chosen this woman to be his Madame du Barry. Like du Barry, *la Sáenz,* an
intriguer and schemer, no doubt hopes one day soon to dictate policies
and appoint government officials. From the reports about the jewels she
displays at the official receptions held in La Quinta, where she has the
gall to act as First Lady of Colombia, she has already looted the treasury
of the nation to bedeck herself in the manner of a King's whore. What
else could be expected from this woman of low birth and lower education? This woman and her slaves, who some say are hermaphrodites?

Madame du Barry was guillotined. In our honorable country we do
not punish our criminals in this manner. But we can expect that when
the tyrant is deposed we can hang *la Sáenz* by her bejeweled neck as
punishment for her insolence, corruption, and degeneracy.

Death to Manuela Sáenz!

It did not surprise me that war had been declared on me as
soon as Bolívar left the city—harassing me, after all, was a
way of getting at him. What did surprise me was the degree of
vitriol. And I had never been called a hermaphrodite. It was
too bizarre.

I got up from the table slowly, shutting my eyes to make
the room stop whirling. I crushed the piece of paper in my
hand.

"How dare they compare me to Madame du Barry! I am not a social climber intent on robbing the people," I said to Jonotás, who looked shaken, too.

"There are hundreds of these, Manuela, posted everywhere," Jonotás said. The black of her eyes looked as if they could strike like lightning. "I removed this one from a wall with my own knife."

"They were not men enough to do this while the general was here. If they think they can slander me in this manner, and that I won't retaliate, they don't know the first thing about me."

"I am at your disposal, *mi coronela*," Jonotás said, calling me by my military rank of colonel. I had not been called that for a long time—not since Peru.

"You are absolutely right, Jonotás. It's time to stop behaving like a lady and start acting like a colonel. If those vultures want to declare war on us, then war it will be. First we must find out who printed this *pasquín*, and then we'll deal with them."

I suspected Santander was behind this action, though he was too shrewd and conniving to get his own hands dirty. As with all his despicable treachery, it would be impossible to trace his actions back to him. Yet I couldn't let his henchmen ridicule me in this manner. Any attack on me was an attack on Bolívar. He could not defend himself while he was away; therefore, I had to show his enemies I could defend myself.

I needed protection, and who better to protect me than the regiments Bolívar had left in Bogotá? I would take my case directly to them. I knew that if I wanted their respect, I must not appear before them dressed as a lady of society. I must meet with them dressed as one of their own. If *bogotanos* thought I was a hermaphrodite, then I'd be one—and rub it in their faces.

Jonotás unpacked my wrinkled, musty colonel's uniform to air and iron it. Just the sight of it brought back memories of when I had fought side by side with *el Libertador* on his campaigns across the Andes, coming to his rescue when he was in danger of defeat. When I went down that mountain, leading the troops and firing on the Spaniards who were decimating our forces, I did not care whether I lived or died as long as I killed a few of the king's soldiers. Firing at them, I felt I was shooting down my father, my aunt, my grandmother, the Concepta nuns, Fausto D'Elhuyar, Quito's society, and James Thorne—for buying me against my will. That moment, those few minutes before we fell on the Royalists, had been the most exhilarating time of my life, the time when I had felt authentic, that I was changing the world.

SHORTLY AFTER SUNRISE, escorted by a cadre of loyal troops, I set off on horseback for the garrison where Bolívar's other troops were stationed. I wore my black three-cornered hat, red jacket, blue pants, and black patent-leather boots, complete with the gold spurs that I had had specially made in Lima. I armed myself with a pistol and, from Bolívar's collection, chose one of his sabers. Across my breast, I affixed the velvet band on which hung the Order of the Sun.

Jonotás and Natán, dressed as soldiers, led the way, carrying the tricolor Colombian flag snapping in the wind as we galloped along the emerald grass carpeting the streets of Bogotá. Onlookers stopped to watch us go by, trying to figure out what this could be about.

I had timed my arrival at the garrison to coincide with the troops' morning review. My friend, Colonel Croftson, whom Bolívar had left in charge of one of the two regiments in Bogotá, received me. I had sent word that I planned to address the troops, that I needed a show of support. I did not tell him the reason why; I knew Croftson would not deny me this request. Sharing a mutual allegiance to Bolívar and his ideals, we had forged a strong bond. I admired Croftson's passionate temperament, the way his Irish blood boiled at the mention of the general's enemies. On more than a few nights we had stayed up into the morning hours, playing billiards and downing glass after glass of whiskey as we discussed plans to crush the general's enemies.

Mounted on his horse, and speaking in the heavily accented Spanish I found so amusing, Colonel Croftson addressed the regiment: "Soldiers, patriots, loyal members of General Bolívar's battalion, I need not introduce to you Señora Manuela Sáenz. You well know the place of trust and affection she holds in the heart of *el Libertador.* Señora Sáenz has proven on many occasions her complete devotion to the ideals we share. With admirable valor she has fought with you on the battlefields of the Andes, where she proved herself to be one of you, and one of the people. Today she has come here to ask for your help. I want you to listen to what she has to say and to promise her your unconditional support, because in Bolívar's absence, she *is* Bolívar!"

An expectant hush fell on the troops. Even the horses stopped snorting and stomping the ground. I knew I could not hesitate, that a favorable outcome depended on the authority with which I seized the moment. From my horse, I made my voice as loud as I could. "My fellow soldiers! I've come to you as your *coronela*, and your friend, to ask for your help. I stand in front of you to reiterate my promise to continue to fight beside General Bolívar for your freedom, the freedom of your families, and the greater freedom of Gran Colombia.

"My friends, it may have come to your attention that since *el Libertador* left for Ocaña to guarantee that the forces of moderation and reason prevail, Bolívar and I have come under violent attack from his enemies in Bogotá. Here is an opportunity for you to show your love for Bolívar. It is up to you to defend the general's legacy while he is away, fighting for your rights. History will remember you as heroes if you make the right decision. I would willingly give my life for Bolívar, and I know you would as well. You must make certain that Bolívar's shortsighted opponents do not undo what he has achieved for you. Hoping to weaken the general, his enemies are attempting to slander and harm me. I am here to ask for your protection and your loyalty."

I drew my saber and hoisted it above my head. As the tip caught the platinum rays of the morning sun, I cut a hoop of light in the air. Shocked at my own audacity, I shouted, "I say to you, my brothers-in-arms, that our enemies can lop off the head of Manuela Sáenz, but they will never kill my ideals. Long live Bolívar! Long live Gran Colombia!"

At once, the entire garrison erupted in cries of: "Long live *el Libertador*! Long live *la Coronela*! Death to the traitors!"

The soldiers' cheers echoed across the savanna. The next day, in broad daylight, Bolívar's troops began to scrub down the walls and doors of the city, removing the pasquinades slandering the general and me. Then they whitewashed the walls. It was, in effect, a warning shot at Santander, though I knew it would not be enough to ward off a new attack.

Bolívar's letters provided me with what little solace I knew in his absence. I slept well only when the day's mail brought news of him. I wrote to reassure him I was doing fine. I did not tell him about the pasquinade or about my speech to the troops—although surely he had heard. I did not write about the moments when, walking in the garden alone, feeling sad, or lost in my thoughts, embroidering, I was overwhelmed with fear. Or about how my anger with him grew for leaving me behind in a city where I was despised. Above all, I could not write to him about my anger at myself for falling in love with a man who was married to an ideal, or about how I hated myself for behaving exactly like the sort of conventional little damsel I was always mocking.

One day a letter arrived describing how the general, instead of going directly to Ocaña, would station himself in Bucaramanga, so that his presence at the convention would not be interpreted as coercion on the undecided delegates. I was overjoyed at this news. In Ocaña, where so many of his enemies were gathered, it would be that much easier to kill him.

Nights at La Quinta were dreary without him. When the fog submerged the gardens, the chilliness of Bogotá's altitude set in, like a sickness of the soul. I needed company. I decided to keep entertaining and invited Bolívar's friends in the city, the British Legion. Pepe París's daughter, my namesake, Manuelita, who despite her youth had become my only woman friend in Bogotá, came, accompanied by her father. She was the only female who accepted my invitations, although at seventeen she was still a child. The soirees were an excellent way of finding out what was going on outside the walls of La Quinta. Besides that, having the house full of soldiers until late at night made me feel safer. Once I was alone in my bedroom, though, I worried. How could I be sure that some of these soldiers were not spies for Santander and his chums? Or of General Córdoba, for instance, a patriot who was jealous of my place in the Liberator's affections, and who would have been happy to see me removed from Bolívar's life.

Every night I kept a candle burning until dawn broke. One morning I noticed dark shadows under my eyes—I looked haggard, exhausted, aged. That was enough for me. Though I knew the servants would gossip, I asked my girls to sleep in my bedroom, just as we had done when we were children. Most nights we sat on my bed in our sleeping garments with a bottle of *aguardiente* and gossiped and smoked and laughed until I became exhausted enough to fall asleep.

As soon as *bogotanos* found out about the three of us sleeping together, malicious rumors flared up. My most vocal enemy was Monsignor Cuervo, who denounced me from his pulpit during daily mass, accusing me of hosting depraved bacchanals in which my slaves and I performed immoral acts and engaged in "the vice practiced by many women in Lima." The monsignor was one of the most corrupt members of Bogotá's clergy, the father of numerous illegitimate children and a usurer who controlled the sale of basic staples to the people.

Jonotás made him the subject of one of her *tableaux vivants*. When I was a girl in Catahuango, she had amused me by impersonating and ridiculing the humorless members of my mother's family. In Lima, she was notorious for her caricatures of the peccadilloes of the society ladies and corrupt politicians. Her antics made James Thorne furious. He demanded that I forbid Jonotás to perform these caricatures. He was afraid they would make enemies for him. I never put her up to it, but clearly I encouraged her by laughing till I cried at her outrageous impersonations. It was one thing when she performed for me in private, or when she acted them out in the kitchen for the other servants. But I had no control over her when she went out in the streets and performed on street corners, or on the steps of a public building, always attracting a crowd and a few coins for her talent.

I was with guests one night in the game room, where we were playing cards and billiards after dinner, when one of my visitors mentioned that the monsignor's most recent attack on me had hinted that I had a pact with the devil and held a witches' coven at La Quinta. Jonotás and Natán were serving drinks and emptying ashtrays as we talked. I never forbade them to converse with my guests—which many criticized me for. They could add to the conversation if they had anything to say. Even so, I was surprised when Jonotás started clapping her hands and asked for a moment of silence.

"Ladies and gentleman," she announced, "Natán and I have taken the liberty to prepare an entertainment for you. We hope you will find it amusing. It is about a certain churchman who has been slandering Doña Manuela. We would like to ask for her permission, and your indulgence, to present our little *tableau*."

"Oh, no, no," I said. "I don't think that's a good idea, Jonotás."

But Pepe París pleaded, "Please, Manuela. This could be amusing. There's no doubt he deserves whatever it is. And we all need a good laugh." The rest of the guests applauded in agreement.

"Fine," I said, thinking we were among friends so I need not worry about news of Jonotás's performance getting back to the monsignor.

"Please continue with your conversation, ladies and gentleman," Jonotás said. "We need a few minutes to get ready."

As she and Natán left the room, a nervous anticipation came over me. Her caricatures could be savage. I lit a cigar and downed a glass of *oporto* to soothe my nerves. When the ringing of a bell was heard, all of us fell silent. The smell of incense reached us as Natán entered the room dressed as an altar boy, holding a bell in one hand and with the other swinging an incense burner. I giggled nervously. Jonotás, wrapped in purple fabric to denote a high-ranking church official, walked behind her. In her hands she held a wooden cross. Her face was impassive.

Natán led Jonotás to a chair and helped her sit, then she sat on the carpet at her feet. Jonotás began to speak in mock Latin in sermon-like tones, reading from a Bible she had fished out of her purple tunic. The theme of the sermon was the sins of Sodom and Gomorrah. She began to enumerate the sins—all of a sexual nature—in which the citizens of Bogotá indulged. She pointed at guests in the room and addressed them by the names of known enemies of the Liberator. "You, Julio Zamora, you patronize filthy prostitutes and gave syphilis and ticks to your saintly wife. That is why she gave birth to children with four feet and two heads." Whenever she mentioned a person's name, Natán would get up, turn to the audience, beat her breasts, pull her hair with both hands, and bawl, "*Mea culpa, mea culpa, mea maxima culpa.*"

"In the name of the Father, the Son and the Holy Spirit," Jonotás continued, "I condemn you to hell, to thousands of years of burning flames." Natán threw herself on the floor, thrashing and screaming. Jonotás continued her sermon, calling out the names of other citizens and accusing them of other depravities. After concluding the homily she offered her parishioner communion. Pulling a pewter cup from under her wrap, she motioned to Natán to receive the host. Natán approached on her knees. When she opened her mouth, Jonotás raised her skirts in a quick motion, producing a small crucifix, which she shoved in Natán's mouth, simulating an act of fellatio. Meanwhile, Jonotás held a rosary, which she started saying aloud, with her eyes shut, her prayers interrupted by her loud moans of pleasure.

Just as quickly they stopped and, as they ran from the room, sprinkled the guests with "holy water."

I had been holding my breath throughout most of the performance. When I turned around to look at the faces of my guests, I saw they were stunned; pale, in fact, as if they could not believe what they had seen. Even for a room full of friends, the satire may have gone too far. Nonetheless, I led off the applause and called back Jonotás and Natán to toast their artistry.

Monsignor Cuervo stopped making me the target of his sermons. But the atmosphere in Bogotá turned so poisonous for me that I could almost breathe toxic vapors in the air.

THE BROADSIDES AGAINST me were replaced by newspaper flyers attacking Bolívar. They appeared in El Conductor, a newspaper published by Vicente Azuero, a santanderista. The flyer

inserts incited the people to stage an assault on the garrisons
where the troops were stationed and to wrest control of the city
away from them. These pamphlets declared the time was ripe
for an uprising, hinting that in other Colombian cities the
troops were ready to rise against the general and defeat his an-
tifederalist ideas. Bolívar was accused of being a "praetorian
dictator" who had plans to become emperor before the convention in Ocaña was over. Still other pamphlets stated that the
Liberator was near death, and invited the general's troops to
surrender peacefully and swear allegiance to Santander as the
new president in return for mercy. Fortunately, I knew from
Bolívar's letters that his health remained stable.

I missed riding. It had become too dangerous for me to go
riding in the savanna, and the idea of going for a ride accompanied by a regiment was not appealing. Riding was freedom
to me. How could I feel free with dozens of armed men following me? Knitting provided a temporary respite from my worries, but I needed fresh air, exercise, to relieve my anxiety. I
began to feel trapped in La Quinta. Even its gardens had begun
to seem to me like nightmarish labyrinths with no escape.

THE ARRIVAL OF Colonel Andrés Fergusson from Ocaña provided some contact with the world outside. He rode into La
Quinta early one afternoon to meet with the general's ministers. Their meeting in the library lasted hours. After it was
over, I sent word requesting an audience with him.

Evening had fallen by the time Andresito Fergusson came
into the room where I was knitting with Natán and Jonotás. I
immediately put my knitting down and ran to embrace him,
then motioned to my girls to leave us alone.

"Colonel, tell me the truth about the general's health," I said, looking straight into his clear blue eyes.

He took a chair and held my gaze. "*Coronela*, the general's health is the same as it was when he left Bogotá. He asked me to tell you he hopes to return soon. He worries for your safety." Andresito paused. "How are you doing, *mi coronela*? Is there anything I can do to make your situation better?"

Over whiskeys I told him about the broadsides attacking me and how they had been replaced by the inflammatory pamphlets against the general printed by Vicente Azuero.

"We have to stop the man," Andresito said, his face reddening with anger. "Give me your blessing, *Coronela*, and I'll put a bullet through his heart."

"No, Andresito," I said, "don't take rash action you will later regret. You are too valuable to the general and me to ask you to do something so foolish. I do agree with you that we need to send a strong message to Azuero. Let me try a plan of my own first. If it doesn't work, then I will ask for your help."

We drank late into the evening. Andresito described the atmosphere in Bucaramanga, and gave me the details of what was happening in Ocaña. He considered it a good sign that José María Castillo, a loyal supporter of Bolívar, had been elected president of the convention. I was happy to have a true friend back in Bogotá.

The next day I instructed Alejandro, a Venezuelan lancer, a gigantic black man who had fought with the general in many campaigns, to find Vincente Azuero, give him a sound beating, and order him to stop publishing the scurrilous pamphlets at once. I was somewhat alarmed later when Alejandro reported to me that, consumed by his fury, he had broken the fingers of Azuero's right hand.

"Don't worry about it, *Coronela*," he tried to reassure me, "he was lucky I didn't cut off his fingers to feed the dogs."

BECAUSE NOTHING ESCAPED Jonotás's espionage network, I heard right away that General Córdoba had let it be known he was appalled by what he considered my act of censorship against a free press. Apparently, he was planning ways to discipline me.

I was pondering whether to write to General Bolívar denouncing Córdoba's treasonous conduct, when news arrived in Bogotá that one of Santander's men, Admiral Padilla, had launched a rebellion in Cartagena.

Padilla, a mulatto who had fought heroically during the Wars of Independence and later turned against the Liberator, had a reputation for brutality and bloodthirstiness. This revolt could signal to Bolívar's enemies that the time had come to rise in arms against him. I desperately wanted to join the general in Bucaramanga, to be by his side at this moment. However, staying in La Quinta meant I could continue gathering valuable intelligence for the general about what was being plotted in Bogotá. My situation was more difficult than ever: I had to fear harm not only from Bolívar's enemies, but now from his friends as well. I could take care of the latter, but the former, led by Córdoba, were too many and too powerful for me to do anything about them.

I wrote to Bolívar:

Sir:

In my last letter to you I said nothing about the events in Cartagena to spare you disagreeable news. Now I congratulate you because the traitors failed. Santander is responsible for this, as if all he had done before was not enough reason for us to shoot him. May God look favorably upon the death of the evil Santander and Padilla. It will be a great day for Colombia when these vile men die. This is the most humane solution: may ten men die in order to save millions.

If this letter fell into the hands of my enemies, it would be my ruin. Yet I was certain that the only advantage we had at this point was the element of surprise—to strike before our enemies did.

Astonishing news reached us: Gran Colombia still lived! Bolívar had ordered his delegates to walk out of the convention, dissolving it for lack of a quorum. Santander and his followers had lost this round. Bolívar would be returning to Bogotá soon, and I could stop looking over my shoulder every second of the day.

I longed to see the general, to hear his voice, be held in his arms again. Without him by my side, living with him the daily turmoils of the nation, the relentless assaults on his dream of unity, life was reduced to the banality of political intrigues, and cold, lonely nights.

Even before leaving Bucaramanga, the general's first action was to vacate the position of vice-president, thus demoting Santander. The newspapers announced that the scoundrel had been named Ambassador to the United States, which meant he would leave Colombia soon and be too far away to represent an immediate danger to the general.

My elation at these events was dampened considerably when I received a rather formal letter from the general saying that for reasons he could not explain on paper he would not be returning to live in La Quinta; he would take up residence in San Carlos Presidential Palace. I was well past the point where I would interpret this as a sign that the general did not want me by his side. I no longer needed reassurances of his love for me, even though a rumor had reached my ears that the general was planning to crown himself king of Colombia upon his return to Bogotá, and that to solidify his position he would marry a princess from one of the European monarchies. It was said that *el Libertador* would never again be my lover, making of me what Napoleon had made of Josephine.

I refused to believe a word of this rumor. It was meant to harm me, I was convinced. If it was true, I would have to hear it from Bolívar's lips. No matter what, I would remain the general's most loyal subject, friend, and lover. I would rather continue as the general's mistress, the second woman in his life, than go back to Lima and Thorne.

23

Natán

Manuela and all of Bolívar's followers applauded his decision to declare himself Dictator of Gran Colombia. Nothing good could come of it, I thought. If he wanted to win the trust and affection of Colombians, it seemed the wrong way to go about it. It's possible Bolívar was so drunk with the total arrogance of absolute power that he thought he did not need the people's love in order to rule them.

To prepare the people for the news, Colonel Herrán, the governor of Bogotá, came up with the foolish idea of parading Bolívar's portrait through the streets of the city. From a corner, I watched members of the Municipal Council carrying the portrait. Gold ribbons were attached to the four corners of the painting, and other members of the council held the ribbons as they walked the streets, praising Bolívar and shouting his accomplishments, as if he were a god. No crowds followed the procession to acclaim the image of the general.

There were even some people who heckled the portrait as it went by.

This procession was Herrán's first step in preparation for the formal announcement of the general assuming extraordinary powers. The next day, the colonel, accompanied by at least a thousand soldiers, held a public meeting at the Customs House. I was there, too, at the request of Manuela, who had sent me and Jonotás to bring back a full report. Colonel Herrán announced at that meeting that General Bolívar, to protect Colombia from chaos, had been persuaded by illustrious patriots to assume the dictatorship of Gran Colombia. Herrán took the opportunity to announce that the mandate of the representatives elected by *bogotanos* the year before had been revoked. To silence the opposition, he added that Bolívar was reluctant to accept the dictatorship and the resolution approved by the Council of Ministers, who had pleaded with the Liberator to accept it in order to maintain unity.

This resolution became known as the Act of Bogotá. If the procession of the portrait had been received without enthusiasm, the new resolution was like a slap on the faces of *bogotanos*. People congregated in small crowds in the public spaces of the city, and it was obvious that some sort of popular resistance was being planned. Herrán wasted no time ordering Bolívar's garrisons out on the streets to make clear to the populace that the military was ready to do whatever it took to enforce the resolution.

Simón Bolívar, Dictator of Gran Colombia, reached Bogotá on June 24. The victory parade felt more like a funeral procession, as the people locked themselves in their homes when the troops entered the city. *Bogotanos* were unhappy to see Bolívar again. They knew that whenever the Liberator showed up in the city, war was not far behind.

The night before Bolívar addressed the people in his new role as dictator, he sent for Manuela. Jonotás and I accompanied her to the palace. We stood outside the closed door of the general's bedroom, from where we heard Manuela vehemently reminding Bolívar of the importance of his words the following day, imploring him to change the tone of the speech, to make the people of Bogotá the true saviors of Gran Colombia. "You have an opportunity right now to win their affection and their trust," Manuela had shouted. "If you want to continue ruling, you need them as your allies." After much loud arguing, Santana was sent for. It was well past midnight, when a new draft, one that had more popular appeal, was completed.

Jonotás and I were with Manuela during the ceremony, which basically amounted to Bolívar's coronation. Manuela had to content herself with watching the ceremony from the balcony of a government building overlooking the Plaza Mayor, in front of the cathedral. She took care to hide her face from the populace. Both those who loved the general and those who hated him showed up. I know Manuela would have given anything to be next to him on the dais when he addressed the people of Bogotá. I could not help but think—and the memory was bittersweet—of all that had happened since the time when, from the balcony of her house in Quito, and when they first laid eyes on each other, she had hit him with a laurel wreath.

After Colonel Herrán welcomed Bolívar to Bogotá, and thanked him effusively for once more helping to preserve order in Gran Colombia, the Liberator addressed the members of the Council of Government, who accompanied him on the dais. Bolívar had returned from the convention looking wan, but that afternoon, in full military dress, he looked splendid. He delivered his speech with a conviction I had not glimpsed since his victorious entrance into Quito. Manuela's eyes brimmed with the adoration she felt for him. I was happy for her, for this moment of triumph.

"The Republic of Colombia," the Liberator cried out, extending an arm in the direction of the stone-faced members of the Council sitting on the dais, "which was left in your charge for several months, has preserved, thanks to you, its glory, its freedom, and its happiness in a way that seemed inconceivable to those who lack nobility of thought." He went on to say that when dangerous storms threatened our lives, the wisdom of the Council had helped to protect our freedom. Then he turned around and faced the crowd and praised its collective wisdom, and thanked them, too, for preserving our freedom. Future generations would be grateful to them, and would forever sing their praises, he said, for the wisdom they had shown, to ensure the safety of the nation. "The will of the nation is the supreme law that all rulers must obey," he proclaimed. "To submit to this supreme law is the first duty of every citizen, and I, as one of them, submit myself to it."

This was the finest performance I ever saw Bolívar give. It was the only one in which he recognized the masses, realizing perhaps for the first time that, if he wanted to govern, his wisdom alone was not enough, that he needed their loyalty, their support, and their love.

"It is the will of the nation that is our true ruler, the only ruler whom I serve," he went on. "Whenever the people stop giving me their support, whenever they feel the time has come to deny me the powers they've entrusted to me, I want you to tell me so, and I will gladly submit to the popular will and sacrifice to you my sword, my blood, even my own head. That is the oath I make in front of this cathedral, in front of the members of the Council, and, more important, in front of the people of Colombia."

The earnestness of Bolívar's appeal for their support, stirred *bogotanos* from their usual torpor, and they cheered the Liberator at the moment he became their dictator.

24

It was to be expected, immediately after he became dictator, that the general's enemies would accuse him of establishing himself as the South American Napoleon. These shortsighted mediocrities failed to see that the only way to prevent an imminent civil war was to have a strong central figure in charge of the deteriorating situation. Bolívar alone had the moral authority and foresight to do that. I was sure of it.

To help repair the ill will that had been created against him by becoming dictator, the Liberator took many steps to win the support of the masses. He needed the complete support of the military to stay in power. So his first act was to pay their back wages, to pension off the soldiers who had fought in the battles of independence, and to raise the salaries of all members of the armed forces. Next, to appease the rabid Catholics who called him an apostate, Bolívar decreed his support for the role of the Catholic Church in government. I wasn't happy with this decree, but I kept quiet because I understood how important it was to have the Church on his side if he wanted to remain in power. Colombians did not mind going hungry as long as the Catholic Church was prospering and could continue to promise them justice in the next life.

I WAS HAPPY for this moment of triumph, when it looked like the general had defeated his enemies, but I was sad we lived in separate homes. La Quinta without Bolívar no longer felt to me like an idyllic refuge. I had to content myself with visiting him at the palace after nightfall, though never staying until morning. I had become a woman in the shadows.

Bolívar had returned from Ocaña looking frail, his nerves raw, exhibiting the excitability of the tubercular. The three months on the road had inflicted further damage on his body. He would never learn how to rest. When he was not on the battlefield, anxiety would overcome him. Without me to make sure that he ate well and rested, it fell to Palacios to take care of him, but Palacios always deferred to his master. He did not dare tell him what to do. Only I could do that, and now we were living in separate domiciles.

In my worst moments I pondered whether this physical distance was temporary or would become permanent. In any case, I had to make my role clear to the people of Bogotá, to let everyone know that I had in no way been demoted. I was still the only woman in his life, and I had his full protection. One night at the palace I broached the subject of his approaching forty-fifth birthday and asked his permission to celebrate it at La Quinta.

"Absolutely not," he said. "I'm not well enough for public celebrations. What I need is rest."

He said this with a finality that indicated the discussion was closed. I, however, was not ready to concede. I needed to be selfish, even if I risked his displeasure.

"Forgive me, my general, but just this once I need you to think of me," I began. He raised an eyebrow, irritated, but I was determined to be heard. I got up from the table where we had been dining and began pacing about, an uncontrollable excitement overtaking me. "You must admit that as a lover, I don't ask much from you," I said. "If you say, 'Manuelita, go,' I go; if you say, 'Manuelita, come to me,' I come to you; if you say, 'Manuelita, stay,' I stay, and stay, and stay. I do all that happily, because I'm honored to be your mistress. But just this once, I ask you to indulge me."

I paused, hoping for a response. Bolívar remained silent. "Since you came back," I continued, "I have had to live with the rumors that you're planning to make an alliance with a European royal house and marry one of its princesses; and I do detect, in the people around me, a kind of pity for me, as if you had already left me for another woman. Don't you see? If I give a birthday party for you in La Quinta, it will signal to everyone that I'm still in your favor. I think you forget, sir, that I, too, have enemies in Bogotá, and there are many people who would love to get rid of me—and would if they found me in a weak position." My voice was shaking, so I said no more. I got up to leave the room.

"Manuelita, where are you going?" he said. "Come here, please."

I stood still, tears flowing. Bolívar got up from the table and took me in his arms. "Stop crying, my sweetness," he said, stroking my neck. "Of course, you're right. Go ahead, plan the birthday celebration, just make sure that it stays small."

The next day, I started making plans for the celebration. I designed an invitation, had them printed and sent to all the important personages in the city who were friends of the general. I tried to keep the guest list as small as possible, as he requested, but even with the elimination of many names it still meant that almost a hundred invitations were sent.

I became consumed with the preparations for the birthday celebration. The day of the party, I was overseeing the final touches when I received a message from Bolívar: he was too ill to attend his birthday party. I did not hesitate or wait for an escort. I got on my horse and rode to the palace. I found Bolívar in bed with a high fever, coughing blood, almost delirious. "Señor," I told him, "I'm canceling the celebration."

"If you want to make me happy, Manuelita," he said, "have your party tonight. It will give me pleasure knowing you're enjoying yourself. I know how much you love to entertain."

"I would not think of hosting a party while you are so ill, my general," I said. It was true, without his presence at La Quinta I wanted no part of the celebration. "You need me here, by your side, to care for you."

"Manuelita, this is an order. I am not talking to you as your lover, but as your general. Go ahead with the celebration. Just make sure you save me a piece of the cake. And I expect a full report tomorrow morning. To make sure people understand you are doing this with my sanction," he added, "I have arranged to have a battalion conduct military drills in front of La Quinta as a welcome for the guests."

25

Natán

I helped Manuela dress in the black and gold velvet gown which her seamstress had made especially for the occasion. When she added the necklace, bracelets, and earrings made of the finest Muzo emeralds, she looked absolutely regal.

Manuela had always been aware of the effect her physical attributes had on men. Now she knew how to use them to her advantage. As a young woman she had been very pretty; as a woman of thirty-one, she had gained an allure. The aura of power made her irresistible. As I helped her adjust her bodice so that her breasts were revealed just enough to tantalize men, Manuela said, "Natán, I'd give anything to have the general by my side tonight. Knowing he's ill... it's hard to hide my sadness."

Everyone who was invited—members of the general's Council, as well as the highest authorities of the Church, even Monsignor Cuervo, who had publicly vilified Manuela—came to La

Quinta that night. No one dared slight the general, because they knew that the following day Manuela would give him a report on who attended. Despite the absence of the Liberator, the birthday celebration was a joyous event, and it would have been Manuela's greatest triumph in Bogotá, had it not been for an unfortunate late-night party prank.

Manuela would be the first to admit that she loved her sherry. When people remarked on how much she could drink, she laughed, saying that she drank like a man. A few glasses of sherry had the effect of making her more fiery than usual; and sometimes her behavior could become reckless. On the day of the party, she had started sipping early. Once the guests arrived she led toast after toast to the general's health and the future of Gran Colombia.

The celebration went on for hours. The crowing of roosters was starting to be heard nearby, but a score of stragglers and Manuela were still drinking under the tent set up in the garden; by then she was quite inebriated. At her table someone brought up the name of Vice-president Santander. Loud hissing was followed by toasts to his appointment as Ambassador to the United States, which we all applauded as his exile from Colombia. It was then that another reveler cried, "He doesn't deserve to become ambassador. What that traitor deserves is the firing squad."

There was a moment of stunned silence, until I heard Manuela loudly announce, "This will be our birthday present to President Bolívar. We'll give him Santander's corpse."

Everyone laughed and cheered. Manuela asked Jonotás and me to get an empty potato sack from the kitchen and stuff it with rags and newspapers. In the kitchen I said to Jonotás, "She's taking this too far. She's asking for trouble." Jonotás, who could never find fault with Manuela, and who loved to play her own pranks, replied, "Natán, why are you always so serious? We're just having a good time. It's a fiesta. Have a drink and try to enjoy yourself for a change."

When we brought out the stuffed sack Manuela asked one of the officers to loan her his military jacket and asked another one for his two-cornered hat, similar to the one favored by Santander. While she was dressing the figure, she asked Jonotás to fetch a piece of charcoal from the kitchen and give it to Muñoz, an officer who enjoyed sketching caricatures.

Manuela was delighted with her scarecrow, which had the face of Santander. She asked the men to stand him against the wall. Now I got the idea—Santander the scarecrow was going to be shot by a firing squad. Someone in the crowd suggested that Santander should be given a chance to repent for his sins. It didn't take much persuasion to get a drunken priest to administer the last rites to the scarecrow. As the priest went through the motions, we knelt and assumed prayer positions. An intoxicated guest slurring his words suggested that Manuela should be the one to pull the trigger. Even in her condition, she had enough sense to refuse the offer. But events had taken on a life of their own. Seeing Manuela's bewilderment, Colonel Croftson took over. He ordered a makeshift firing squad of half a dozen soldiers to assume ready positions. For a moment, there was a tense silence, broken by Croftson's stern command to "Fire!" The salvo rang thunderously in the still night. A chorus of dogs barked and howled in the distance. The scarecrow, in flames, collapsed in a heap. The guests clapped and hooted and offered many toasts celebrating the Liberator's triumph and Santander's demise. I knew this prank could have grave consequences for Manuela.

26

By the time I rose from bed with an excruciating hangover late the morning following the party, General Córdoba had already been to the palace to see Bolívar and had given him a full report of our joke. My palace spies reported overhearing Córdoba saying, "My general, I know the high regard you have for Manuela Sáenz. Regardless, it's my duty, as a loyal soldier and friend, to point out to you that she's become an embarrassment to you, and a liability to your government. She's a woman out of control, sir. And it's in your best interest that you sever all ties to her." I was relieved to hear that Bolívar had replied that he could not control me, and that he would not send me away. Nonetheless, later that day the general sent me a note declaring that under no circumstances should I set foot in the palace—until he asked me to.

A week later, his secretary, Santana, hand-delivered another letter with Bolívar's order to move out of La Quinta as soon as possible. No explanation was offered, and none was necessary. This was the price of my mocking Santander. I rented a house on Calle de la Carrera, a block away from the Presidential Palace. I furnished it in a manner that was befitting if not to the First Lady of Colombia, then to Bolívar's mistress. I billed it all to the national treasury. I expected to come under criticism for this, but I was determined not to appear in the eyes of the world as if I were no longer a personage of high rank. It was painful for me to accept the precarious nature of my position. I was sure Bolívar would give me another chance. I would just have to be more thoughtful from that moment on.

A chilly distance grew between the general and me. My only consolation was my fervid belief that this impasse was temporary. My enemies among Bolívar's followers, especially General Córdoba, made it known that I would be tolerated and allowed to remain in Bogotá only on the condition that I never appeared in public with the general again. If this was the only way I could remain close to Bolívar, I was willing to accept this situation.

Weeks passed before I saw him. During that time, I did not entertain and kept a low profile. When I was finally summoned to the palace, I was allowed to go only late at night, a shawl wrapped around my head so people would not recognize me. I nurtured the hope that someday soon our former, more public, relationship, rather than this covert one, would be resumed. I knew that despite the political damage I had caused, Bolívar was not ready to part with me. Perhaps he no longer loved me with the physical passion of our first years, but I was still his best friend, the only person in whom he could trust completely, and I could still be of value to him.

My house on Calle de la Carrera became a salon where my

friends from among Bolívar's intimates came to visit me. At
that point, the most I could do for the general was to use Jonatás and Natán and their friends to continue gathering rumors
in the cesspool of Bogotá. More and more stories were circulat-
ing about plans to assassinate the general. As the rumors mul-
tiplied, the plots became more ominous. Santander, that fetid
excrescence of humanity, claiming that he needed more time
to get his affairs in order, delayed his departure for the United
States. Bolívar knew, I knew, we all knew that Santander was
plotting against the general, but the cunning rat was very
clever at leading a double life. I remained alert; sooner or later
we would catch him in the act of conspiracy. Then he would
not go to the United States—but straight to hell, where he belonged.

On August 10, to celebrate the anniversary of the Battle of
Boyacá, the battle in which Colombia had achieved its independence from Spain after Bolívar had defeated General Morillo, a masked ball would be held at the Coliseo, across from
the Presidential Palace. Bolívar would attend, which meant
that I could not.

The prospect of being captive in my house while the ball
was taking place at the Coliseo, so close by, was unacceptable.
The night before the ball, after a pleasant supper together, taking advantage of Bolívar's jovial mood, I said, in a tone of sup-
plication, "My general, since it is a masked ball, and nobody
can see me, please, please, give me permission to attend."

He smiled. "Manuelita, you look so enchanting tonight, I
could not deny you anything. You have to give me your word of
honor that you will attend alone, without Natán and Jonotás,

so you won't be recognized. What's more, you have to promise me you will not talk to anyone."

Leaping from my chair, I put my arms around his neck and kissed him. "I give you my word of honor, my sweet general."

"Palacios will personally deliver an invitation to your house tomorrow. This will remain our secret, understood?"

THE NEXT DAY, I spent hours selecting a mask until I found one that covered my face entirely; I tried on many costumes until I settled on one that covered my arms and neck and hid the shape of my body. That night as I was about to put on my mask as the finishing touch of my disguise, Jonotás knocked on the door of my dressing room. "This just came for you, Manuela. The woman who delivered it said it was extremely urgent, a matter of life and death."

I took the envelope and opened it. "Señora Manuela," it read, "I am a friend of the general who must remain anonymous. There is a plan to murder His Excellency tonight at the ball. Ten men will be coming at 11 o'clock with the express purpose of killing the Liberator. Please, señora, if you can send word to the general, do so without delay." The note was signed: "Un amigo."

My reflection in the mirror was ghostly white.

"For heaven's sake, Manuela, what is it?" Jonotás asked.

I handed her the note to read. Since I had come to Bogotá I had received many warnings about plots to murder the Liberator, so this note was not unusual. Yet, something told me that unless I acted quickly, the general's life was truly in grave danger.

What could I do, though? I had given Bolívar my word of
honor that I would remain anonymous at the ball. "Bring me a
pen and paper," I said to Jonotás. "I must make sure he gets a
message from me, without delay."

As I finished writing the note, I heard the crowds outside
the Coliseo calling the Liberator's name. He had arrived at the
ball. "I must go at once," I said, putting on my mask. I left the
house, using the servants' entrance in the back, just in case
spies were watching the front door.

Inside the Coliseo I had to push my way through the throngs
of masked guests. I recognized many of them by their voices,
but I spoke to no one to keep my identity concealed. The Liberator was seated on a velvet-covered dais built for the occasion. Prominent members of the government, many of them
accompanied by their wives, surrounded him. I felt a pang of
anger and regret that I could not be seated next to him, where
I belonged. A line of soldiers cordoned off the dais. The protection around the general did not reassure me; it was possible
that some of his guards were among the conspirators.

The clock at the top of the stairs struck ten o'clock. It was
difficult to get close to the dais, and when I did, the soldiers
ordered me to step back. The speeches began. General Urdaneta read an endless homily in commemoration of the Battle
of Boyacá and its heroes. The clock was ticking and the conspirators were probably already in the vicinity of the Coliseo.
When Urdaneta was finally finished, Bolívar rose to speak. He
looked weary, uncomfortable. The usual resonant authority in
his voice was missing. Did he have a premonition of the impending danger? His words had none of his usual eloquence;
he tersely thanked those in attendance for coming together to
celebrate such an important anniversary and then sat down

again. Colombians love pomposity, and the Liberator's lackluster speech was received with perfunctory applause.

The orchestra began to tune their instruments. The crowd started to clear a circle so that Bolívar could take the floor for the first dance. He walked over to Pepe París's wife and she took his arm. It was a quarter to eleven. There was no way I could cut through all the people and hand him the note. There was not a minute to lose. I would rather lose Bolívar as my lover than see him murdered. As the general and Señora París made their way out onto the dance floor, and the first notes of a *contradanza* began to play, I removed my mask so the guards would let me through. As soon as I got close enough, I cried, "General, ten men are on their way to kill you! I implore you, sir, leave this room before they get here."

A startled Bolívar looked uncomprehending. The orchestra stopped playing, and for a moment there was total silence. Without a word of thanks to me, Bolívar took Señora París by the hand and rushed toward the platform. Confusion broke out. Bolívar's guards made a tight circle around him and led him out a back way. In the ballroom the celebrants stampeded toward the exit to the street. I put on my mask again and followed them. Natán and Jonotás were waiting for me outside. Word had spread in the crowd of an assassination plot and the people were already chanting "Death to the traitors!" "Long live Bolívar!"

Back home, I worried aloud to my girls that the General would never forgive me. I had broken my promise not to make my presence known at the ball. But—had I not saved his life?

"Stop your moaning, child," Jonotás said. "Of *course* he'll forgive you. The general's no fool. He knows you couldn't have saved his life and your behind at the same time."

I laughed, and we all relaxed. We stayed up all night, drinking *aguardiente*, singing and smoking, hoping to receive a word of reassurance from Bolívar, but none came. The following day, I was seized by a terrible anxiety. What if the note had been a hoax? How many times could I embarrass the Liberator in public and still remain in his good graces? My despair grew as the hours passed and not a word came from the palace. Time passed at an agonizing crawl until late in the afternoon, when Jonotás, who had gone out to see what people were saying, returned with the news that one of the conspirators had gotten drunk in a *cantina* after the attempt was foiled and began to brag about the plot to kill Bolívar. "The man's in custody," Jonotás said, "but he's named none of his fellow conspirators yet."

That night he named names. Bolívar ordered a public execution of the traitors the following day in the Plaza de San Carlos. I knew then I would be vindicated; that Bolívar would forgive me for not keeping my word.

Two days later, I was in the kitchen, discussing with the cook what to make for dinner when suddenly I heard a commotion in the house, boots marching across the patio. Before I had time to react, Bolívar entered the kitchen. "My general!" I cried, in a mix of confusion and happiness. I began to smooth my hair. Without saying a word, Bolívar took me in his arms and kissed me in front of the servants, kissed me as he had not kissed me since our days in Lima. He took me by the hand there and then and, without saying a word, led me to my bedroom upstairs where we made love for hours, until night fell and we passed out on my bed from exhaustion, just like we had done in the old days.

GENERAL CÓRDOBA AND the *bolivarianos* who disliked me had been dealt a setback in their plan to separate me from the general. Bolívar did not ask me to move into the palace with him after I saved his life, but I could now come and go in plain view of everyone, at all hours, and he began to receive friends and foreign dignitaries, with me acting as his hostess.

One night in late September I was at the palace, reading to Bolívar from Marcus Aurelius's *Meditations*, a book that always consoled him. He had been in bed for a few days with a bad cold. As I finished reading a section where Aurelius talks about the "Ruler within you," Bolívar sat up on the bed.

"Read that passage again, where he talks about always being ready." He reminded me of a child at times like this, a boy asking his nanny to reread a passage from a book he could not get enough of.

I read: "In a word, anything that distracts you from fidelity to the Ruler within you means a loss of opportunity for some other task. See then that the flow of your thoughts is kept free from idle or random fancies, particularly those of an inquisitive or uncharitable nature. A man should habituate himself to such a way of thinking that if suddenly asked, 'What is in your mind at this minute?' he could respond frankly and without hesitation."

"See?" he interrupted, pulling his blankets aside. "That's why I must not worry so much about my enemies, about Santander's intrigues. If I want to be a good ruler of Gran Colombia, all my thoughts must be about what I can do for the good of the nation. No wonder I'm not a good ruler. I let my mind be crowded by conspiracy and petty politics."

"My general," I said, "Marcus Aurelius is talking about an ideal. I doubt if he himself was able to achieve what he preaches."

"That's one great difference between the Romans and us, Manuelita. Marcus Aurelius's teachers were philosophers. For him these are not unattainable ideals. These are precepts he tried to live by."

I was about to reply that the Romans had had their share of rotten rulers, when there was a knock on the door. An aide entered and said that a woman at the front door insisted she had to see me on an extremely urgent matter.

Bolívar frowned. "Never a moment's peace. Tell the woman to come back tomorrow."

"No, wait," I said to the aide. This could be important. It was a mystery woman who brought a note to my house the night of the Coliseo ball, and that had saved his life. "You just stay in bed and I'll continue reading when I get back," I said to Bolívar. I got out of bed, put on my slippers, and wrapped a shawl around my shoulders.

She was a woman of the people, unknown to me, dressed humbly, her head covered by a black shawl. Two guards flanked her.

"Forgive me, Doña Manuela, for coming to you like this," she said. "I asked for you, hoping you could lead me to see the general. I have an important message for him, and time is of the essence." She stole a glance at the guards, who had already searched her for weapons.

I asked the woman to follow me into a small drawing room. "All I ask, Doña Manuela," she began once we were alone, "is that my name not be mentioned. Otherwise, I fear not so much for myself, because I am doing a patriot's duty—but I have concern for my family."

Realizing the importance of her mission, I asked her to wait for me in the room while I went to relay her message to the general.

Bolívar was in bed, already asleep. I tapped him on his shoulder and told him I had a woman with a message for him.

"I'm not feeling well enough to see anyone right now, Manuela," he said. "Please find out what she has to say."

I went back downstairs to explain, to excuse the general. "Then I have no choice but to tell you," the woman said. "I know how much you love the general, and that you have already saved his life once." She paused; in the light of the candles, I could see a tremor in her lips. "There are men plotting against the Liberator, Doña Manuela," she whispered, even though we were alone in the room. "They are well armed. Their plan is to kill him."

My heart sank. My hope had been that, at least for a brief time, we would not have to worry about another conspiracy. "Who are these men? Do you know them?"

"They are enemies of the general who want to see Gran Colombia dissolved. They meet at different places across the city, even in the House of the Treasury. There are many of them, señora."

"Who is the leader of these men?" I asked, although I was already sure of what her answer would be.

"Vice-president Santander leads them. He doesn't attend the meetings, but he's kept informed of every step they take." She paused, then added, "General Córdoba is also one of them.

He knows about the conspiracy. His friends pass on information to him, bit by bit."

This accusation against one of the Liberator's closest confidants would come as a terrible blow to the general. I told the woman to wait and ran back upstairs to deliver the news to Bolívar.

He was skeptical. "You must have misunderstood what the woman was saying, Manuelita. I have complete faith in Córdoba. He is a patriot who has proven his valor and loyalty many times. Call Fergusson up here," he demanded.

When Andresito Fergusson appeared, the general said: "Interrogate the woman in our dining room. I need to ascertain whether Manuela has misunderstood her." I think the general already knew what the answer would be, but it was just too painful for him to accept that a man he loved and trusted could be his enemy.

Andresito returned, repeating what I had said, and adding even more details.

The general said: "Tell the woman to go. It is a disgrace to blacken the name of a patriot as valiant as General Córdoba."

I was angry with the general but said nothing. I could not believe he would rather put his life at risk than think ill of someone he considered a friend. Nonetheless, I understood why he did it. If he couldn't trust his friends in a land where he was hated, whom could he trust?

A FEW NIGHTS later, I was at my house when Bolívar sent word that I should come to the palace immediately.

It had been raining all day, and the streets were wet and

cloaked in darkness. The Liberator was taking a hot bath when I entered his suite. He seemed more preoccupied than usual, in no mood to talk. Whenever I found him in a state like this, I tried to keep quiet. I was planning to pick up my embroidering and sit there to keep him company, but he asked me to read to him while he bathed.

When he finished his bath, he went to bed and fell immediately into a deep sleep. He had taken no extra precautions other than keeping his sword and pistol in the room. There were no extra guards. Bolívar was content with the reassurances of Colonel Guerra, his chief of staff, who had assured him everything was under control.

While Bolívar snored, I lay in bed, fighting off sleep. The bells of the cathedral had just tolled midnight when the general's dogs began to bark. I heard strange noises, a scuffle downstairs, although no firearms went off. I lit a candle and nudged Bolívar on the shoulder. "Sir, please wake up. Something's wrong." He leaped out of bed in his pajamas, picked up his sword and pistol, and marched toward the door. "I beg you, my general," I said, "please don't go out there." I locked the door from the inside. "Put on some clothes," I told him, seeing he was still in a daze. He dressed quickly. His eyes showed fear, weariness, almost resignation. He looked old and frail. I feared he was too tired to fight back and was considering surrendering. Footsteps were marching up the stairs. I had once heard him say to Pepe París that the window in his bedroom would come in handy if he ever had to escape in a hurry. I said, "If you want to live, the only way out is through the window."

"I think you're right," he said.

I went to the window, opened it, and looked out. At that moment there were men running beneath it. They reached the front door of the palace and began to force it open. I embraced Bolívar, trying to control my agitation. The general said, "Don't worry about me, Manuelita. I know where I can hide. It's you I'm worried about."

"I'm a woman," I replied. "They won't harm me."

"If anything happened to you, I'd never forgive myself. Perhaps if I stay..."

"Please go," I said, standing by the open window.

The general picked up his gun and saber, and then leaped from the balcony to the street. To give him time to escape, I grasped a sword, unlocked the door of the bedroom, and ran down the stairs, ready to strike anyone in my path.

A pack of armed men stopped me at gunpoint. "*Señora*, drop the saber or we'll shoot," one of the conspirators yelled. I dropped the saber. "Where's Bolívar?" another one asked.

"He's in the Hall of the Council," I said, trying to buy time. Among the men I recognized the Frenchman Augustín Horment and Carujo, a Venezuelan officer. He was Córdoba's teacher of French and English. The woman who had implicated Córdoba had been telling the truth. All the men were young, wearing their first mustaches, and I could smell liquor on their breath—as if they had had to drink to muster the courage to carry out their villainous plot.

They dragged me back upstairs and went into the general's suite. One of them pointed to the open window and exclaimed, "He's escaped."

I said again, louder, "If you want to find the general, he's in the Hall of the Council."

Horment, who seemed to be the leader, asked, "Why's the window open?"

"I opened it when I heard the noise downstairs."

A conspirator approached the bed and placed his hand under the blankets. "She's lying," he said. "The bed is still warm. He was here not long ago. He must be nearby."

The general's life was in the balance. "I was reading in bed," I said, trying to appear calm. "I was waiting for the general to return from the Council."

"*Puta!*" Carujo shouted and slapped me with such force it sent me reeling against the wall.

"Come with us and show us where the Hall of the Council is," Horment said.

I did not know the layout of the new building. "I have never been there," I said. "It's in a new wing of the palace."

"Come with us, *perra*," a traitor said. I became so terrified I could not move. He hit me in the face with the butt of his gun on my jaw, then pointed the gun at me. The pain was excruciating. I tasted blood.

"Lopote, we don't kill women," Carujo said. "She's not worth one of our bullets."

I was pushed down the stairs, where I found Ibarra, wounded in the chest. I got on my knees and applied my shawl to his wound, trying to staunch the flow of blood. He asked in a whisper, "Have they killed the Liberator?"

"No, Ibarra," I replied, "the Liberator lives."

A man they called Zuláibar grabbed me, pinned me against the wall, and started firing more questions at me. My answers did not please them, so they started to drag me back to the bedroom. I pleaded with the men to take Ibarra with us, not to leave him dying on the stairs. Two men helped me carry him up the stairs and put him in the general's bed. A few men were left guarding the door, and the rest ran off.

I sat on the bed, holding Ibarra's hand, encouraging him to

hold on. Hearing the sounds of cleated boots, I went to the window. The full moon wore a new, golden coat that night. Colonel Fergusson was running toward the entrance of the palace. Andresito spotted me at the window and stopped.

"Where's the general?" he yelled.

I replied I didn't know where he was, that he had escaped, that I couldn't speak freely because of the guards. "I implore you, Andresito. Please go back," I said. "If you come inside, they will kill you."

"*Coronela*," he shouted from the street, "if the bullets of the traitors kill me, I will die doing my duty." He ran through the door and then I could not see him. Two shots rang out. I held my head in my hands and, for a moment, I felt as if two bullets had gone through my heart.

All the noise and gunfire had attracted the attention of the neighbors. Many windows along the street were opened, and people holding lighted candles and lamps began to shout questions at passersby. As loud voices approached in the street below, the conspirators guarding my door vanished. I threw a shawl over my shoulders, and ran downstairs, where I found Andresito wounded in the chest. His eyes were closed, but he was still breathing. Part of the skin of his skull had been sliced off. Afraid that Andresito would choke on his own blood, I folded my shawl and placed it under his head.

I ran to the wing of the palace where Dr. Moore, the general's official doctor, lived. He had been sound asleep but woke up when I banged and banged on his door. "There's been an attempt on the Liberator's life, Dr. Moore!" I blurted out when he opened the door. "Come with me downstairs. Fergusson's dying."

Dr. Moore grabbed his instruments and, still in his nightgown, followed me downstairs. At that moment I remembered Don Fernando, the general's nephew. He must have slept through the commotion. I ran to his apartment and banged on his door until I heard him stirring. "Fernandito," I yelled, "there's been an attempt on your uncle's life. But he escaped. The conspirators are still in the building. Please arm yourself."

Don Fernando woke up immediately and came out with two guns—one of which he handed me. "Please, please, God," I prayed, as we rushed downstairs, "if you hear me, save Andresito." It was the first time in many years, not since I was a child, that I had prayed to God.

By the time we got downstairs, the general's guards were fortifying the palace. The conspirators had fled in the darkness. Though I was desperate for news of Bolívar, I served as Dr. Moore's nurse as he tried to save Andresito's life.

WORD OF THE ATTEMPT spread through Bogotá. Soon after the palace was secured, General Urdaneta and Colonel Herrán and other friends of the Liberator arrived. I was inconsolable: Andresito Fergusson, one of my dearest friends, was dead. And I did not know if the general was alive.

Jonotás and Natán arrived at the palace. Seeing the state I was in, Natán made me an herbal potion to soothe my nerves. Dr. Moore was now trying to stop the bleeding that was draining the life from Ibarra. It looked as though another valiant patriot would be a casualty of the attempt. I was sinking into total exhausted despair when word arrived that the Liberator had escaped unharmed and was in the Plaza de San Carlos, addressing his troops. I burst into tears. Natán made me finish the tea to calm me. When I was more collected, I said to my girls, "I'm going to the plaza. Come with me."

"Let me clean your face," Jonotás said. She took a towel from the general's bathroom, poured a little water on it, and rubbed some of the blood off my hands and face. "That's better," she said. "You would have given the general a heart attack if he saw you covered in blood."

I was racing down the cobblestone street that led to the plaza when I realized I was still in my nightgown—I didn't care. Let the curious stare.

That moment when I saw the general mounted on Paloma Blanca was the happiest moment of my life. He was talking to Córdoba and another man on horseback. It was Santander. I recognized him instantly. There he was, my greatest enemy, and the first thing I thought of was how handsome he looked. He was in civilian clothes. It didn't look as if he had dressed in a hurry to go out, which I interpreted as proof of his knowledge of the conspiracy. He had probably been home fully dressed, waiting for news of the general's death. He wore a round hat, a black jacket, green velvet pants, and laced boots. His mustache, his eyebrows, and the eyes below them were raven black. He was nodding his dimpled chin as the general spoke. My first impulse was to borrow a gun from a soldier and shoot him. A shred of sanity held me back. It was harder to refrain from screaming, "They are your enemies, my general. Have them arrested and shot!" I told myself that there would be plenty of time in the future to punish them. I swore then that Santander and his followers would pay for everything that had happened that night.

When Bolívar spotted me in the crowd, he dismounted and rushed to my side. I ran toward him and threw myself into his

arms and began to weep. I wept for all the times I had wanted
to in the years since I had met him; for all the times I had been
left behind; for all the times I had feared for his life; for all the
times my own life had been in danger; for all the dark times
that undoubtedly lay ahead of us.

I was shivering in the night chill. "Manuelita, *mi Manuelita*,"
Bolívar repeated over and over again, kissing my cheeks, my
forehead, my hair, my hands, my lips still bearing the blood of
Andresito and Ibarra. Taking me by the hand, he led me to the
middle of the circle made by Santander, Córdoba, and the military members of his staff who had begun arriving at the
plaza.

"Gentlemen," the Liberator said loudly, addressing the men
surrounding us, "I am alive because of the courage of Manuela
Sáenz." As he said these words, I stared at Santander with hatred. He blanched when our eyes met, but his features remained imperturbable. Still speaking in a loud voice for all to
hear, the general anointed me a new name, "Manuelita," he
said, "you are the liberator of the Liberator."

It was daylight when we returned to the palace. The general was burning with fever. Though there had been many difficult nights in the years we had been together, I could say
with all certainty that that September night was the most horrible night of my life; and that dawn, when I dressed the general's scratches, put him to bed, and kissed him good-night,
was one of the happiest.

BOLÍVAR AND I began to sleep together again. One night, not
long after the attempt, I could not sleep. The fear of men coming in the dark to kill us while we slept kept me awake many

nights. That fear would persist for many years to come, and it would not be until my old age in Paita that I finally slept in peace, knowing that there was no one in the world who wanted to kill me. Feeling restless, I got out of bed while Bolívar snored, lit a candle, and went into his study to smoke a cigar. An unfinished letter on his desk caught my attention. It was a letter to his friend José Fernández Madrid, Colombia's chargé d'affaires in Paris and London. I skimmed the letter until I came to the last paragraph:

> *A man fighting against all others cannot do anything.*
> *My past efforts have exhausted my energy. This fight has*
> *left me overwhelmed, and I am alive not because I have*
> *the strength to go on or any desire to do so. No, my*
> *friend, I go on in this world out of habit, like a dead man*
> *who cannot stop walking.*

In Paita, where I had nothing to do for twenty years but re-member, I blocked any thoughts about that painful night and the period immediately following the September conspiracy. I blocked it out because, although Bolívar had survived the attempt, his heart—as this letter to Fernández Madrid made clear—had been shattered by the betrayal of Córdoba and the people he loved. Bolívar could never understand why, though he had given up his fortune, his health, and his happiness to give freedom to Colombians, all they wanted in return was to see him dead. The conspirators had failed to kill him in his body, but the Liberator's spirit had indeed been murdered.

27

Natán

The September conspiracy was the beginning of the end. Even though *el Libertador* felt vindicated, because he finally had proof that Santander and his followers were actively trying to assassinate him, the attempt on his life robbed him of his will to live; he became less than half the man he had been. Bolívar made no effort to hide his unhappiness, and life seemed to hold few joys for him.

A council of war headed by Croftson was convened to deal with the conspirators. It came to light that the group of young traitors, in order to meet without creating suspicion, had formed a group they named the Philological Society. They met regularly, under the pretense of studying literary works and foreign languages.

The conspirators were convinced that the ultimate goal of the Liberator was to become emperor of the Andes, and they detested monarchy. They were *santanderistas*, believers in democratic institutions. The government of the United States of America was the model Santander wanted to adopt for Colombia. The university students were disgusted with the ruthlessness of the general's military, and how, in the name of keeping public order, the armed forces crushed any sign of discontent.

As head of the council of war, Croftson published an edict threatening death for anyone found harboring the conspirators. Croftson was constantly on the verge of letting his military influence run unchecked, and now there was no one to restrain him.

Bolívar's power was absolute, and Manuela reigned as his empress.

She thought nothing of giving orders to drag the men accused of conspiracy from their homes or jail cells so she could interrogate them.

One morning I was in Manuela's bedroom tending to her because she had a cold, when Croftson came in accompanied by a prisoner and guards. Croftson informed Manuela that the prisoner's name was Ezequiel Pérez. He was a scrawny boy, no older than fifteen, with peach fuzz on his chin. His eyes bulged with fear. Manuela received him with all courtesy and asked him to sit down. The boy's legs trembled uncontrollably. His fingernails were bloody, as if he had been chewing his nails raw. Manuela said, "Ezequiel, I understand you worked for General Santander as his page, that you were present when the conspirators discussed their heinous plot to assassinate the general. I give you my word of honor that if you tell me the names of all the conspirators, including that of General Santander, your life will be spared."

The terrified boy answered that it was true he had worked for Santander, but that the vice-president had never taken him into his confidence, and that he had not been present at any meetings where plans were made to assassinate the Liberator. His voice cracked a couple of times as he spoke.

The boy's reply made Manuela angry. She motioned to me. "Go downstairs and tell his mother to come up."

I found the woman in the patio and asked her to follow me. She was dressed in clean but ragged clothes; she was probably a domestic. When she came into Manuela's bedroom, she embraced her trembling son.

"*Señora*," Manuela said, addressing Ezequiel's mother, "if you want your son to live you must order him to tell the truth and reveal General Santander's part in the conspiracy."

"Please, Ezequiel," the woman pleaded, "do as Doña Manuela says. If you love your mother, tell her everything you know."

"But I can't, *mamá*," the boy replied between sobs. "I can't."

"Be a good son, Ezequiel, and make your mother happy," Manuela said.

I could only imagine what that boy felt as he saw the gleam in her eyes. To understand Manuela, you would have to see her eyes, because they revealed who she really was. They were her most striking feature, and she was well aware of it. All those years in Lima, when she walked out of the house with her head covered except for one eye, taught her the power of a single eye. She had mastered her glare. Her eyes could entice and caress you, like a feather, or they could make you feel worthless, or slash you like a knife.

"I cannot do what Your Grace asks me to do, Doña Manuela," the boy said still sobbing. "I cannot name General Santander as a conspirator, because I was not present at the meetings Your Grace is talking about."

Abruptly Manuela said to Croftston, "Take him away and shoot him with all the others."

Ezequiel's mother knelt on the floor at the foot of Manuela's bed, as though she were praying. "He's my only son, Doña Manuela," she pleaded, sobbing in a way that made me want to run from the room. "He is my whole life. His two older brothers, my husband, and my own brothers were killed fighting the Spaniards. My son is all I have left. Please, Doña Manuela, I beg Your Merciful Grace as only a mother can."

"*Señora*, please get up," Manuela said softly. "Believe me when I say it breaks my heart to do this. I don't want to cause you pain. I would love to spare your son's life. May God forgive me for what I'm about to do. But your son must die with all the other conspirators. If I let him live, the Liberator will never be safe." With a nod of her head, she said to Croftson, "Take him away."

The two of us were left alone in the room. I stood staring at the floor, waiting for her to tell me what to do next. When I looked up, Manuela snapped, "Why are you giving me that accusing look? You think it was easy doing what I had to do? Get out of here. Leave me alone. I don't want to see you the rest of the day."

I closed the door behind me and stood frozen. It was an instant reflex. Eavesdropping was something I had been doing all my life, something all house slaves did. Since our lives depended on the whims and actions of our masters, and we were always the last ones to be informed about decisions that affected us, very early on in our servitude we learned eavesdropping was one of the few ways for us to get some control of our lives. When I remembered there was no one else in the room with Manuela, I began to walk away. Before I had taken two steps, I heard Manuela wailing in pain. I had never ever heard her make such a sound.

I often heard the Liberator say, after he was criticized for an authoritarian act, that in war the ends justify the means. That day it became clear to me that if Bolívar and Manuela had stayed in power, they would have become as cruel as the most bloodthirsty of the Spanish tyrants. No one who took part in the epic of independence could claim not to have blood on their hands.

LATER THAT WEEK, a man named Florentino González gave a full confession implicating General Santander. Although the vice-president declared from jail under oath that he had had no knowledge of the conspiracy, he was stripped of all his possessions and sentenced to die by firing squad.

The massacres, uprisings, and wars that followed the arrival of the conquistadors had made the people of Colombia bloodthirsty—like those jaguars that, once they have eaten human flesh, can never be sated again. Human life was cheap. When so many people have died, a single human life has no value. Large massacres barely raised an eyebrow. Colombians constantly looked for excuses to spill more blood. Whose blood it was, it made no difference. The shedding of blood became a main source of entertainment, a never-ending, gory spectacle everyone could afford. Colombian crops were fertilized with rotten flesh and blood. Sometimes it seemed that more blood than water flowed down the streams and rivers of Gran Colombia. No one in Gran Colombia—whether rich or poor, Spanish or *criollo*, free man or slave—could claim innocence. There was no family in Gran Colombia that was not in mourning for the death of a relative killed in battle, or executed, either by the Spaniards or the *criollos*, or jailed and tortured, or exiled for life. Orphans, widows, childless parents made up the bulk of the population of Colombia. This was the result of the Wars of Independence—a nation of people with uncharitable hearts, a place where hatred was what made hearts beat. A nation of people blinded by anger, a race of vicious beasts indifferent to human suffering. People lived for vendettas and revenge. It was not the end of suffering that was sought but its continuation.

On September 30, at noon, in Bogotá's Plaza Mayor, the conspirators who had been caught—with the exception of Santander, whose death sentence was commuted—were shot in front of hundreds of cheering *bogotanos*. Orders were given that they should be left tied to their chairs, still bleeding. Pools of blood gathered in front of them for the rest of the day as a warning to any who might consider plotting against Bolívar in the future.

THAT NIGHT HAIL as big and hard as large stones fell on the city, cracking and breaking many tiles on the roofs of the houses and shattering stained-glass windows in the churches and public buildings. Some people caught in the storm died of brain concussions. Afraid of the intensity of a storm that would undoubtedly kill livestock and destroy all the crops growing on the savanna, *bogotanos* began to pray. All through the night, a mournful prayer echoed all over Bogotá, mixing in with the cracking sounds of the hail that pelted the roofs of the city. I had heard similar prayers in Ecuador when a volcano near Quito threatened to erupt, and people took to the streets carrying images of the saints, begging for clemency; and I had heard the same in Lima, after a devastating earthquake that left looting and pestilence in its wake.

In the morning, when I left the house with my baskets to go to the market, all of Santa Fe de Bogotá, including the red clay roofs of the buildings, looked unsullied and white. The mountains ringing the savanna looked as if they were made of solid ice. As I reached Calle de la Carrera and began to cross it, I glanced in the direction of the Plaza Mayor—and gasped. The day before the plaza had been drenched in the blood of the conspirators. This morning the plaza, too, was sheeted in ice. But as the sun rose behind Monserrate, the layer of ice over the coagulated blood made the plaza look like a frozen lake made of the crimson juice of the corozo fruit.

28

You would think that the period after the September con-spiracy, when the traitors were executed and Santander was thrown into a dungeon in Cartagena, and then exiled to Europe, would provide some peace for the general. But the Colombians—out of sheer stupidity, out of a narrow sense of nationalism—simply did not want Bolívar to govern them.

Congress demanded a new election—and Bolívar agreed to it. One of Santander's minions, Joaquín Mosquera, was elected as president of Colombia. Bolívar fell into a deep melancholy, and despite my best efforts he refused to take care of his health. Soon he was coughing and spitting up blood again. Following Mosquera's election, large groups of *bogotanos* began to parade on a daily basis in front of the Presidential Palace carrying placards ridiculing Bolívar's frailty, "Go back to Venezuela, you shriveled sausage," they chanted. "Bring back Santander."

This conduct was so infuriating, I finally said to Bolívar, "*Señor*, you must send the troops out to disperse that rabble."

He shook his head. "The last thing I want to do, Manuelita, is to start behaving like a tyrannical viceroy. It's true they don't like me, but they are my people. I cannot forget that."

Bolívar was no longer listening to me but to a voice he alone heard that prodded him to plan his departure from the city, even before Mosquera was due to move into the palace. Most nights he stayed awake pacing his room. The virulence of his coughing fits left him breathless and listless, and I became afraid that his days might be coming to an end. Much as the notion terrified me, I came to accept he must go abroad, someplace where he could recover from the ingratitude of the people who owed him their freedom.

So it was that after a long day in which the protesters outside threw stones at the windows of the palace, and he spent the night coughing blood, I said to him, "My general, we must begin to prepare for your departure without delay." I did not ask him to take me with him. For the first time in many months I saw something like a smile cross his face.

"I want you to come live with me in Italy," Bolívar said, quelling my fears of being left behind. "But we cannot leave Bogotá together. Once I reach the coast, you can follow me."

I had been left behind many times before, and we were always able to reunite, so I seized this ray of hope for a future away from political intrigue, a future in which we would grow old together, enjoying the small pleasures of life.

Bolívar all but started counting the minutes until he could leave Bogotá, and then Colombia altogether. However, his travel plans depended, in large measure, upon the sale of his

silver mines in Venezuela. Unfortunately, legal troubles delayed the sale to a British syndicate. In the meantime, Bolívar
was short of cash. In a feverish desperation, the general sold
his silverware, his jewelry, and his finest horses at a fraction
of their value to raise funds for the journey.

ONE GRAY AND bleak dawn, just like every dawn of his leaving me behind, he rode out of Bogotá, accompanied by a small
group of loyal officers. As I watched his figure fade into the
morning fog, a coat of numbness so complete wrapped around
me that I felt neither sadness nor pain, just a numbness that
said to me that all the coming mornings of my life, when I
awoke in my bed and opened my eyes, I would find myself
alone. Years and years went by before that numbness wore off,
before I began to feel the ice in my veins beginning to thaw.

A few days after his departure, as if to reassure me that he
was thinking of me, the general wrote me a letter from Gua-
duas that, in years to come, I would recite aloud whenever I
felt I wanted to give up:

My darling:

I have the pleasure of informing you that my journey goes
well, except for the sadness we both feel that we cannot be together. I love you very much, you are my beloved, but I will
love you even more if now, more than ever, you behave with
prudence. Be careful of your actions; should anything happen
to you, it will be too much for me to bear.

Always your most loyal lover,

Bolívar

I put this letter in the little mahogany chest where I kept all the letters he ever wrote me, the letters that were proof of his love for me. I held on to these letters for the rest of my days.

MANY OF BOLÍVAR'S men who had stayed behind were murdered. The exiled conspirators began to return to Bogotá, welcomed as heroes. Whenever I heard about a traitor's return, I wanted to grab my pistol and shoot the coward. With the help of the few friends I had left, I went back to writing broadsides—denunciations of the corrupt new government—to paste on the city's walls. Doing that much made me feel that perhaps not all was lost.

I lived each stage of Bolívar's journey, as he traveled down the Magdalena River to the coast, leaving the mountains behind, and entering the jungles of the tropics. I found consolation in the thought that he was traveling through a place where the air was warm, the nights fragrant and luminous, where the vivid colors of the flowers and the greenness of the trees were a feast for the eyes. He could only be regaining his health in such a realm, closer and closer to the life-giving Atlantic Ocean.

Yet the reports I received about Bolívar's health dampened my hopes. I heard that he could not climb a flight of stairs without help; that he continued to be his stubborn self, ignoring his doctor's orders even as he coughed blood; that his temper tantrums had become more violent; that he was often delirious; that he suffered from a debilitating insomnia; that he talked to himself all the time.

Each new report made me want to leave Bogotá without his permission and join his party so I could nurse him back

to health, as I had proven so many times I could do. I wrote
to him:

> Señor, *please, I beg you. Let me come to your side and I*
> *will make you all the sweets you love so much. I am told*
> *you are hardly eating. I worry about you day and night.*
> *Not to see you, not to be by your side, is the hardest pun-*
> *ishment of all.*

My letter went unanswered.

THEN, JUST DAYS before the New Year, a rumor spread
through the streets of Bogotá that Simón Bolívar had died in
the Quinta of San Pedro Alejandrino on the outskirts of Santa
Marta. I told myself this was vicious gossip started by the
santanderistas. It was unimaginable that his brilliant light had
gone out. A world without the nobility of his vision, life without his selflessness, seemed inconceivable.

I had to swallow the truth when a letter arrived from Péroux
de Lacroix, the physician who had tended to Bolívar when his
death was imminent. I read de Lacroix's letter over and over
again, hoping to find a hidden message in it, something that
would change its terrible last line,

> *Allow me, my kind* señora, *to add my tears to yours in*
> *this immense loss.*

AFTER HIS DEATH, I saw the general as I crossed the streets,
as I sat down to a plate of soup, as I lit a cigar, as I brushed my

hair, as I blew out the candle on my night table. In my dreams his image was so lifelike, so throbbing with life, so revealing of his soul, that I knew he was appearing to me in this manner so I could engrave him in my mind forever.

I spent days, weeks, months, years, decades, thinking of things I would have done differently. How was it that I was never able to call him Simón, as any woman would address the man she loves? It was always "My general," or "*Señor*" when we were alone, and "Bolívar," "the general," or "the Liberator" when I mentioned his name in the presence of others. In our moments of passion, I would sometimes grab his member and call it "*mi palo santo*," my holy rod, but not once was I ever able to say, "Simón, come here" or "Simón, look"…or even just plain "Simoncito."

Who had he been, this lover of mine? Man or hero, man or monument, man or chimera? I was unable to separate them. I had loved them all. He had been like a comet traveling through my life with such speed and heat that it was impossible to think of him as a mere mortal. After he died, when I was destitute, nationless, without a family, with the rest of my life devoted to thinking of my days with him, I was not so sure whether loving the multitudes that Bolívar was had been best—perhaps I had loved a mirage, not a man.

LATER IT WAS SAID by the people that I took a *mapaná* viper, the most poisonous of all Colombian snakes, and tried to get it to bite my breast—as if he had been my Marc Antony and I his Cleopatra; that I roamed the streets of Bogotá at night like a lost soul doing penance, calling out loud his name—the Co-

lombian version of Mad Joan; that I went on shooting ram-
pages, attacking government soldiers who had erected a
mocking effigy of Bolívar; that I resisted arrest with my sword.
Not one of those stories even approached my desolation, because I myself did not know its depths. It was as if the earth
had stopped turning around the sun and I was left suspended
in midair, encapsulated in a stationary bubble. Everything I
did, everything I tasted and saw, everything I touched reminded me of Bolívar. For a while I would wake from my
dreams, smiling, happy, thinking he was still alive, sleeping
beside me. The smile vanished as soon as I opened the windows
and let the daylight into my bedroom.

A crusade to erode his glory and tarnish his legend soon began. I would like to say that I stayed in Bogotá to fight to restore his name, or because I hoped to see his detractors revealed
for the reactionary cowards they were. The truth is, I stayed in
a city I despised, surrounded by people I loathed, because I had
no other home to which to return. I wanted to go to Ecuador to
join my brother, who was now a general, and who had joined
forces with other bolivarianos to continue fighting for the ideals
that the Liberator had left us as his legacy.

José María sent word discouraging me from traveling to Ecuador to join him. The man who delivered the news said that
my brother and his men were always on the run and that they
operated in a terrain so inhospitable that no woman could endure it for long. The messenger, however, made it sound like
my brother's forces were becoming stronger, that he had the
support of the people and that it was just a matter of time before the reactionaries were defeated. I began to allow myself
to dream of the day when I would join my brother, and then

reclaim Catahuango. The idea of growing old around my brother was appealing. At that point all I wanted was to live in peace for however many days I had left on earth.

The situation in Ecuador became only more turbulent and inauspicious. I heard reports that José María and his men were in hiding, and launching attacks from the vicinity of the volcano Imbabura. But among his soldiers there was a traitor who betrayed him. When José María, wearing a disguise and accompanied by his servant, descended to a village to buy provisions, his enemies were waiting for him. Realizing he had fallen into a trap, my brother tried to flee, but his horse tripped and José María was thrown to the ground. His servant, Zaguña, raised his arm, holding a white flag, as a signal of surrender. José María was taken prisoner by a certain Captain Espinosa, in whose custody he remained until a Lieutenant Cárdenas arrived with orders that José María was to be shot without delay. This unspeakable act was carried out. My grief at learning of the cowardly murder of my brother, and my bitterness at seeing my last hope dashed, became unbearable. I shut myself in my house and stopped receiving visitors. All I wanted was to nurse my pain. It was all I had left. Without my bottomless grief, I was nothing.

ROSITA CAMPUSANO, WITH whom I had lost contact after I fled Peru, heard the news of José María's death and wrote me a long letter from Lima. Earlier, when I had tried to discover her whereabouts from Bogotá, I discovered she no longer lived above the National Library in Lima, but no one could say where she had gone. A consolation was that she could not be dead, otherwise the news would surely have reached my ears. During those years, my affection remained undiminished for the friend with whom I had shared both miserable schooldays and the splendid moment of glory when San Martín liberated Lima.

One afternoon I was embroidering on the patio when Jonotás brought me a letter. I indicated that she should set it on the table, but Jonotás said, "I think this might cheer you up, Manuela." I immediately recognized Rosita's familiar handwriting. Rosita's letter opened with a heartfelt expression of sympathy on José María's death. She knew I had stayed in Bogotá after the Liberator's death and had been thinking about contacting me for a long time, she wrote, but for a time her own life had been so full of uncertainty that she didn't want to burden me with her travails. She was close to destitution, living with a series of friends who could make room for her in a corner of their homes, when news arrived that her father had died, leaving her an inheritance. The amount of money was not sufficiently large to support her comfortably for the rest of her life without working, the letter explained. But it was enough to start a business. So she opened a school for the daughters of families of modest means. It would be an alternative to the punitive education that most Peruvian girls suffered at the hands of the nuns, as we had, and which in any case were open only to girls from rich families. She talked in her letter about a new curriculum she had devised concerned with freeing the imaginations of her students. For example, they all had to learn to play chess, as preparation for the games of logic in life. This made me smile. It was so like Rosita to come up with something as Quixotic as that. There was also an annual competition, she continued, involving hiking up the mountains behind Lima. "Dearest Manuela," she wrote, "nothing would make me happier than to have you join me at my *escuelita* as a teacher and partner. You could teach the girls about the history of independence, about General Simón Bolívar, and you would be an example to them of what women can do with their lives. You and Jonotás could live at the school. Nothing would give me greater joy, Manuela, than the two of us spending our last years on this earth living under the same roof."

I wrote back immediately, expressing my immense happiness at hearing from her and my deep gratitude for her kind invitation to come teach at her school. That she had made a useful life for herself and did not have to depend on anyone's help was the best news I could imagine. But although her invitation was tempting, I said I was not ready to leave Bogotá yet. Perhaps in the future.

Rosita and I corresponded for years. Later, when I was living in Paita, once in a while she sent me a novel (though by then I had lost my appetite for romantic novels), and I sent her packages with the pineapple, papaya, and guava sweetmeats I made. This went on for many years, until one day a letter came from one of the teachers at Rosita's school, informing me that my oldest friend had died.

COULD IT BE I stayed in Colombia to learn a lesson from the women of Bogotá, the same women I had ridiculed so many times behind their backs as banal and empty-headed? It was the women of that city who came to my defense when the government repeatedly tried to jail me. It was they who, in a broadside posted on the walls of the main buildings of Bogotá, reminded the citizens and authorities that when I had been

the most powerful woman in Gran Colombia, I used my power
to help our soldiers.

When the *santanderistas'* demands for my punishment continued to escalate, these same women of the Liberal Party
drafted an even stronger document, reminding *bogotanos* that,
despite my haughtiness, my provocations, my recklessness,
and, above all else, my imprudence, I was not a criminal.
"What heroism she has shown! What magnanimity! If Señora
Sáenz has written or shouted, 'Long live Bolívar,' where is the
law that forbids it?" they wrote. It humbled me that the women
I had dismissed as marionettes forgave me my arrogance, my
hubris, and it moved me to discover that I had been admired
by my own sex from afar.

What else might I have misjudged, to what else had I been
blind when I had been the empress of the Andes? Had I remained in power, I might well have become unfeeling and un-
just, like all the tyrants I abhorred. Perhaps tyranny was no
more than the extreme expression of a heart gone cold. And
one could become a tyrant even if one worked selflessly to undo
the evils of the world.

29

Jonotás

Manuela drank a lot to numb her pain after the Liberator's death. In time she stopped drinking excessively, but she still seemed to be in a trance, as if her soul had been snatched by her enemies. She had lost everything but us.

"Jonotás, I wish I'd taken my life when I heard the general was dead," she confided to me. "I don't know if I have the guts to do it now."

We slaves learn to be patient. I knew that fate was the ultimate master and liberator, that time was the best healer, that eventually the situation would change and Manuela would rejoin the world of the living. I did not want to die yet, even if sometimes I felt my only reason for living was Manuela. This much I knew: if Manuela died, I would not want to go on without her. What kind of life could I have on my own, even if I were free? After I lost my parents, I had wanted only one thing—to be with Manuela.

Staying in Bogotá became too dangerous. We were convinced that sooner or later there would be an attempt on Manuela's life. Except for the few jewels she had not sold, Manuela was virtually indigent. So she rented a *casita* in Fucha, a village outside the city. There the three of us spent our time embroidering tablecloths, sheets, pillow covers, and ladies' handkerchiefs to support ourselves. Natán and I sold these items in the market, or going door to door.

Around this time I began to dress as a man, at first because men's clothes were cheaper, then because wearing men's clothes made me feel like I could protect Manuela better than I could as a mere slave woman. I became so used to wearing pants and shirts that I took all my dresses to the market and sold them, every one. I kept my hair bushy, out of what little female vanity I had left. One day an irresistible urge came over me and I took a pair of scissors and cut my hair off. Not content with the way it looked shorn, I went to see a barber and told him I was sick and tired of getting lice and wanted my head shaved.

When I returned home, Manuela laughed and commented, "You look good, Jonotás." From then on, once a week I sat on the floor at her feet and she shaved my head. After a while, people began to forget that I was a woman and addressed me as "*muchacho*," if they were prejudiced; or as "*señor*," if it was another Negro talking to me; and years later, in my old age in Paita, as "*viejo*." I never corrected them.

I made up my mind that I would stay with Manuela, as long as she wanted me by her side. Natán, on the other hand, was full of resentment that she could not join Mariano in Lima.

She concealed this from Manuela, but not from me. Natán was a noble creature, enough that she felt it was her duty to stay with Manuela so long as Manuela's future was so uncertain. But she was biding her time until the right moment came along when she could ask again for her freedom to start a family of her own. I wanted this for Natán, too, but I wondered how and when her freedom would arrive.

WE HAD BEEN LIVING for three years in Fucha when in early December, 1833, news reached us that Santander had returned to Bogotá. He had returned in triumph, which was devastating to Manuela. To see the Liberator's enemy return as Colombia's savior was too painful an insult to bear. For days, she sat on her chair on the patio, smoking cigars and staring at the mountains and tracking the journey of the clouds. She only spoke to us to answer a question.

Finally, she rallied and started taking her meals with us. One day we had finished eating when Manuela said she had something to tell us. "*Mis niñas,*" she began, "Santander's not the forgiving type. I've been thinking that it's time for me to leave Colombia. I'm a poor woman now and cannot afford to keep you. Tomorrow we will go into town and I'll draft the documents to set you free. I will go on to Jamaica to stay with old friends of the general, and I will wait there until my aunt dies and I can sell Catahuango. That is, if I don't die before she does."

Immediately I said, "I will stay with you, Manuela. I can help you in Jamaica."

"We may be even poorer there than we are here, Jonotás."

"I don't care about that. I want to go wherever you go."

I knew, and I suspect Manuela knew, too, what Natán would say. She thanked Manuela profusely for making her a free woman. "I will go to Lima to be with Mariano," she said. "He's still waiting for me. In the meantime, I don't want to be a burden to you, Manuela. I'll wait here until Mariano sends me the money for the trip."

"No, I wouldn't dream of letting you stay here by yourself," Manuela said. She got up from the table and beckoned us to follow her into the bedroom. There, Manuela asked me to pull from under the bed the mahogany chest where she kept the few jewels she had not sold, the documents the Liberator had left her for safekeeping, and all the letters he had written to her. "Here it is," she said, pulling out from under a packet of letters tied with a blue ribbon a medal—the Order of the Sun! "It's solid gold," she added, holding it up for inspection, as if to assure herself it was still gold. "This will pay for Natán's trip. I knew one day it would come in handy."

Then the three of us embraced and cried as we hadn't cried since we were children living with the Aispurus.

THE FOLLOWING MORNING, Natán and I accompanied Manuela to the home of Pepe París, who had remained a loyal friend in her adversity. He purchased the medal, in addition to an emerald necklace the Liberator had given her as a birthday present. Later that day she signed the papers making us free women. Unlike Natán, who was beaming with happiness, I felt sad. Manuela and Natán were my family. And now my family was breaking up.

We devoted ourselves to preparing Natán for her journey.

Barely a week after she became a free woman, Natán left Bogotá with a convoy heading south to Lima.

I thought I would never see Natán again. How poorly we
can guess what the future holds for us. Many years later, in
Paita, of all places, we were reunited.

In the next few years, we wrote back and forth, from wherever we were. Natán had worried that she had waited too long
to get married, that it be might too late for her to have a family. Fortunately, within two years she gave birth, first to a boy,
Mariano Nemesio, named after her husband and her father;
and the following year to twin girls, Julia Manuela and Julia
Jonotás, named after her mother, and after Manuela and me.
Though she knew of our dislike of the Catholic Church, we
were asked to be the girls' godmothers. We accepted, even
though it was understood we couldn't be at the christening. It
was a source of puzzlement to Manuela and me that Natán had
turned out to be a devout Catholic, and even more puzzling
that she chose two atheists to be the girls' godmothers.

For years after we arrived in Paita, on the far northern
coast of Peru, Natán spoke in her letters of her desire to come
visit us. Manuela always wrote back, saying how much we'd
love to see her again, that our home was her home. But the
visit was always postponed—one year because money was a
problem; another year because one of the children fell ill
around the time of their departure; still another year because
business was so good she couldn't tear herself away from her
bakery. I started to think I would never see Natán again, or
ever lay eyes on my goddaughter.

Finally, twelve years after Manuela and I settled in Paita,
Natán and her children got off a boat in early January. They

arrived with a big trunk full of presents for us. From her letters we knew that Natán and Mariano had done well for themselves. Natán, still modest, put on no airs despite her prosperity. She must have spent a small fortune on ladies' accessories for Manuela, and pants and shirts for me.

Natán also brought us two oil lamps, pots and pans, a set of beautiful china, English linen, and a lovely porcelain water jug and washbowl. Manuela was too proud to ever mention in her letters how poor we were, and Natán clearly seemed disconcerted at first observing our reduced circumstances. The children, who must have heard many stories of Manuela's grand past, seemed perplexed. But Natán and Mariano had done a superb job educating them, and they had beautiful manners. The girls did not complain about the straw mattress on my bed. They were very much Natán's children.

We could barely accommodate so many guests in our little house, but Manuela would not hear of Natán's suggestion that they stay at a boardinghouse in town, the only one that accepted Negroes. So the three of us slept in Manuela's big bed, just as we used to do when we were girls, the two Julias sharing my bed, and we hung a hammock for Mariano in the parlor.

The two weeks they spent with us were the happiest times I had in Paita, in all of my old age. Each night, with the balcony door open to a patch of starry sky, Manuela, Natán, and I would stay up until well past midnight, smoking, drinking *pisco*, and reminiscing. We'd laugh and laugh about our adventures until tears ran down our cheeks, then fell sound asleep, exhausted from so much talk and laughter.

The children called us Aunt Manuela and Aunt Jonotás. Though I had not seen them grow up, I felt a love for them far beyond the affection I felt for the children to whom I sold candies in Paita. These two girls and Marianito were like my own blood family.

Natán took over the kitchen, where she did not tolerate the presence of Manuela or me or the children. She woke up before anyone in the house and at breakfast fed us bread so warm that when you cut it to butter it, the butter would instantly melt into a puddle of gold on our plates. Among the delicious meals she cooked for us, our favorite was her thick *parihuela* soup, its fish and mollusks simmered to perfection. She also prepared coconut rice and sweets, such as coconut paste—Manuela's favorite—and baked cookies and cakes. Natán tended the oven fire as if it were a sacred shrine and she was its priestess, in charge of keeping it going all the time.

"*Muchacha*," Manuela would say, "take a break from that kitchen before you end up cooking yourself."

At the end of the day, before supper was served by the Julias, Natán would go to the bathing room at the back of the patio and wash herself for a long time, singing songs from our *palenque* that brought back painful and happy memories. She came out of the bathhouse placid, smelling of lavender.

While Natán spent her days in the kitchen, the rest of us hired horses and went on excursions to nearby towns to look at the ruins of churches and fortresses built by the conquistadors when they first arrived in Peru. One day we rode all day through the desert to reach the oasis near the Indian ruins of Narihualá. We went to the bay at least once a day. The children amused themselves playing games in the water. Manuela and I sought refuge from the heat in the scant shade of a coconut tree, from which we watched after them.

In the evenings, before supper was served, Manuela sank

into her rocking chair, and the children gathered around her to ask questions about the old times with their mother, or they told us what they learned in their schools. They had studied Simón Bolívar and his great triumphs. They were fascinated that their mother had actually known someone who was written about in books. The children wanted to know whether it was true that Natán had participated in military campaigns and fought in a battle.

"As peaceful as she is, your mother is as brave as the bravest soldier in the Wars of Independence," Manuela told them.

Marianito had many questions about the Liberator in battle. "Did he ever talk about the Battle of Boyacá, the battle that freed Colombia?"

"Are you interested in the military?" Manuela asked.

"Yes, aunt," Marianito said, bright-eyed. "I want to fight for our nation, to defend her against our enemies."

"Listen to me, Marianito," Manuela said, frowning. "If your Aunt Manuela ever hears about you joining the army, she will sail straight to Lima and give you a good public spanking. If you don't want to break my heart, or your parents' hearts, you'll stay away from the army."

"But Aunt Manuela," Marianito replied, full of fervor, "if the Liberator were alive, what do you think he would have said?"

"I'm not going to presume to know what he would have said. But let me tell you a big secret, Marianito. The Liberator hated war and the destruction of human life. He told me that one night shortly after we met, when my head—like yours—was full of dreams of military glory. If you want to do something for your country," she added, her tone softening, as she ran her fingers through the boy's curly hair, "you will be a man of peace. You will wage your battles with your words. The last thing our poor countries need is more wars."

Shortly before they went back to Lima, at the children's insistence Manuela opened the mahogany chest that contained the love letters the Liberator had written to her. She chose a few passages to read for the awestruck children. Natán and I were no less awestruck. We had never heard what these letters, which she had carried and protected so ferociously, contained.

WE DID NOT have time to mourn the loss of Natán. That same afternoon, Manuela received a note from Santander, ordering her to appear in his office in the Palace of San Carlos the following morning at ten o'clock.

"This will be my final humiliation in this hateful country," Manuela said. "After tomorrow, we will make preparations for our trip to Jamaica."

For the first time since Bolívar's death, she smiled. It was as if her veil of sadness had been lifted. The prospect of leaving Colombia for good was liberating.

After the Liberator died, Manuela didn't care anymore about her physical appearance. She avoided looking at herself in mirrors, and there were none hanging on the walls of our house. No longer young, and a little plump, she was still beautiful, and she would be beautiful in old age, too, because of her charcoal eyes and her clear, porcelain skin.

Yet Manuela gave a good deal of thought to what she should wear to her meeting with Santander. Not that she had much to chose from. She had sold all her elegant gowns. There was enough vanity left in her, however, that she did not want to appear disheveled in front of the man who had crushed Bolívar's most cherished dream—Gran Colombia. More than Fausto D'Elhuyar, more than her father, and more than James Thorne, Santander had made her unhappy. Manuela chose a pale-yellow silk dress she had not worn in years.

Though it was a sunny January morning when we rode to the palace, neither one of us could enjoy the horseback ride. Our mood was dark and apprehensive. Manuela must have been boiling inside as we entered the palace, the same palace that on so many occasions she had entered freely to see the Liberator. The palace where she had so often served as hostess was now Santander's home.

"What's the worst he can do to me, Jonotás?" Manuela had said on the way to this appointment. "To be deported from Bogotá is no punishment, and I suspect that's what this meeting will be about."

I hoped she was right. I could not forget that after the September conspiracy Santander had been locked up more than a year in a dungeon in Cartagena. I had no doubts but he had heard of Manuela's public vows to shoot him. Surely he remembered these stories.

We sat in the receiving room outside the presidential offices for hours, as people came and went. Fortunately, I had thought to bring the knitting bag with our yarn and needles. We passed the time making scarves we would try to sell before we left Bogotá.

It was mid-afternoon before Manuela was summoned. During those long hours of waiting we barely spoke to each other, except to comment on how our knitting was coming along. She kept her thoughts to herself. One thing was clear to me: our destiny was in Santander's hands.

"Jonotás, come with me," she said as she got up and started smoothing her hair and fussing with the pleats of her dress. "I cannot do this alone."

As we were admitted to his office, Santander rose from his desk. He glanced at me, and started to gesture as if to ask me to leave, but then changed his mind. Perhaps there was a flicker of compassion in that dog's heart. He could afford to be kind in her hour of humiliation.

Colombia's president greeted Manuela and offered her a chair. I stood behind her. Manuela looked around the room as she seated herself, as if searching for signs of Bolívar. There were none.

"I apologize that you had to wait so long, Señora de Thorne," Santander began. "But matters of importance demanded my attention." I saw Manuela's shoulders tighten. Nobody addressed her by her married name anymore. Was this the rat's way of denying the existence of Manuela Sáenz?

A woman came in with a coffee tray. Manuela accepted a cup, but Santander did not. He was telling her their meeting would be brief.

"Since I doubt we'll get another chance to meet in the future, Señora de Thorne, I invited you here today to inform you that you must leave Colombia without delay," he said. "I wished to say good-bye to you in person before you left." He paused to clear his throat, then continued: "Although great animosity has existed between us for many years, I wish to remind you that there was a time when General Bolívar and I were close friends, as well as brothers-in-arms. I would have gladly given up my life to protect his. This is why my later disagreements with him were so painful. I always admired the general, in every way, in everything he did. I will forever be grateful to him for his great service to the nation. Without the general we would still be subjugated by Spain."

"The Liberator would have been happy to hear you say this," Manuela said. Her tone was mocking, but Santander seemed unaware of it. The old Manuela would have said something like "Why didn't you tell this to the general when he was alive? Before he died of a broken heart?"

"Believe it or not, I am also full of admiration for you, *señora*," Santander went on. "I admire you for your selfless devotion to the general, and for demonstrating your love for the people of Colombia when the Liberator was president. I take this occasion to say that I also deeply admire you as a woman— your example has shown the women of Colombia what it's possible to achieve."

Could he mean a word of what he was saying? Did he think Manuela was a fool to believe him?

"Thank you, sir," she said. "You're most gracious."

"Graciousness has nothing to do with it, Señora de Thorne. I'm certain that in the future history will remember you as one of our heroines of independence. And although you have caused me great personal suffering, what happened between us is the past."

Perhaps that was so. I was convinced that until her dying day Manuela would despise him. As I would.

"Despite my admiration for you, Señora de Thorne, you're to be deported from Colombia and exiled for the rest of your life. You have continued to voice your opposition to the government. That I find unacceptable. And make no mistake about it, should you return, on any pretext, *señora*, you will be executed. Since the general's death you have refused to accept that Gran Colombia is defunct, that the Liberator's legacy died with him, that his ideas have been rejected by the people, that it is time for this new nation to move forward."

Manuela took a last sip of coffee, stared at the inside of the cup as if she were trying to read her future in the patterns created by the coffee grounds. Then she placed the cup squarely in the center of the small table next to her chair and stood to address Santander.

"Mr. President," she said, "the reason Your Grace hated the Liberator so much was because deep down, no matter how much the people preferred you to him, you knew that you would never be half the man he was. Even after all these years, it must torment you to know that history will remember you only as a footnote in the story of Simón Bolívar."

As she turned to leave, and walked toward the door with me following her, I heard him say, "*Bon voyage*, Señora de Thorne. May God be with you."

LATER THAT NIGHT, when we were sitting in our parlor, smoking our nightly cigar, Manuela said, out of nowhere, "His looks are vastly enhanced by his elegant clothes." It took me a moment to realize she was speaking about Santander. "Clearly, he learned to dress like a gentleman during his stay in Europe. But, you know, Jonotás, despite the cosmopolitan aura of power he projects now, he will never be a natural prince like Bolívar. I'm proud of myself, though. Last night I had decided that no matter what happened during our meeting, I would not apologize for the past." She paused. "Jonotás, had I stayed there another minute, the scoundrel would've sworn he'd had no part in the September conspiracy. My only regret is that he was not shot with the other conspirators." She let out a prolonged sigh, took a long puff of her cigar, exhaled, and added, in a tone so wounded it broke my heart, "They've erased the Liberator from history, Jonotás. It is as if he had never existed. And if Bolívar didn't exist, I'm nothing but a ghost."

30

It was the dry season in the cordillera. At this time of year the Falls of Tequendama broke into mere threads of water, but rain had fallen over the savanna late in the afternoon the day before, a sudden, violent pelting of heavy raindrops, and today the Bogotá River was swollen, furious. The clamor of the falls filled the spaces between the mountains, producing an endless echo that sounded like a crowd cheering a victorious general entering a liberated city.

Our party—two Indian porters to lead the mules loaded with my trunks, eight soldiers assigned by the Colombian government to escort me out of Bogotá, and Jonotás and myself—had stopped for the night in a clearing near Tequendama.

Jonotás dismounted first. Tonight, the expression on her face was severe, her features rigid, as if carved in stone. She was dressed in a dark-green hussar's uniform, complete with saber.

I wore my colonel's uniform: a three-cornered hat, a royal-blue jacket—now without the medals I had been forced to sell, one by one—and red velvet pants. It had been years since I'd donned my military uniform, and I no longer felt comfortable in it, as if it were a skin I had shed long ago. The night before, after the trunks were packed, the only question remaining was what clothes to leave out for the journey.

"There's no question what I'll wear," Jonotás said, "I'm leaving dressed as a soldier."

Until that moment, I had not given any thought to my attire. "That settles it," I said. "Let's dust off my colonel's costume." We decided to depart Bogotá dressed this way in order to affront one last time a society and a people the two of us despised.

After securing the horses for the night and posting two soldiers as sentries, our party descended the narrow path that led to the clearing that jutted out over the chasm at the top of the falls. At dawn, the convoy would take the road leading to Honda, fifteen miles away, on the shore of the Magdalena River. The government decree specified that from Honda I must travel downriver to the town of Arjona on the Atlantic Coast. From there I would be taken to Cartagena as a prisoner and held till a ship bound for Jamaica would remove me from Colombian soil.

We divided into three groups for the night. The soldiers camped by the road. In the clearing, the Indian porters huddled around a fire, where they roasted yellow potatoes and ears of corn still wrapped in their green husks. Jonotás and I were ordered to set up camp closest to the falls. She chose a mossy spot at the edge of the wood, where a knot of oaks provided shelter from the mist that the falls created as it hurled its waters into the temperate zone.

While Jonotás gathered twigs and dry logs for a fire, I wandered off to be by myself. Below me, thick fog hugged the rock at the top of the falls on which stood the Virgin's shrine. At the wooden railing built at the edge of the precipice, I picked up a small stone, cast it into the open space and tried to follow its course, though the shifting body of the mist quickly swallowed it. My eyes traveled over the huge gap of the gorge. I wanted to memorize this moment, this place. I leaned on the railing and caught a glimpse of the river hundreds of feet below, propelling itself over rocks and boulders before it disappeared in the twilight. Tequendama's icy drizzle sprayed my face, yet I felt as if I were burning.

Tonight, the roar of the waterfall produced an urge to become part of its mystery. In pre-Columbian times, the Chibcha Indians of the savanna used Tequendama as a sacred entrance to the world of the ancestors. My Indian servants in Bogotá claimed that the ground around Tequendama was haunted by the souls of the hundreds who sighed in the pool at the foot of the waterfall. The Indians insisted that on tranquil nights they could hear the cries of the dead as far away as the city. On sunny, clear afternoons, when I hiked in the mountains with my girls to gather herbs and wildflowers, the hazy plume of the falls rising in the sky was visible in the background. And with it rainbows, often double rainbows, which made perfect arcs over Tequendama just before sunset. At those moments, I forgot I lived in Bogotá—I dwelt in a magical land.

A part of me wanted to leap into the void before me. Four agonizing years had passed since Bolívar's death. Only his memory anchored me to life, and I was, as always, steadfast in my determination to defend his name against those who vilified it. If for nothing else, I must live long enough to see the day when the general's name would be restored to its full glory. If I did this, then my existence would be vindicated.

Half a decade earlier, at one of my nightly *tertulias* in the house I had taken across from the Presidential Palace, in view of the fine summer weather we were having in the savanna I had proposed to my guests a picnic the following morning at the Falls of Tequendama. The exclusively male company—members of the British Legion, officers from Bolívar's army, Irishmen and Frenchmen who had come to South America to fight for the cause of liberation—accepted my invitation with alacrity. As a young woman in Quito, I had dreamed of visiting the waterfall that Alexander von Humboldt had made famous in his book *Personal Narrative*. "Let's go easy on the drinking tonight, gentlemen," I said to my guests, "so we don't oversleep and wake up hungover." Despite my appeals, the *tertulia*, as usual, went on until well past midnight.

The following morning we gathered in front of Captain Illingworth's home. The sun bathed the mountains surrounding Bogotá in a bright white light. Although we had agreed the night before to dress as civilians to avoid curiosity upon leaving the city, at the last minute I changed my mind and dressed in my colonel's uniform. To further amuse myself, I put on a mustache made of the hair of Spanish soldiers killed in the Battle of Pichincha.

It was a pleasant outing. Upon arriving at the falls we spread the linen tablecloth Jonotás had packed, and I laid out cheese, ham, olives, bread, sweetmeats, silver goblets, and bottles of French champagne. The ride, in such sunny weather,

had made me warm, and I imbibed goblet after goblet of champagne to cool off. Later that afternoon, inebriated, excited by
the talk of the men about their travels in Europe and their adventures in South America, the battles they had fought and
their romantic conquests (I noticed they talked about the ladies as if I were not present, and this flattered me), I wandered
to the top of the falls. The chilly waters rushing right next to
me were enticing and I dipped my toes into it, unaware of how
close I was to slipping and falling in. Two men from the party
saw me, came from behind, and pulled me away from what
would have been a certain death.

THE LIGHT was fading fast. I took off my hat, removed the pin
holding my hair in a chignon, and shook my head to let my
hair cascade to my shoulders. I tossed the hat toward where
Jonotás was preparing our bed for the night.

I turned to face the torrent and pulled from my pants pocket
a copy of the letter the government had sent ahead to the authorities in Cartagena, stating the reasons for my expulsion
from Nueva Granada, as Colombia was known once more. I
propped my arms on the railing to examine the crumpled piece
of paper I had read and reread since I received it.

COLOMBIA. *Member country of Nueva Granada.*
Secretary of the Interior and Foreign Relations.
Bogotá, 7 January 1834.
    To His Excellency the Governor of Cartagena:
    The office of the Governor of Bogotá, in accordance with
current laws, has ordered the departure from this capital of
Señora Manuela Saénz, who has chosen the port of Cartagena

to leave Colombian territory. The scandalous history of this woman is well known, as is her arrogant, restless, and bold character. The political chief of this capital has had to resort to force to remove her from here, because this *señora*, hiding behind her sex and her haughtiness, gave herself permission to mock the orders given by the authorities, as she has done from 1830 to the present.

The Executive Power has ordered me to inform you of this occurrence so that you can be aware of any breech of conduct on the part of this woman, and be ready to force her, without excuses of any kind, to depart from the territory over which you govern, in accordance with the passport she bears, and prevent any turmoil she could create in political affairs. She boasts of being an enemy of the government and, in 1830, used her powers to contribute to the catastrophic revolution of that year.

Also, His Excellency orders me to warn you that under no circumstances should you allow said *señora* to remain in Cartagena. If there should be no ship ready to sail with her as passenger, she must then be detained in Arjona, ensuring she is scrupulously watched, and ensuring that not even courtesy visits by any official of the army should be allowed.

May God grant you good health.

There followed the signature of Lino de Pombo, a government bureaucrat, an enemy of Bolívar, and a filthy swine. I crushed the letter in my fist and hurled it into the gorge.

The chill of the Andean night crept across my skin. At the horizon the sky glowed scarlet from the smoking volcanoes to the south. Stars throbbed in the sky like fireflies. Directly above me the Southern Cross blazed. Shooting stars, fat with light, ripped the cobalt vastness, but I had no wishes to make, not one. From childhood, I had loved the Andean sky after nightfall, even preferred it to daylight. As a young woman, the solitude and quiet of nighttime conferred a sense of freedom. I had often stayed awake watching the firmament until dawn bled its darkness. Tonight all this beauty and promise was lost to my misery.

A tap on my shoulder startled me. It was Jonotás, wanting to drape an alpaca shawl over my shoulders. "Come, *niña Manuela*," she said, her voice full of concern. "You need to get some nourishment. Tomorrow we have a long way to go." The last time Jonotás had called me *niña* was when I was a child in Catahuango.

We had cheese, bread, chorizo, and wine, which I drank from my wineskin, and then I lay down on the pallet Jonotás had prepared for us on the cushioning moss. I buried myself under thick *ruanas*. Though I was not sleepy, I closed my eyes and drifted off. Some time later, I awoke. Jonotás, asleep next to me, was snoring in a purr, her soft skin brushing my face.

"Tomorrow, tomorrow," I said under my breath. Tomorrow I would awake and start the voyage down the river, toward the coast, all the way to the Atlantic Ocean, where Bolívar had died and was buried. Lines by the Spanish poet Jorge Manrique came to mind: "Our lives are the rivers that flow into the sea of Death." At sunrise tomorrow, night's darkness would be dispelled for another day. But not for me. Not for me. Not for as long as I lived and remembered. Ahead of me, in a future full of tomorrows, I saw nothing but an unremitting darkness—no moon, no stars. Yet the oncoming darkness did not frighten me, because I knew it would never lift, would never change, would never trick me with a new beginning in which there might blossom again the promise of love, in which happiness would turn to grief. I would float down the river until the day I entered the sea, a dead woman on a raft, en route to eternity. As I closed my eyes, I knew that if I chose to live, I would have to go on and on until I met the pitch blackness beckoning at the end of the long road ahead. In the meantime, tonight, I was relieved and thankful that I could not foretell what was ripening for me in time's dim, unknowable womb.

book

FOUR

The Years by the Sea

31

PAITA

1 8 3 6

I stood on the prow of the barkentine *Santa Cecilia* as the screeches of a swelling tide of seagulls, frigates, pelicans, and cormorants pierced my ears. *Tijeretas* hung suspended between the water and the sky, their long black-and-white tails drooping like supple scissors fanning the air. The mass of birds swelled above the sails, darkening the pallid sky, the color of the desert.

As the ship entered the bay of Paita, the waters carpeted with whorls of dark-green algae, the town's name stuck on my lips. Paita made me think of other words equally unpleasant in Spanish, all of them starting with "p": *puta, perra*—the whore, the bitch I had been called over and over again, in many cities and countries. It also sounded like *pedo*, which is what I came to call Paita—the world's fart. I arrived in Paita to die. I was barely forty years old, but my life was over. Six years had passed since the Liberator's death, and now I was beginning my interment alive.

Paita reeked of putrid fish. A slaughterhouse where sperm whales were dragged ashore, quartered, and boiled to illumine the world's darkness.

Petrified Paita. Its squatting port nestled in a bay walled in by barren, chalk-white mountains. Its ashen sky, unperturbed by clouds, the colorlessness of the landscape and the white sands of the streets made me feel I was entering my own mausoleum. I had arrived at a fishing port that was more like a desert island.

I arrived in Paita after I had fought all my wars, except for two. I wanted to stay alive to reclaim my mother's estate. More important, I wanted to live to see Bolívar's enemies die, one by one, and to see his name restored to its former glory; restored after his name had been besmirched time and time again in the years following his death.

IN JAMAICA, WHERE we had settled after our expulsion from Colombia, penury's grubby hand had knocked louder and louder on our door. Jonotás and I survived by selling my few remaining jewels. Before we left Bogotá, my aunt had agreed to buy Catahuango with the understanding that she would send me the interest on the yearly profits for two years, at the end of which time she would buy me out for 10,000 pesos. Two years later Ignacia had not sent a peso due from the interest nor the 10,000 promised, and Catahuango was auctioned in Quito. It was bought by a man who signed promissory notes to me that would become due within the year.

I became desperate to return to Ecuador and collect on the

promissory notes the man had signed. Many obstacles arose preventing our departure. The memory of José María's long and ferocious war against the current regime in Ecuador was fresh. Rocafuerte's government feared that I wanted to return to rally José María's followers, who were clamoring for revenge. After permission was given for me to return, and I had finally arrived in Ecuador, my enemies prevailed and I was forbidden from setting foot in Quito and told to immediately leave the country or else face execution. Peru was the logical retreat and Lima's government allowed me to enter the country with the condition that I did not move from Paita, a port near the border with Ecuador, except to go abroad. We were able to sail to Paita thanks to a loan of 300 pesos, which my friend General Juan José Flores had given me.

I rented a small two-story house with bamboo walls, with a balcony and a good view of the harbor, and settled down to write letters. Every week I sent Jonotás down to the beach to hand off my letters to the ship sailing for Guayaquil. Months passed with no word from General Flores, whom I'd put in charge of collecting the money that was owed to me. To someone who had waited all my life—for my aunt to die, for Bolívar to come home in three countries—waiting had become a way of life.

After the 300 pesos General Flores had loaned me were gone, a bar of soap became a luxury for us. I forgot what red meat tasted like. There was nothing I could do but wait it out and hope for a return to Ecuador to collect the money from the sale of Catahuango.

Drunken sailors, gamblers, schemers, political exiles, prostitutes with lips and cheeks painted crimson, Indian shamans from the mountains bringing potions that promised to cure bad health and bad luck, in business and in love—these were the citizens of Paita, my new neighbors.

Each day in Paita began with a gray haze over the Pacific that hid the sun until mid-morning, when it blazed above our heads. I felt imprisoned, trapped between the vast ashen expanse of the ocean and the scorching sands of the desert that lay beyond the outskirts of town. I felt as if my soul were being squashed out of me.

Two winds met in Paita, the hot one blew in strong from the desert toward the Pacific, carrying with it sand and spiders, snakes and scorpions that rained down over us like a punishment from the heavens. The pests slithered or oozed through the crevices of the house, lurking with their poison in dark corners. This wind blew as if desperate to immerse itself in the waters of the ocean to cool off. The other wind blew into Paita from the opposite direction, from the ocean toward the desert. Redolent with the aroma of ripe fruit and inebriating tropical flowers, it blew all the way from the Polynesian islands, bringing along an invitation that seemed to chant, "Come, come with us, don't die there on that scorching coast. Come, let us wrap you in a lush green garment." This wind filled my heart with melancholy, the melancholy of remembering how much beauty the world contained beyond the confines of this hellhole I had come to live in.

To distract ourselves, often late in the afternoon Jonotás and I would ride our burros up the hills overlooking the bay. Below us spread the desert that separated Paita from Piura, the nearest thing to a city in this desolate country. We would sit on a blanket spread on the ground and smoke a cigar, with our backs to the sea, as we watched the sun set behind the Andes. On very clear days, it was possible to glimpse the charcoal

plume of an Ecuadorian volcano. It was one of the few pleasures we had in Paita.

Other days all we could see was the desert. During the hot-
test months of the year, its sands became so parched from lack
of moisture that they baked until they turned hard as clay. The
algarrobo trees, the only trees in that thirsty soil, would sweat
their resin to the point that they combusted on their own, as if
fire were a means to get release from the heat. The sparks of
the flaming trees landed on the dried-out balls of *matorral*
tossed about by the hot winds, setting them to spiral across the
desert, burning every twig, dry leaf, and insect in their paths.
The flames leaped so high that the birds, roosting in the tall
cactuses, flew from their nests ablaze, like miniature comets.
We sat on top of the hill at dusk on many days, in the roasting
heat, mesmerized spectators at the gates of hell.

Paita's brief rainy season, when it poured all day long,
brought a brief respite from the suffocating heat. When it
rained harder than usual, the clay hills hugging the bay crum-
bled, unleashing a tide of wet earth to flow into the town,
burying everything in its path. Paita cried in an avalanche of
mud.

That was Paita. So far away from anywhere, so remote that
no matter what conflagrations were taking place in the world
I could live in peace; where I could finally stop dressing as a
soldier, carrying weapons, and fearing for my life; where I did
not have to fight anymore to have the same powers as a man;
where I could be just a woman, a woman without control over
anyone's life.

Paita was the final destination of many exiled *bolivarianos*.
The Peruvian port town had a large colony of those who refused to give up their belief in an ideal which history had

defeated. The main occupation of these lost souls was to wait, and wait, for an auspicious moment to return to their homelands and continue the fight for a Gran Colombia. Now here I was, in that purgatory, to join them in their waiting.

The news spread that Manuelita Sáenz, the Liberator of the Liberator, had settled in Paita. I shut myself inside the house. *Bolivarianos* soon came knocking on the door. I instructed Jonotás to say I was indisposed. I wanted quiet and time alone to think. I was sick of talking about politics. The *bolivarianos* wanted to turn me into a symbol of their resistance—I wanted no part of it. My main occupation became fending off the morbid curiosity of people who arrived in Paita, wanting to see in the flesh a living curio of the past.

This was our home, the last home I would know on earth. At first, I occupied myself with writing to General Flores, who had put a man named Pedro Sanín in charge of my affairs. When Sanín didn't reply to my letters or send any money, I wrote directly to General Flores to ask him to pressure Sanín, whom I was beginning to suspect was unscrupulous. I began to entertain the idea that if I could collect on my birthright, the money that had been cruelly withheld from me, perhaps I could move to Lima. After so many years of separation, I was sure James would leave me alone. Natán and her family lived in Lima, and we would be able to see them, so Jonotás and I would not feel so alone.

Sometimes, gripped by despair, I rehearsed the idea of ending the state of suspension my life had become with a bullet through my head. Yet I had a responsibility toward Jonotás. She was a free woman, but she was growing old, and there was nothing of any value I could bequeath her. Not even enough for a trip to Lima, where Natán would be happy to take her into her family.

Often I wrote letters in a hurry, when I heard there was a boat ready to depart for Guayaquil. In my missives, I begged General Flores for reading materials; for copies of the writings of Bolívar; for anything that would relieve the monotony of life in Paita. But months would go by before I got even a line or two in return from the general. Indeed, few letters arrived addressed to me. Convinced my mail was being intercepted, I took a pseudonym: María de los Angeles Calderón. No letters addressed to Señora Calderón arrived, either.

After a wait of almost two years, a letter arrived from the owner of Catahuango explaining why he had not been able to meet the schedule of payments. He had suffered severe losses from a hailstorm that had destroyed most of the livestock and all the crops. He had been ruined and begged me to have compassion for his predicament. I threw up my hands. What else could I do? It was almost as if there was a curse on my inheritance, and it might take a miracle to ever see a *peso* of it. I realized that the endless wait for my money was making me dull and bitter. No matter how much I tried to be patient, it was impossible to live for years on hope alone.

So JONOTÁS AND I started again to knit shawls and embroider linen. Jonotás was not very adept at this skill—she was happier running errands in town—but was always helpful. We knitted in earnest, to stave off starvation.

Eventually I warmed up toward the locals. *Paiteños* were an amusing people. One day they believed in one thing, the next in another. Their opinions changed with the winds that swept Paita. Poor Peru! Its morally bankrupt populace had forgotten what it was like to live for an ideal dictated by the purity of the heart. Instead, everything was done out of greed or fear. Peru had become a country of buccaneers, which made me feel more patriotic about Ecuador. I was appalled by Peru's drive to annex more and more Ecuadorian soil. Deep down I disliked myself for caring about Ecuador as a single country; it meant that some part of me had accepted there would never be a Gran Colombia.

DAILY ABLUTIONS IN the sea became my consolation. In the early morning and late afternoons, the tides brought venomous stingrays, but from noon to four o'clock, as the tide receded, the water was freed of the frightening creatures. Then I could immerse myself all the way to my neck in the bay's still coolness. As schools of small transparent fish swirled around my body, I was transported to a more innocent state and in that moment shed the hardships of my life.

Embroidering and knitting did not bring enough money, so, making the best of our circumstances, I started a business—the sweets Natán had taught me to prepare many years before. In the late afternoon, a tray of these confections balanced on her head, Jonotás went from house to house, selling my little sugared animals and *cocadas*. The profits were insignificant, but we had gotten used to living like poor women, thus any amount of money was welcome. Besides, making candies cheered me up. Many hungry children came to our door to beg for sweets we had not sold that day. To Paita's children I became "*La dulcera*," which made me proud.

IN PAITA, WHERE I—the only woman who ever rode into battle by Simón Bolívar's side, wearing my colonel's uniform, and the red, blue and gold colors of Gran Colombia, wielding my saber or firing at the enemy—was destined to lie in my humble house, so still, so quiet that I could hear the termites gnawing the thin walls of mud and bamboo, my days and nights became interchangeable in their sameness, like the unmoving sea of Paita. I had nothing but memories to keep me alive. And so, now that I was no longer powerful, young, or beautiful—in the unhurried humiliation of sinking from wealth and power to indigence and anonymity—I finally came to understand the workings of the world. And I was grateful for the truth of things, for a knowledge that became as unnecessary as it was bitter.

In that old age, when we were so poor, and my diet consisted of the sweets I made sitting in my rocking chair, by the charcoal fire, with the coins earned I let Jonotás buy fish, so we had fried fish for breakfast, dinner and supper, sometimes accompanied by rice; and when there was a little water in the *tinaja*, and a tomato or two, fish soup thick with the fruits of the sea. Then I would remember hand-picking vegetables for the Liberator's table from La Quinta's garden, selecting the tenderest endives, the thickest cabbages, the firmest carrots, the reddest tomatoes and juiciest, sweetest onions.

And as I breathed the saltpeter in the air of Paita, which cracked my lips, made my throat dry and my skin brittle and lined like onion paper, when I longed for the taste of fresh fruit—other than the white flesh of the coconut and its refreshing milk—I recalled the trays on the dining table of La

Quinta heaped with mangos, maracuyas, chirimoyas, caimi-
tos, juicy curubas, oranges, fleshy guavas, peaches, pears,
plumb tangerines, pomegranates, and the other fruits Bolívar
loved because they reminded him of his childhood in Caracas.

Late afternoons in Paita, when twilight invaded my room,
and a bat the size of a pigeon swooped past my hammock as if
on a trapeze; when I had no visitors, and Jonotás was in the
kitchen finishing her chores before daylight was extinguished,
before a candle would be brought to my room, in the chiar-
oscuro of my bedroom, I would feel lonely and yearn for conversation, for human company.

In Paita, where my old age seemed to be longer than the rest
of my life, there were many days when I would look at myself
in the mirror in my bedroom and see an indigent invalid living in a town that was the latrine of the world, "where the
mule shits," as Jonotás used to say, and I wondered whether
that other Manuela, who had lived at the center of power of a
great nation, who was wealthy and famous, powerful and
feared, loved and hated, beautiful and desired, was the same
old woman swaying in a worn-out hammock in a hot, termite-
infested dark room. Then my own life seemed to me like a history book I had read about a woman named Manuela, another
Manuela, living in a brighter, more exciting world full of hope
and dizzying ideas, and all I had to do was close my eyes, holding my two dozing hairless dogs against my withered breasts.
If I kept my eyes closed long enough, long enough to forget
about my present circumstances, then it would all come back,
freshly alive and fragrant in my dusty room—the leafy cool
haven, the sprawling beds of vivid flowers, the pirouetting
hummingbirds, the transparent rivulets. It made me, Manuela Sáenz—whom history would dub the Liberator of the Lib-

erator because I had risked my life once to save his, because I made his heart glad with love and freed it from bitterness when Bolívar was dying, broken, rejected, and hated by so many ingrates—it made me thirsty just to think of La Quinta in Paita with its inert sea, a desiccated, arid hell where a jug of drinking water was more precious than pearls.

IN A LIMA NEWSPAPER already two weeks old when it arrived in Paita, I read the awful news that James Thorne had been murdered on February 16, 1847, in the hacienda of Huayto by unknown assassins. James and the woman who accompanied him (who I assumed was his mistress) had been hacked to pieces. After the shock wore off, I grieved for him the way one grieves the death of a dear friend. I regretted that James and I did not have a chance to meet again in the years since we had become friends.

As James's legal widow, I retained the services of an old acquaintance in Lima, Cayetano Freire, to claim in my name the dowry of 8,000 pesos that my father had given James. Don Cayetano wrote to inform me that in his last will and testament James had bequeathed the 8,000 pesos to me. However, should the funds not be liquid at the time of his death, which they were not due to the nature of his export business, the executor of his estate was to send me annual interest of six percent, until I was paid in full.

James's will also supplied answers to questions I had not presumed to ask in our correspondence. He had fathered two daughters and one son, born to a woman named Ventura Conchas, and to each of them he left the sum of 2,000 pesos. The Anglican Church received the remainder of his estate.

Don Cayetano suggested that I gather documents attesting to my dire circumstances, which might spur the court to release more of the funds. For a time I dared to dream that my years of mendicancy might be at an end. Jonotás was growing old, and I wanted to hire a younger maid to take over the heavier chores. But I was being naïve: I had forgotten how much I was still despised in some circles in Lima. The executor of James's estate, a man named Escobar, raised an objection to my claim on it and went to court to void the will. He argued that at the time James made his will, he was not in possession of his reason. Furthermore, the money James had left me was merely a gallant gesture, not a legitimate debt because I had forfeited my rights as a lawful wife when I abandoned him for Bolívar. Thus the bequest was null and void.

Don Cayetano tried to get the courts to release the money due me, but it was a wasted effort. The judge ruled that I had indeed lost all my rights as James's wife when I committed adultery.

I grew philosophical as a defense, slowly accepting that money was not to be my inheritance in this life, but the riches that resided in my heart and mind. These were the riches of my days and nights with Bolívar, of those eight glorious years when I was loved by the greatest man born in South America, and when I loved him in return with a burning fire that time—destroyer of so many things—could not touch.

NOT LONG AFTER James's death, I fell going down the stairs of my house. I thought it was just a matter of time before the fracture healed and I could walk again. I followed the doctor's instructions, staying in bed for weeks, but when I tried to get

up, and put my foot on the floor, the pain shot through me like
a knife. Jonotás moved my bed to the parlor so I wouldn't be
confined to my bed upstairs. Eventually, I got strong enough to
sit in my rocking chair until my siesta, when Jonotás helped
me onto the hammock, where I also slept at night. My hip had
healed but it was frozen. I could not walk. Still, I continued to
believe that one day I would walk again. Thus I became an old
woman and a cripple in Paita. From then on, I lay a large portion of my days in a hammock to alleviate the pain in my hips,
my dogs at my side providing body heat to relieve my aching
arthritic bones.

My only distraction was to sit in my rocking chair outside
my house at dusk, the way many *paiteños* did to enjoy the cool
evening breezes before they turned in for the night. One afternoon an old, lanky man on a decrepit donkey approached my
house, looking for all the world like Don Quixote. The donkey
came to a halt a few yards from my rocking chair. The man's
black eyes sparkled. I was surprised when he said, "Doña Manuelita Sáenz?"

"What's left of her," I said. "How can I help you, my
friend?"

"I am Simón Rodríguez."

Bolívar's teacher was still alive and sitting atop a donkey
next to my chair? How had he found me?

"My dear professor," I welcomed him. "My house is your
house." He tried to dismount the donkey but was having great
trouble doing so.

I called Jonotás, who was in the parlor, doing chores. "Please
help Don Simón Rodríguez dismount from his donkey."

"Thank you, kind lady," he said to Jonotás as she helped him
down. He tottered in my direction.

"Forgive me for not getting up," I told him. "A problem with my leg."

"Doña Manuelita, Your Grace," he said, grabbing my hand and bending over to kiss my parched skin.

Jonotás brought out a chair and helped him sit. Then she went to fetch him water.

"I've traveled a long distance to come meet you," he said, after he had had a long drink of it. "I didn't want to die without having the great honor of meeting you. I've come to you, Doña Manuelita," he added, "because I cannot yet go to join Simoncito."

It was as if the Liberator in his pantheon had sent him to me as a gift to sweeten my old age. I did not want to lose Don Simón.

"As you can see, Professor," I said, "I am no longer a woman of means, but my humble home is your home. And where there's enough food for two, three can eat. I know this is what the Liberator would have wanted. Nothing would make me happier than the pleasure of your company. Jonotás and I don't have many friends here in Paita, and certainly no old friends."

Don Simón accepted gladly. We spent days and nights talking. He had just finished a tour on his donkey of the entire American continent, spreading his philosophy that the book of nature was "the only book worth studying. Besides those of Rousseau, of course."

Professor Rodríguez must have been in his nineties at that time. His earthly possessions consisted of his donkey, Brutus, who tried to kick anyone who approached him from behind, and a threadbare bundle in which he carried a change of clothes and a few worn-out volumes of Rousseau.

"Can you believe the backwardness of our people?" he exclaimed, during one of our conversations. "I've been chased out of many towns just for insisting on teaching anatomy lessons in the nude, and for saying to my students, 'Children, the walls of this school are a prison. It is time to tear down the walls of the schools so you can contemplate reality.'"

Professor Rodríguez regaled me with anecdotes from Bolívar's youth. Not only about their early years in Venezuela, but about their trip to Europe to complete Bolívar's education. So much time had passed since the Liberator's death that we could talk about those times without sadness.

Don Simón satisfied my curiosity about what it was like to have been in Rome, at the top of Mount Aventino, when Bolívar, still a youth, vowed to liberate the South American continent from the Spanish Crown.

"Tell me, Professor, what was it like to witness the most important moment in the Liberator's political awakening?" I asked.

"Doña Manuelita, I do not consider it the most important moment. It's the one historians have popularized and the people have embellished, certainly, but the defining moment came much earlier, when he was thirteen years old and heard the story of the great Indian chief Tupac Amaru. I remember that morning so clearly, how his eyes shone with pain and disbelief when I told him how in 1781 the chief of Pampamarca raised twenty thousand soldiers with slings and sticks and machetes to fight the mighty army of Spain. You should have seen the sorrow in his eyes when I told him how Tupac Amaru had been betrayed and then hacked to pieces with an ax, though not before the noble chief witnessed the Spaniards beat his wife and his son to death. 'See, Simoncito?' I said. 'The oppressors can cut off our heads and fry them in sizzling oil, but the ideas in those heads will survive.' It was on that day he swore to raise an army of tyrant-slayers, even if they had to fight the tyrants with slings and rocks. It was then, you see, that he understood that the great men in history become so by fighting against the tyrants, even though they risk losing their wealth, their health, or their very lives."

It developed that the professor was too frail to manage the stairs to the bedroom, so, after a few weeks with us he went to live with his friend Don Julio, the priest of Amotape, a tiny hamlet a stone's throw from Paita.

"Have you become religious?" I asked him when he told me of his plan. "I thought you and I shared the same anticlerical sentiments."

"We do, of course, Doña Manuelita. But Don Julio is my friend—we both love Rousseau, and so we overlook each other's defects."

Not long after he left, the altar boy of the priest of Amotape came by our house to deliver the news. Don Simón Rodríguez, the Liberator's teacher, had died. "Father Julio asked me not to forget to tell you, Doña Manuela," the boy said, "that the professor's dying words were: 'I'm proud to leave behind nothing but a trunk full of ideas.' Father Julio wanted you to know that he buried him in the chapel of the church because, though Don Simón professed to be an atheist, he was more a man of God than most clergymen Father Julio knows."

The appearance of the professor in my life made me think again of politics, of the cause we had fought for. Paita was a good place to contemplate the unfolding of history in the nations of the Andes. From this vantage point I'd seen them plunge into the protracted civil wars that Bolívar had predicted would result after the dissolution of Gran Colombia. I found perverse pleasure in knowing that history had proven the Liberator right. It was only a matter of time, I hoped, before history would absolve me as well.

What was the main difference between the time when the Spaniards ruled and now? During my years in Paita, I'd often pondered this question. What good had our independence brought? No one wants to see his motherland ruled by foreigners. We fixed that. Yet I was afraid that the same injustices perpetrated by the Spaniards were now perpetrated by us *criollos*. The Negroes and the Indians and our poor were now oppressed by their own countrymen.

One day, thinking about the whole of my life, I found that the anger in my heart had subsided: I'd forgiven Ignacia, my father, and even Santander—my mortal enemies. When I thought about the past, now it was not my motherless childhood in Catahuango, nor my mistreatment by the nuns, nor my unhappy, stunted life in an arranged marriage I thought about. Instead, I remembered my days with Bolívar, the happy times as well as the unhappy ones, and my grief lifted at last. One day it struck me that even though I was old, an invalid, and forgotten, I was finally free because the poisonous scorpion that had dwelt in my heart for most of my life had died.

I KNEW MY end was approaching when Bolívar began to appear in my dreams. I grew closer to him than we had been in life. No enemy and no campaign could come between us. Now he belonged to me alone. To summon his presence, all I had to do was to think of him, to wish him by my side to share a confidence and, regardless of the hour, he would be there, as he had never done when he was alive. His presence became almost corporeal, as tangible as Jonotás's when we sat on the patio, smoking a cigar and gossiping about our neighbors. I never felt alone again. When Jonotás went out to do errands, it was the general who kept me company, not the little dogs on my lap. We talked about our years together, and took walks through his family's hacienda in Venezuela, or through the fields of Catahuango, and indulged in the games we had played as children. Always I would bring him up to date on the news that reached Paita about old friends or enemies. More and more, I looked forward to the time when I could join him on the other side, when we could be two naked souls together in eternity, never to be separated again.

32

⊼

1856

Over the years, the ships that docked in Paita brought with them many diseases and plagues. As soon as the authorities announced the arrival of a pestilence, Jonotás and I made sure we had enough supplies to last us for a while. Then we would shut ourselves in our home until the scourge ran its course.

One morning in November, Jonotás came back from the market with the news that a ship had arrived that day carrying two sailors stricken with uncontrollable coughing. The men died hours later in the infirmary, after a dreadful agony. Word of the illness spread through town immediately.

Without losing a minute, we filled all the *tinajas* in the house and made plans to ration our consumption of water to no more than a *totuma* per day—which could hold us for a couple of months, if necessary. We stocked up on salted fish, rice, lard, salt, sugar, and candles. To supplement these essentials, we filled shelves with jars of the sweetmeats and pickled fruits that we prepared. We made additional purchases of wood and charcoal for cooking, incense to purify the air, and a good supply of cigars, which were the only real pleasure left to us in our old age. Finally, Jonotás sealed up the windows and doors, and we settled down to wait for the cloud of disease to pass over us.

As the plague felled scores, I heard from my hammock the *paiteños* imploring God's mercy for their loved ones. Late at night, lamentations pierced the quiet, like ululations of the souls trapped in purgatory. I was reminded of the cries rising from the battlefield after darkness fell, the moans of the wounded as they prayed to be rescued—or prayed to die a quick death. Each night, shortly after the bells of Paita's church tolled midnight, the squeaky wheels of the wagon and the snorting of the mule announced the transport of the dead to the communal grave outside Paita, where they would be buried before dawn.

We made sure one of us was awake late at night so we could answer the knock of the cadaver collector who went from house to house to confirm that there were people still alive inside. As the days passed, I began to think that if we stayed inside and did not let anyone in the house, and kept the windows and doors shut—despite the suffocating heat—we might outlast the scourge. Our house was like an oven, not just from the lack of ventilation but from the heat outside produced by the fires set all over town to burn the homes and the possessions of the victims of the plague.

Late at night, Jonotás would open the door to the patio to let the dogs out just long enough for them to relieve themselves, and for her to empty our chamber pots in the latrine. Before she opened the door to do any of this, she wrapped her nose and mouth in a shawl soaked in camphor to protect herself from the malevolence in the air.

One morning Jonotás woke up coughing, and she continued coughing as she lit a fire to boil water for coffee. When she came over to my hammock to help me use the chamber pot, she complained of a tightening in her throat, a dryness, and difficulty in breathing. "You probably haven't been drinking enough water," I said. "The sand of Paita has stuck in your throat." Jonotás took a long drink of water, but she did not feel any better. "Ay, Manuela," she protested, "there's something blocking my throat."

"Come over here and let me take a look inside your mouth," I said. Jonotás held a candle near her face and opened wide. On the roof of her mouth I saw a thick fibrous spot the size of a small starfish, and the lining of her throat was red and swollen. I noticed, too, whitish membranes had almost sealed her nostrils. She had only hours to live.

Jonotás sat in the chair by my hammock, rocking slowly, her eyes closed. She started humming an African song. Something she had not done in a long time. But I remembered it; it was a song of leave-taking, of good-bye. When her coughing intensified, she announced, "Manuela, I'm going to leave the house. I'll close the door behind me."

"I know what you're thinking, Jonotás," I said. "But it's too late. It's just a matter of time before I come down with it, too. The least we can do is die together."

We stared at each other, no longer able to speak. The plague had robbed Jonotás of her garrulous nature. Every sound she uttered seemed to cause her pain. This was a time to seek comfort praying to God, but we were atheists. Jonotás and I were old women, and I had been an invalid for ten years. The future was not something I anticipated with any pleasure. If anything, I had lived too long and now I was curious to find out what would happen to us after we left the earth.

"Let's smoke," I proposed. Jonotás got up with great difficulty, lit two cigars, and we sat beside each other in silence, puffing and blowing smoke. Jonotás was halfway through her cigar when her coughing became intense. She started to get up, gulping for air. She collapsed on the floor and fell into a fit, making gagging noises. As I watched her, a whitish foam poured out of her open mouth, like something that kept growing inside her even though she was no longer alive. I had lived practically all my life with Jonotás—I did not know what it was like to live without her by my side. I had seen too much destruction and pain and experienced too much loss—all my tears had dried long ago. I felt cobwebs starting to grow in my throat, becoming thicker and thicker until the air was cut off. I could not breathe. I had made up my mind to remain in Paita no matter what so I could die by the sea, like the Liberator. My only regret was that the plague did not wait until December—the month he had died.

I placed my hand over my heart. It had stopped beating—I was dead.

That night, the bats that usually glided over my hammock when darkness fell did not come. For years Jonotás had fought these winged rats, chasing them with a broom, catching them in a net, searching for their hideouts during the day to kill them, sealing the gaps in the bamboo walls they came through from the outside—all to no avail. It would have been easier to keep out the sand of Paita than to keep out the bats. Every evening, as soon as the candle was snuffed, the bats would arrive.

As my eyes closed, the tips of their wings chilled the fuzz on my cheeks. After years of trying to get rid of them, we gave up. When we did, I began to welcome my nightly visitors, the only visitors I had during Paita's long nights. But tonight no bat came, as if the plague had claimed the bats, too.

The candle Jonotás had lit the day before had burned down, but in death I could quite clearly see Jonotás lying on her back, her toothless mouth agape, her eyes glazed, the top of her head covered with a cap of white hair, her old gnarled fingers placed on her breasts as if she were reaching for her throat to open the passage for air. The dogs sat by Jonotás as if they were expecting her to wake up soon and let them out onto the patio. What would become of them? So long as our corpses were found the following day, Santander and Córdoba would not die of thirst.

But Jonotás and I were no longer of this world. My body lay in the hammock, head to one side, ears, nostrils, mouth coated by cottony membranes. Yet my soul remained inside my body, as if waiting for permission to leave. Or waiting to be told where to go next.

From my hammock I could see the mahogany chest containing Bolívar's letters. Waiting for the plague to move on to another town, I had asked Jonotás to bring the chest near my hammock, and although I knew each letter by heart, I began to read and reread them silently, hearing his voice in my ears, the honey of his words, his whispered terms of endearment, his declarations of love. For two decades I had guarded this chest as if it contained my own life. What would happen to it now?

In the twenty-six years since Bolívar's death, my name had not rated as even a footnote in the official history of the Liberator's life. For a long time I refused to think about what would happen to the letters when I was gone. In recent years, I had thought of sending them to my dear friend General Flores, who would have guaranteed that the letters would be preserved for posterity. But I had delayed acting for too long, perhaps because once I let go of them I would be admitting the world had defeated me. Now the letters would be destroyed, and I, Manuela Sáenz, the woman who had loved and comforted Simón Bolívar in the last eight years of his life, the woman who had shared with him not just his glory but his decline, would be forgotten. It would be as if I had never existed.

Suddenly men with torches burst into the house, picked up our corpses, and threw them on top of the pyramid of cadavers in the mule wagon. Then my spirit began to exit my cold flesh. It was a strange sensation to be weightless. As our bodies were transported through the sandy streets to Paita's outskirts, I desperately searched for Jonotás's soul, but she had left my side for good. Maybe she had gone back to her origins in San Basilio, and maybe she was glad to be her own mistress at last.

I was not done with Paita. I knew I had to return to my house for one last time. I watched as a man with a lighted torch set my house on fire, creating a vortex of red flames. In minutes the fire consumed everything except a shred of brittle, yellow paper that escaped the flames and swirled up to the sky, flying toward me. I could see Bolívar's handwriting on it. I read—"Come to me, come soon, come sooner."

A powerful wind engulfed my spirit in a fast-traveling cloud. The sky above me glimmered as a full moon emerged from the mouth of a volcano. I recognized the shape of Cayembe. I had returned to Ecuador and was flying over the lus-

cious fields of Catahuango, my ancestral land, the inheritance
that never came to me and had caused me so much pain. I was
finally free of it, free of a place that should never have belonged to me in the first place. It would always belong to the
Indians, who had always belonged to it, because the land and
the Indians were one.

As the moon spilled rays of light over the landscape, a wide
view opened up, revealing an avenue of snow-crowned volcanoes. Tiers of stars sparkled in the frosty sky. The moon climbed
higher, and a burning white splendor swathed the topmost
peaks. The light kept spreading until the white landscape became a crystal cordillera against the charcoal line of the horizon. A deep brooding hush hung above the scene, until I heard
faintly, as if approaching from afar, a swoosh—the sound
made by the wings of a condor.

I had returned to my place of birth so that my spirit could
be buried in one of the sacred volcanoes, as the Indian legends
promised to the people born in the valley. I flew over the mouth
of Tungurahua where, in olden times, the ancient dwellers of
Quito hid their emeralds deep inside, away from the rapacious
conquistadors, until Tungurahua's crater became a verdant
mirror.

I was but a speck of dust in the fierce wind that carried me
over the boiling ruby mouth of Cotopaxi, its entrails brothers
and sisters killing each other in civil wars that lasted hundreds of years—the great spilling of blood that would harm
and enslave in the name of hatred, draining the nations of the
Andes of their best people, and of hope, until the five nations
forming Gran Colombia became one delta of blood.

Indian drums echoed across the valley, followed by the
piercing horn sound of the *bombo leguero* and the mournful tuba

notes of the *tru tru ca*, the most ancient of all the flutes. These instruments were playing the music of my own funeral march. I was entranced by this music, the glow of the valley, the caressing ruffling sound in the air. It was the sound of my wings, the same sound that all solitary, dying condors make as they begin their descent into the mouth of Cotopaxi, Lord of Terror, where all the creatures of the land of the volcanoes eventually return to be consumed until nothing is left of us but the ephemeral trail we have made in this world that we unwisely call *ours*, and even *home*, but which is nothing more than a beautiful, and often painful, resting station; a place where we fight with desperation to create, to control, to change, to hold on to things, people, power, glory, beauty, and even love, without understanding that they are given to us on loan, forever and ever being passed on to those who come on our heels, whether master or slave—all the fools who inhabit the earth, dreaming the dreams of which we are made.

MY THANKS

AMONG THE BIOGRAPHERS, historians, and memoirists I must acknowledge and thank for opening the way for me, my largest debt of gratitude must go to Victor von Hagen, for his romantic biography *The Four Seasons of Manuela*, which made me fall in love with Manuela's story many years ago. Other books that illuminated for me the era and the characters are *Selected Writings of Bolívar*, compiled by Vicente Lecuna and edited by Harold A. Bierck, Jr.; *Bolívar* by Indalecio Liévano Aguirre; *Bolívar* by Salvador de Madariaga; *Santander* by Pilar Moreno de Angel; Jean Baptiste Boussingault's *Memorias*; Péroux de Lacroix's letter to Manuela Sáenz, dated December 18, 1830; Carlos Prince's *Lima Antigua, La Ciudad de los Reyes; La Guía del Viajero en Lima* by Manuel Atanasio-Fuentes; *Tradiciones Peruanas* by Ricardo Palma; and, of course, the writings of Manuela Sáenz herself: *Manuela Sáenz, Epistolario, Estudio y Selección del Dr. Jorge Villalba F.S.J.* My description of the events of the attempt on

Bolívar's life is based on Manuela's famous account, which she wrote for General O'Leary and which is dated August 10, 1850. One literary debt in particular I must acknowledge: the last few pages of my novel were inspired by the ending of Alejo Carpentier's *The Kingdom of This World*, where Ti Noel is transformed into a goose. That is my homage to an author and a novel I love.

I also owe an immense debt of gratitude to many old friends, and to the new ones I made in the writing of this novel. My thanks to my friends in Paita: to Don José Miguel Godos Curay, who shared with me his knowledge of Manuela's life and his insights into her personality, and who made available to me hundreds of pages of writings he has collected about Manuela; and to his son, Juan de Dios, who insisted I get in touch with his father.

Other friends heard me talk about this project for years and read endless drafts of the novel, making invaluable contributions. My thanks to Nicholas Christopher who, one afternoon in late December 1999, said to me, "What's holding you from traveling to Paita?" The next day I purchased a ticket, and that was the beginning of this journey. To Kennedy Fraser, my writing buddy as I started writing the book; to Maggie Paley and her writers' group, where I workshoped an early draft of the novel; to Mim Anne Houk, my college teacher, who read an early version and made me realize how far off the mark I was; to Jessica Hagedorn, who said to me, "What are these slaves doing here?" It was after her reading of that early draft that I began to write in Jonotás's and Natán's voices; to Connie Christopher, who said to me, "You have to make me believe that Manuela really loved Bolívar;" to Edith Grossman, who after reading a late draft said, "I need to understand how Manuela became the woman she became"; to my agent, Thomas Colchie, who early on said to me, "I think you're onto something here"; to Shepherd Raimi, who heard me tell and retell the story hundreds of times; to Robert Ward, for his assistance preparing the manuscript; and to Bill Sullivan, who read countless drafts, and never complained. But I am most grateful to two people in particular: to the freelance editor Erin Clermont, for her inspired and exacting copy- and line-editing of the novel. And to my fellow teacher and novelist, Marina Budhos, who helped me find the structure and the shape of *Our Lives*, after I had been writing for four years. It was only when I began to listen to her suggestions, that the novel finally fell into place. Last but not least, I wish to express my gratitude to my insightful editor, Rene Alegría, for many valuable suggestions and for embracing my novel with passion.

This book is dedicated to the memory of Josefina Folgoso, whom I met in Barranquilla, Colombia, when I was fourteen years old. She became my mentor and my teacher. For forty years, we maintained a close friendship that distance made all the more precious. From the moment I began to write this novel, hardly a week went by without a call from Josefina from Barranquilla to inquire how the novel was progressing. After a while, it became apparent to me that she saw the writing of my novel about Manuela as the vindication of her own life. Like Manuela, hardship had befallen her in her old age.

Then, on August 13, 2004, as I was writing the last pages of this book, I received a call from Josefina's sister saying she had died of cancer the day before. She added that Josefina had been ill for four months but had kept the illness from me so I would not be distracted from finishing my novel.

A BRIEF CHRONOLOGY

1783   Simón Bolívar is born in Caracas, Venezuela.

1797   Manuela Sáenz is born in Quito, Ecuador.

1801   Simón Bolívar, age eighteen, travels to Spain to study.

1802   Bolívar marries María Teresa del Toro, who dies, eight months later, of yellow fever.

1808   Ferdinand VII, king of Spain, is deposed by Napoleon Bonaparte. Napoleon's brother, Joseph, is crowned king of Spain.

1811   Bolívar begins his military campaigns for independence in Venezuela.

1815   The Spanish government in Venezuela exiles Bolívar to Jamaica.

1815   Manuela Sáenz, while a student at the school of the Concepta nuns in Quito, elopes with Lieutenant Fausto D'Elhuyar. Shortly afterward she returns to her father's house in humiliation.

1817   Manuela marries James Thorne, an Englishman, in Lima.

1819   Colombia achieves its independence in the Battle of Boyacá. Bolívar creates the Republic of Gran Colombia.

1821   The Argentine general José de San Martín liberates Lima.

1822   Manuela Sáenz is made a Knight of the Order of the Sun for her efforts on behalf of Peruvian Independence.

1822   Manuela Sáenz meets Bolívar in Quito, and they become lovers.

1823–27 Manuela and Bolívar live openly as a couple in Lima.

1827   Bolívar leaves for Bogotá and Manuela stays behind in Lima. There is a coup against the general; Manuela is arrested and exiled from Peru.

1828   Manuela Sáenz arrives in Santa Fe de Bogotá and joins Bolívar at La Quinta. In September, Manuela thwarts an attempt on Bolívar's life.

1830   Bolívar is exiled from Colombia and dies in San Pedro Alejandrino, a plantation on the outskirts of Santa Marta.

1834   Manuela Sáenz is exiled for life from Colombia. She goes to Jamaica.

1835   Manuela Sáenz settles in Paita, Peru, after the Ecuadorian government denies her permission to return to Quito.

1847   James Thorne is assassinated by unknown assailants.

1856   Manuela Sáenz dies of an epidemic that ravages Paita. Her house and its contents are burned. Manuela Sáenz is buried in an unmarked grave on the outskirts of Paita.